PRAISE FOR *A LONELY MAN*

"Power . . . smoothly blend[s] prosaic day-to-day events with Robert's fictionalized renderings of Patrick's disclosures. But gradually the 'le Carré stuff' Robert saw merely as material presses in from the edges, and . . . consolidates for a killer payoff ending."

—Sam Sacks, *The Wall Street Journal*

"Power develops a tense and unsettling narrative, part John le Carré's *The Spy Who Came in from the Cold* and part Janet Malcolm's 1990 study of the ethics of journalism, *The Journalist and the Murderer* . . . *A Lonely Man* is a gripping novel that balances political intrigue with personal danger."

—Hannah Rosefield, *New Statesman*

"*A Lonely Man* is an uncanny novel in the best sense possible. The mystery comes in readers' efforts to untangle the many disorienting layers of narrative, asking themselves whether anything in this compelling world is authentic, and whether that's the right question at all."

—Dwyer Murphy, *CrimeReads*

"An exhilarating literary thriller about the nature of fiction itself . . . With a deft and subtle hand, Power structures his novel in such a way as to draw out the kind

of tantalizing ambiguity that only precise writing can produce . . . Exploring the shifting borders of fiction and reality, *A Lonely Man* locates peril in the disputed territory between the two."

—Theo Henderson, *Shelf Awareness*

"An elegant, atmospheric story of shadows and half-truths . . . *A Lonely Man* soon reveals itself as a taut, subtle, postmodern literary thriller written with an exacting command over its form . . . The final fifty pages are so tense, I found myself both too stressed to go on and too stressed to stop, a total captive to the story."

—Johanna Thomas-Corr, *The Sunday Times* (London)

"Power's talent lies in the narrative blend of psychological struggle and wider international espionage . . . The interweaving of Patrick's investigations and Robert's writing culminates in a gripping finale."

—Zoë Apostolides, *Financial Times*

"The last third of *A Lonely Man* is so tense, so full of jeopardy, that it makes many thrillers feel underpowered . . . Elegantly written, accomplished."

—Robbie Millen, *The Times* (London)

"Well-constructed spy stories about lost and lonely men are a rarity these days . . . John le Carré and Roberto

Bolaño are acknowledged, but unobtrusive, influences on this slippery, ambiguous thriller . . . An all-too-plausible portrait of the lengths to which both states and individuals will go to seize ownership of a story."

—Claire Allfree, *Daily Mail*

"Power holds in a state of suspension two distinct narrative modes. There is the le Carré–esque, Russian spy plot centred on Patrick, involving shady figures stealing computer hard drives and stalking street corners; and there is a looser, elegant literary flâneurism, reminiscent of Ben Lerner . . . This balancing act is expertly handled; both styles are refreshed and made strange by their contact with the other . . . Power unsettlingly resurfaces the theme of false memories, and the narratives we construct for ourselves from the truth."

—Lamorna Ash,
The Times Literary Supplement

"Chris Power's striking debut novel, *A Lonely Man* is first-rate . . . Bursting with potent, beguiling prose."

—Martin Chilton, *The Independent*

"This is an intricate and elegant story, and cleverly metatextual. *A Lonely Man* is an exploration of the creative process, and the sacrifices that are made in real life in the pursuit of art."

—Sarah Gilmartin, *Irish Times*

"A classy page-turner . . . Unbearably tense, the intricate narrative delivers electric drama as well as thought-provoking reflections on storytelling ethics."

—Anthony Cummins, *Mail on Sunday*

"Power's understated style abets the tension, creating gaps and unanswered questions that pull the reader along, recalling Hermione Lee's description of Penelope Fitzgerald's prose as 'plain, compact, and subtle' . . . An entertaining literary thriller that traces intrigue from the writer's mind to the latest headlines."

—*Kirkus Reviews* (starred review)

"In this beguiling literary thriller about the ethics of storytelling, Power (*Mothers*) examines the plundering tendencies of oligarchs and writers." —*Publishers Weekly*

"Chris Power writes with masterful dexterity, and this novel reveals his genius for subtle misdirection and pulsating tension. *A Lonely Man* is a delicate snare of a novel, and by the time you realize that the characters are trapped in a lethal game, you are also trapped and powerless to resist its hold."

—Brandon Taylor, author of *Real Life*

"A thrilling, unnerving novel following an international conspiracy and domestic solitude, *A Lonely Man* is one of those rare books that's as entertaining as it is perceptive, a page-turner with exacting syntax and emotional heft." —Catherine Lacey, author of *Pew*

"Is it possible to spin a thriller, a real thriller, out of the deep and bitter mysteries at the heart of the creative process? With *A Lonely Man*, Chris Power shows us that it can be done, and done beautifully. This is a thinking person's novel of suspense—and also one of the most vivid and unsparing accounts of the expatriate writer's life that I've encountered. Power writes with genuine daring."

—John Wray, author of *Godsend*

"I loved this taut, graceful literary thriller in which domesticity is as riveting as the threat of criminal entanglement. In *A Lonely Man*, family life—and love—is the beating heart of the story, creating an absorbing, menacing interplay between home, ambition, and (self-)deception."

—Megan Hunter, author of *The Harpy*

"*A Lonely Man* is a remarkable debut; an accomplished and intricately plotted story that manages to be both thrilling and deeply considered. If you're a fan of existential crises, family dramas, Putin-era paranoias, and Bolaño-style multiplicities, and want to see them woven into one taut novel, you're in the right place. A lonely triumph."

—Jon McGregor, author of *Lean Fall Stand*

"*A Lonely Man* manages to set an unlikely premise alongside extraordinary events, while speaking honestly about the overwhelming, mundane things of fatherhood and being a friend and husband. A very deft literary act."

—Cynan Jones, author of *Stillicide*

"*A Lonely Man* entrances with its ingenious structure, haunting mood of paranoia and intrigue, and games of literature and violence played out in a seductively rendered Berlin. I savored every page."

—Rob Doyle, author of *Autobibliography*

"A portrait of a man and his dawning, imperfect realization that his connections with others have been facile, even superficial, *A Lonely Man* is an unsettling portrait of contemporary masculinity."

—David Hayden, author of *Darker with the Lights On*

"Such grand themes as wealth, power, greed and truth itself are explored in an impressively deft and discrete way. Here a bottle of beer or an illicit kiss feel as subtly significant as the death of an oligarch or a mysterious man on the run. *A Lonely Man* is a tense and taut work that's utterly European, and all the better for it."

—Ben Myers, author of *Male Tears*

© Eva Vermandel

Chris Power

A Lonely Man

Chris Power is the author of *Mothers*, which was long-listed for the Rathbones Folio Prize and short-listed for the Edge Hill Short Story Prize. He lives in London.

Also by Chris Power

Mothers

A
Lonely Man

A Lonely Man

Chris Power

PICADOR
FARRAR, STRAUS AND GIROUX
NEW YORK

Picador
120 Broadway, New York 10271

Printed in the United States of America
Originally published in 2021 by Faber & Faber Limited, Great Britain
Published in the United States in 2021 by Farrar, Straus and Giroux
First paperback edition, 2022

The Library of Congress has cataloged the Farrar, Straus and
Giroux hardcover edition as follows:
Names: Power, Chris, 1974– author.
Title: A lonely man : a novel / Chris Power.
Description: First American edition. | New York : Farrar, Straus and
Giroux, 2021.
Identifiers: LCCN 2020053582 | ISBN 9780374298449 (hardcover)
Classification: LCC PR6116.O9536 A5 2019 | DDC 823/.92—dc23
LC record available at https://lccn.loc.gov/2020053582

Paperback ISBN: 978-1-250-84909-0

Our books may be purchased in bulk for promotional, educational, or
business use. Please contact your local bookseller or the Macmillan Corporate
and Premium Sales Department at 1-800-221-7945, extension 5442, or by
email at MacmillanSpecialMarkets@macmillan.com.

Picador® is a U.S. registered trademark and is used by Macmillan Publishing
Group, LLC, under license from Pan Books Limited.

For book club information, please visit facebook.com/picadorbookclub or
email marketing@picadorusa.com.

picadorusa.com • instagram.com/picador
twitter.com/picadorusa • facebook.com/picadorusa

1 3 5 7 9 10 8 6 4 2

for Sofia

A Lonely Man

They met in Saint George's in Kollwitzkiez, both reaching for the same book. 'Sorry,' they said together, drawing back their arms.

'Please,' Robert said.

'After you,' said the other man.

His speech was slurred. He stank of alcohol. 'Don't worry,' Robert said, turning away. 'I've got it, I just wanted to look at the cover.' It was an edition he hadn't seen before. He would wait until the man had gone. He heard a cough behind him, then a gruff, 'Here.' He turned and saw the man smiling a little stupidly, angling the cover towards him. He looked at it and nodded. 'Thanks,' he said.

The man flipped the book over and studied the back. Robert watched him sway.

'Any good?' the man said.

'Most people like the later stuff better but I think it's great. I like everything he did, though, so maybe you shouldn't trust me.'

The man made no response, just stared at the back of the book. He yawned widely and scratched his cheek. Robert wondered if he could even read the words he was looking at.

'He died?'

'About ten years ago.'

The man grunted and opened the book. Robert went back to scanning the shelves. He wasn't really looking for anything, just killing time before the reading started. Saint George's was a twenty-minute walk from his apartment and over the past couple of years, since moving to Berlin, he had become a regular there. Sometimes he brought his daughters and set them up with colouring books on one of the cracked leather couches in the back room, while he browsed the second-hand books in the front. Tonight they were at home with a babysitter and Karijn was going to meet him for dinner after the reading. She had suggested recently that they make an effort to spend some time with each other away from the children.

'Would everyone take their seats, please?' a bookseller said. Robert moved towards the back room, along with a few other browsers. Feeling a hand on his shoulder he turned and saw the drunk, still clutching the same book.

'What's the event?' the man said. They were about the same age, Robert thought, with a shared accent: London, or nearby.

'Sam Dallow.'

The man looked back at him expressionlessly.

'He's a writer? He's talking about his new novel.'

'I'm a writer,' the man said.

'Great,' said Robert.

The man's boozy stench was even stronger now he was sitting beside Robert on one of the folding metal chairs set out for the reading. 'Is this Dallow any good then?' he said, loudly enough for the rest of the small audience to hear him.

'I've not read it,' Robert whispered. 'It's had good reviews.'

The interviewer was an English journalist who once chaired a panel Robert had sat on in this bookshop, his first and, as it had turned out, only Berlin event. 'Thank you everyone for coming,' the journalist said, 'to hear from one of the breakout voices of 2014, one of the most exciting young writers at work in Britain, and indeed all of Europe, today.'

Robert studied Dallow, a thin young man with short black hair, pale skin and red-blotched cheeks. He looked at ease, idly flipping the pages of his novel and pretending to grimace while the journalist read out strings of adjectives from book reviews. Robert guessed Dallow was still in his twenties, much younger than Robert was when his first book, a collection of stories, had been published four years earlier. There had been some good reviews, a small prize and negligible sales. Now he was two years late with a novel he had started and abandoned so often as to lose count.

Robert tried to listen to the reading, but the words slid off him. He pinched the bridge of his nose and squeezed his eyes shut to refocus on Dallow's voice, but was distracted again when the man beside him slipped a vodka miniature from his coat pocket, twisted off the cap and upended it into his mouth. Robert sat forward in his seat. Dallow was talking about columns of light falling to a forest's floor. He read well, his voice was strong and steady, but he was being too solemn, handling each word as if it were uniquely precious. Robert's neighbour suddenly stood, his chair squealing against the laminate floor, and almost knocked Robert from his seat as he pushed his way along the narrow row. 'No time for this bollocks,' he said, growling the word. People turned in their seats and Dallow, aware of a disturbance, paused for a moment as he peered at the departing man.

Robert felt embarrassed, as though this stranger's behaviour was somehow his responsibility, but most people had already returned their attention to Dallow. 'On the bare hillside,' he read, with deliberate slowness, 'they stood silently, and apart.' Robert wanted to leave, too, but he remained and Dallow eventually stopped and the oppressive hush of a listening audience eased. Robert pulled out his phone to check the time. Karijn wouldn't arrive for another twenty minutes. He didn't want to stay, but he didn't want to look at any more books, either. Second-hand books depressed him after a while: all those novels and stories that had been laboured over, had for a brief moment been the centre of someone's attention, were now like old blood being pumped around a failing circulatory system. 'Does the family you describe in the novel,' the journalist was asking Dallow, 'bear any similarity to your own?'

'I suppose you could say families are a novelist's greatest source of material,' Dallow began, and Robert had to admire the way he made the question seem interesting, even unexpected. Robert had written one story about his family, based on a childhood holiday in Greece. His parents had hated it, but he quickly realised, after a moment of uncertainty about how to proceed, that he didn't care. 'You're supposed to be writing fiction,' his mother had said to him when she read the story. 'You can't write about us.' She didn't understand when he tried to explain that sometimes actual events were the only thing that gave a story life. They had barely spoken since. He checked his phone again: 20:26. The journalist asked if anyone in the audience had a question. A few hands went up and as the chosen spectator began to ask her question Robert made his way out as unobtrusively as he could. On the street it was almost dark, the sky purple, the temperature still in the twenties. It had been an unusually hot September. Looking up and down the street he saw diners at pavement tables and drinkers outside the pub on the next corner. A group of younger men, caught up in a story, burst into laughter as they passed Robert. Behind them, smiling as she approached, was Karijn.

'How was it?' she said.

'Confusing in all sorts of ways. How was your thing?'

'Great!' She hugged Robert tightly. 'Gregor showed us how to stitch squab pads.'

Earlier in the year Karijn had begun inviting other upholsterers from around the city to demonstrate techniques at evening sessions in her workshop. They always seemed to energise her. 'Good turnout?' he said.

'Full up! I had to stand on a table to introduce Gregor. And he's so pedagogic. He kept that secret.'

'Maybe he can teach that guy in there something about writing,' Robert said, jerking his head towards the bookshop. 'Or me, for that matter.'

Karijn sighed. 'Another bad day?'

He shook his head. 'Are you hungry?'

'Starving. Where are we going?'

'November.' Two years before, when they moved to Prenzlauer Berg, it had been the first restaurant they went to alone, their friend Heidi at their apartment with the girls. They had never been since, and earlier that day Robert had hesitated before making the booking. Last time, when they left the restaurant, they had walked into the aftermath of a suicide. The body was in a blue bag, on a stretcher that paramedics were loading into an ambulance. One of the crowd of people standing watching from the pavement said it was a woman, a neighbour of his. He said she had jumped from her apartment window, four storeys up. As Robert and Karijn walked away the ambulance's lights had made the street flicker blue around them, as if they were walking through a silent electrical storm. 'Horrible,' Robert said. 'That poor woman.' He could still remember, clear as a photograph, the puzzlement on Karijn's face when she looked at him.

'You didn't know her,' she said.

Now they walked slowly down the street, Robert's arm around Karijn and her hand in his back trouser pocket. Outside the bars and restaurants the air was teeming with conversation. Blooms of cigarette smoke ascended. Everyone wanted to be outside for as long as the Indian summer lasted – the Altweibersommer, as Robert had learned to call it.

'I spoke to Greta on the way over,' Karijn said. 'All is well.'

Robert held up a hand. 'Our children have been erased for the evening. We're young, sexy lovers in the greatest European capital. No backstory.'

'Youngish and sexyish,' Karijn said.

They came to where Wörther Strasse opened into Kollwitzplatz, a diamond-shaped park dense with plane trees, surrounded by grand old apartment buildings. 'Let's go through,' Robert said. It would have been quicker to skirt the park, but they had plenty of time and he wanted to see the statue of Käthe Kollwitz. Walking towards the pedestrian crossing that led to the park, they heard angry shouts coming from a bar. They saw a man run from its doorway, stumble and fall heavily to the ground in front of them, his face striking the pavement slab. Three men came after him. The first of them, short and muscular, in drainpipe jeans and a tight, zipped tracksuit top, crouched over the man collapsed on the ground and hauled him roughly onto his back. Robert recognised him as the drunk from the bookshop. As his attacker pulled back his arm and balled his fist Robert stepped forward. 'Entschuldigung!' he shouted and held out his hand to block the punch. 'Entschuldigung, was ist . . .' He didn't have the German. 'Tell them I know this man,' he said to Karijn, who was looking at him in bewilderment.

'Das geht Sie gar nichts an,' the short man said. His head was shaved, his skin tanned. Robert saw blurred blue ink tattoos on the knuckles of his raised fist.

'Bitte,' Karijn said. 'Er ist unser Freund. Wir wollen ihn mitnehmen.'

The man looked at her. His mouth was drawn tight. He was breathing hard through his nose. He shook the other man and shouted something in his face, then dropped him to the ground. He took a few steps away then spun around to face Robert and Karijn. 'Your friend is asshole,' he said. He took a step towards the man where he lay on the pavement. He raised his booted foot above his face. 'Spast!' he yelled, stamping his foot down beside the man's head. He turned away and swept his arms repeatedly, waving his companions back inside the bar.

The man rolled over onto his side. One of his eyes was red, clenched shut, and his lip was bleeding. 'You really know him?' Karijn said to Robert as she knelt down beside the man.

'He was at the reading,' Robert said. He put one of the man's arms around his shoulders and heaved him onto his feet. The stench of alcohol enveloped him. Together they staggered to a bench and Robert helped the man sit down.

He spoke, his voice weak; Robert couldn't understand him. He cleared his throat and spoke again. 'Thank you,' he said.

'I'll get water,' Karijn said, and strode quickly towards a Späti.

The man leaned forward and spat blood onto the road. He seemed to be smiling, although it might have been a grimace.

'What was that about?' Robert said.

'Difference of opinion,' the man said. 'Not so serious.'

'I'd hate to see what you call serious. You almost got your head kicked in.'

'They could have been someone else,' the man said.

He wasn't making sense. He might be concussed, Robert thought. 'We should get you to the hospital, have them take a look at you.'

'No,' the man said.

'I think—'

'No, don't bother,' the man said more loudly, his voice clearer. His good eye focused on Robert. 'Listen, I appreciate the help.' He held out his hand. 'Patrick,' he said.

Robert took his hand. 'Robert.'

Karijn returned with water. She twisted off the cap and handed the bottle to Patrick.

'Karijn, this is Patrick,' Robert said.

Patrick nodded and swigged the water, wincing as the bottle pressed against his lip.

'I was saying we should get him to hospital,' Robert said to Karijn.

'I think so,' she said.

'Really, no. I won't go so don't waste your time trying.'

Despite the reek of alcohol, Robert thought that Patrick didn't seem as drunk as he had been in the bookshop. In fact, he suddenly seemed remarkably sober.

'Let me look at you,' Karijn said, placing her hands gently on the back of Patrick's head and tilting his face up towards her. 'Yes: you look like shit,' she said. He laughed.

Robert saw now that Patrick had an impressive face. Broad and sharply angled. His nose was crooked, perhaps from an old break.

'You'll live, I suppose,' Karijn said, 'if you stop provoking the locals.'

'I've learned my lesson,' Patrick said, putting the water bottle to his cheek. 'Give me your number, I'd like to buy you a drink sometime to say thanks.'

Robert pulled a pencil from his pocket and looked in his wallet for a scrap of paper.

'Robert, give him a card,' Karijn said.

He felt a flash of irritation. His cards, stating 'Robert Prowe / Writer', had come to embarrass him, because when people asked him what he wrote, whatever answer he gave sounded false. It was as if the cards belonged to another man. But he slipped one from his wallet and handed it to Patrick, who looked at it and said, 'Me too.' Robert remembered what he had said in the bookshop.

'I'm sure you'll both have plenty to moan about, then,' Karijn said. She winked at Robert.

Patrick stood and swayed for a moment between them and they both put their arms out to steady him. 'I'm fine,' he said, waving them off.

'Where are you headed?' Robert asked.

Oddly, Robert thought, Patrick immediately turned the question around. 'Where do you live?' he said.

'We're round here.'

A moment's hesitation. 'I'm in Neukölln,' Patrick said.

'You want us to walk you to the train?' Karijn said.

'No, I can make it on my own. I'm fine, really.'

They watched him walk away. 'Should we go with him?' Karijn said.

'I think he'll be all right.'

They crossed into Kollwitzplatz. Sodium lamplight glared off the bronze figure of Käthe Kollwitz, robed and seated, the expression on her face one of mournful acceptance. Although night had fallen Robert saw, across the sandy expanse of the playground, the dim outline of a man pushing a child on the swings. He wondered how many times he had brought Sonja and Nora here.

'An interesting fellow,' Karijn said dubiously.

'If he wanted a fight he should have picked one in the

bookshop,' Robert said. 'He might have won. He was necking vodka during the reading, you know.'

'Now that, I kind of like.'

'Better than listening to it sober, I guess.'

'Was it really that bad? Or do you just hate this man because he wrote a book?'

'Probably that. It was shit, though.' Robert gave a brief, bitter laugh.

'Rob,' Karijn said.

'I know, I know, negativity verboten. I'm very happy to be here with you tonight. Forgive the wallowing.'

'Wallowing is a lot like masturbation,' Karijn said. 'Both should be done in private.'

They left the park and crossed the road, pausing halfway as a cyclist glided by, hands resting on his thighs as they rose and sank. They walked slowly, the night still warm despite the breeze shifting the tall planes that lined the street, drawing a soft hiss from their leaves and making the candle flames on November's crowded pavement tables dance in the darkness.

Leaning back from his laptop in defeat, Robert noticed the espresso he had made an hour before. He drained the cold, bitter liquid, lifted his hands to his face and briskly rubbed as if the friction might knock something loose: a fragment of an idea to work with. It was months since he had written anything worthwhile. The deadline for his novel lay eighteen months behind him and he had nothing to send his publishers. He no longer wanted to write the book described in the outline they had paid for. Or maybe he didn't have the ability. When it came to his writing, he didn't know what he thought any more, except that he didn't like the solitary line on his laptop screen: He returned ten years later, a changed man. The result of the last hour of labour. The stories in his first book had been written over several years. They had grown gradually, naturally. They had come from episodes in his own life and anecdotes told to him by friends, family, and strangers he had met while travelling. People he had been stranded with; got drunk or high with. Back then he was always running into people who had stories to tell him.

He could see now that the book was filled with the longing and disappointment that, without him realising it at the time, had been the dominant currents in his life.

It was Karijn and the girls who had dispelled them. Or, he sometimes thought, redirected them so their existence could, most of the time, be forgotten.

He tabbed to his email and saw a message from Liam, a friend he had worked with at an advertising agency in London a few years before. They hadn't seen each other since Robert came to Berlin, but Liam regularly sent gnomic messages, or unusual clinical papers he dug up in the course of his work as a medical writer. There was one from the *Lancet* attached to this email, about something called penile allotransplantation. All that the accompanying message said was, I'll be in Berlin soon. A beer? Robert replied, Definitely a beer, and a couch if you need it. He sent the message. He knew not to ask for more details, such as when this visit might be taking place. Liam seldom answered direct questions.

Robert tabbed back to Word. He returned ten years later, a changed man. Robert didn't even know who this person was, or what he had changed from and to. He was reaching for something; sometimes it felt distant and sometimes close, but what it was he couldn't say. He only knew he didn't have it. He deleted the sentence letter by letter, his index finger striking the key with increasing force. When every word was gone, he looked at the white page until he could no longer tell how far the screen was from his eyes. He slammed the laptop shut. He stood and stretched, then yanked open the heavy door that led to the postage-stamp balcony. He rolled a cigarette – an action that had taken on a furtive aspect since, to Karijn's disgust, he had restarted smoking after seven years' abstinence – and stared across the Hinterhof at the peeling wall of the apartment block opposite. Four storeys below him, on the ground floor, there was a gym. He saw a woman in black tights and vest top on a running machine. He watched her, watched the cord of her headphones swing and snap in time with her movements. His gaze roamed across the Hinterhof: weather-stained plastic furniture and children's toys, mossed stone pathways, stands of long grass and vegetable beds. There was one tree, a birch, almost as tall as the seven-storey blocks that hemmed it in. Its leaves hadn't turned yet and when the sun shone they made the light on this side of the apartment green, as if the rooms were underwater. Today the sky was grey, the leaves dull, and the tree's peeling bark mirrored the peeling facade of the block beside it. Their own block had been renovated not long before they moved in; its walls were smooth and painted a soft, stately blue. A lift shaft had been added to the back of the building, which had made life with a buggy easier, although Nora, who was three, had almost grown out of it. Soon she would probably be just like Sonja, who was obsessed with riding her bike. The weekend before, having received permission from their landlady, Robert had put up a hook in the hallway to hang the bike from. They would have kept it on the landing, but in the last few months several neighbours had reported thefts: a pram; a scooter; even a pair of muddy football boots.

Robert rolled another cigarette. Might there be a story in thieves prowling the hallways of apartment blocks? Perhaps the objects they stole gave them a sense of the owners. He remembered the Carver story in which a man's living-room furniture – couch, coffee table, TV and record player – was set up on the lawn outside his house, and another that described a couple, asked to keep an eye on their neighbours' apartment, becoming obsessed with spending time there, trying to live a life different from their own. He crushed his cigarette into a small clay ashtray so packed with butts that they stood vertically, like a hedgehog's quills. He began to go inside, but at the sight of his laptop on the table his hand dropped from the door handle. He rolled a third cigarette. As he licked the paper he looked at the runner in the gym. He liked to watch people. Coils of damp hair clung to her face. Her throat and chest were slick with sweat. Her legs, slim and muscled, pumped as she sprinted in place. Her arms cut through the air. When he sold his book of stories it was as if wide avenues stretched in every direction and all he needed to do was decide which one to proceed along next. But each avenue had narrowed to a track and eventually these had petered out into nothing. Robert realised the woman was looking directly at him as she ran. He quickly looked away, turning his head upwards. It was still warm but the sky had grown darker, the grey purpling. There was supposed to be thunder later. He felt the runner looking at him. He didn't want to check to see if she really was. He decided to find somewhere else to work for the rest of the day and went inside to pack a bag.

The nearest coffee shop was just a few doors down from the apartment, but it was too intimate to work in. It was an ascetic space, with only a single blocky pine table facing the counter, and sitting there he always felt he should be talking to the unfailingly happy, long-haired Japanese barista, not staring into a laptop screen. But the barista, who only spoke German and Japanese, made Robert feel he had failed to make Berlin his city, and he thought that would remain true until he learned the language. Sonja was five and her German was better than his, and soon Nora's would be, too. They were becoming Berliners while he moved through the city like a ghost, solitary and largely silent. He continued on to Schönhauser Allee and the anonymity of Balzac. It was a chain, and sterile, but it was also a place where the only conversation he needed to have was with the beggars who sometimes made the rounds until one of the staff told them to leave.

Instead of writing he went online and read the news: football, then politics. He had stopped looking at the books pages a long time ago. After an hour of idle reading he checked his email. The subject line of a message from his agent read: R U ALIVE? He opened it and found that the message was blank. 'Cute,' he murmured. How long was it since he had spoken to her? He entered her name into the search box and saw he hadn't answered her three most recent messages, the last of which was two weeks old. He returned to her new message and thought about what to reply: I'm done, maybe, or, I wrote 8 words today. Instead he typed, Hey Sally, alive and well! Hope you are too. Got an idea that feels promising but don't want to jinx it. Should have something to show you in a few weeks. He read it back, deleted weeks and replaced it with months, then deleted months and restored weeks. As he hit send an email came in from an address he didn't recognise: punsworth221@gmail.com.

Hello, it's Patrick, the one you stopped from getting killed. I was serious about that drink. How about tomorrow night?

Robert began to type a reply:

Hi Patrick, glad you're alive. Things are pretty hectic at this end right now

He paused, his hands above the keyboard. His instinct was to have nothing more to do with this man, whoever he was, but something made him hesitate. He was always encouraging Karijn to see friends or take evening yoga classes while he stayed home with the kids, preferring to be a hermit because seeing people he knew meant being asked how he was doing and what he was up to, questions he didn't want to answer. But Patrick didn't know anything about him, which meant Robert could tell him whatever he wanted. He could get away from everything for a few hours, including himself.

They had agreed to meet at a restaurant in Mitte. Stepping onto the southbound U-Bahn train at Schönhauser Allee, Robert wondered if he was making a mistake. 'It should be you going,' he had said to Karijn the night before. 'You're the one who talked that guy out of smashing his face in.'

She frowned as she looked up from her laptop. 'Why would I want anything to do with somebody like that?' Her eyes went back to the screen, two white bricks in the lenses of her reading glasses. 'Just don't get beaten up. Or arrested.'

'Eberswalder Strasse,' the recorded announcement said. He had nudged her shoulder as she typed. 'What if I do? What if I come home with bloody knuckles and a black eye?'

She continued tapping at the keyboard. 'You don't want to find out,' she said.

At Alexanderplatz he stood, stepped off the train and climbed the steps to the S-Bahn. One drink, he told himself. One drink, then he would make his excuses and leave. He narrowed his eyes against the gust of gritty wind the S5 pushed before it as it pulled into the station. From his seat he watched the city scroll past the window. It had changed so much since his first visit, almost fifteen years before. Berlin then was a nightscape of waste ground he stumbled across, moving between the cavernous dark of Tresor and Berghain, clubs in high rises, in drained swimming pools, in confusing warrens beside the Spree. He remembered bars, squat parties, sunny mornings in parks and a long, strange comedown in a bowling alley. The memories were scrambled; there was a lot he had forgotten, and some he might have invented. He made a couple of German friends that he visited during the World Cup in 2006. He stayed in Berlin for almost three weeks, and that was when he started exploring the daytime city and fell in love for a second time.

The train pulled into Hackescher Markt and Robert stood and waited for the doors to roll open. Amid the crowd of people getting off he went down the stairs from the platform and through the dark underpass to the station exit. On his right was the terrible club, open twenty-four hours a day, where he had gone dancing with his German friends and some Mexicans they had met when Mexico lost to Portugal in the group stage. It had been maybe eight in the morning when they got there, all high and eager to make the night last a few hours more. In the end it had been him and one of the Mexicans, a guy called Alejandro, drinking beers beside the Spree as the sun beat down, surrounded by office workers on their lunch breaks. He had never known when to stop.

He didn't know the restaurant Patrick had suggested,

a place called Sophien 11 that turned out to be solidly traditional: a tile floor, wooden tables, whitewashed walls cluttered with paintings and framed photographs. The air was sharp with the tang of fried onions and vinegar. A large woman dressed in a black skirt and shirt approached Robert. 'Guten Abend,' she said, smiling politely but without warmth.

'Guten Abend,' said Robert, looking around for Patrick. 'I'm meeting a friend. Ich . . . suche meinen Freund?' He spoke the words with the hesitancy that always afflicted his German. Karijn, who had become almost fluent over the last two years, rolled her eyes when she heard it.

The woman waved her arm, inviting Robert to look. 'There is also outside,' she said in accented English, nodding towards a door through which Robert saw a courtyard and tables.

When Robert stepped through the door he heard someone shout his name. Patrick was sitting at a table in the corner, the thick, overlapping leaves of a vine covering the wall behind him. A book lay on the table, a glass pinning it open on one side.

Patrick stood and shook Robert's hand. One of his eyes was black, his bottom lip cut and swollen. 'I haven't ordered yet,' he said as they sat down. 'I was waiting for you. You hungry?'

One drink, Robert had thought, but the smell of frying meat had triggered his appetite. 'I'm starving,' he said.

'Good, it's on me.' Patrick handed Robert a thick black

leather menu. 'Any man who stops me getting my head kicked in deserves dinner.'

'There's no need,' Robert said, but Patrick held up his hand in refusal.

'Nice watch,' Robert said, looking at Patrick's wrist.

'It's a Breguet,' Patrick said, angling it towards Robert so he could take a better look: a thin gold watch on a leather strap, an intricately patterned face with several smaller dials set into it. 'Those dials are engine-turned,' he said.

'I have no idea what that means, but it looks expensive.'

'It was a gift. From someone I used to work for.'

'Good boss. You're a Londoner?'

'No, I grew up in Bracknell.'

'No way! I used to go and see films there when I was a teenager. The Point.'

'That was a nasty fucking place. How old are you?'

'Forty,' Robert said.

'I'm forty-two. We might have been there at the same time. Where did you grow up?'

'Farnborough. No reason you should have been there.'

'I was, a couple of years ago.'

'Really?' Robert felt a childish kind of happiness at the coincidence. 'What for?'

Patrick hesitated for a moment, then shook the watch on his wrist. 'This guy used the airport there. We got in a car and straight on the motorway. I didn't see much.'

'There's not much to see. Where were you coming from?'

Patrick shook his head. 'It's a long story.'

Robert smiled. 'Bracknell, Farnborough, now Berlin. You live here?'

'Yeah,' Patrick said. 'Well . . . sort of. I'm seeing if it suits me.'

A waitress came to the table. She was tall and thin, with bottle-black hair and a pale, deeply lined face. She wore a tie-dye crop top and drainpipe jeans tucked into knee-high platform boots. 'Möchten Sie schon bestellen?' she said.

Patrick looked questioningly at Robert. 'You understand?' he said.

'She's asking what you want.'

'Have you got meatballs?' Patrick asked.

'We have Bremsklotz,' the waitress said. 'Big meatball.'

Patrick nodded. 'A big meatball, great. Danke.'

The waitress looked at Robert and arched a thin, painted eyebrow.

'Ich möchte . . .' Robert began, scanning the menu, 'Putengeschnetzeltes, bitte.'

'Gerne,' she said.

'And a beer, please,' Patrick said.

'Zwei,' said Robert.

'Vielen Dank,' the waitress said, taking the menus and striding away.

They sat in silence for a moment. An elderly man and woman took the table beside them. Patrick looked them up and down as they sat. 'Whereabouts were you in London?' he said, still looking at the couple.

'Hackney. You?'

'I moved around.'

'Where?'

'Hammersmith, Tottenham. Other places.'

'So why the move? Work?'

Instead of answering, Patrick picked up the book that was lying in front of him. 'I read this,' he said.

Robert laughed when he saw it was *Antwerp*, the book they had both reached for in the bookshop. 'What did you think?'

Patrick flipped a few of the book's pages. 'It was,' he said slowly, as if still deciding, 'interesting. It's more of a mood than a story, isn't it?'

'That's a good way of putting it. It's definitely not conventional, but that's one of the things I love about him. He wanted to break the forms, you know?'

'How?'

'In all kinds of ways,' Robert said. 'He took what he read, and things he did, and other things he made up, and' – he clapped his hands – 'mashed them together.'

'Isn't that what all writers do?'

Robert shrugged. 'I guess, but all his books talk to each other – the more you read, the more connections you can make.'

'What, so I've got to read all of them to get it?' Patrick sounded unimpressed.

'Not necessarily. But, well, yeah. If you really want to get it.'

Patrick dropped the book onto the table. He looked

unconvinced. 'Isn't it a bit, I don't know, juvenile? Poets and femmes fatales.' He pulled a pack of cigarettes from the jacket that hung on his chair. He offered one to Robert and lit it for him. 'Did he live the kind of life he writes about in here?' he said, narrowing his eyes as he lit his own cigarette. 'Crime, rough sex, all that?'

The waitress threw two beermats down on the table, each emblazoned with a black bear, and set the beers down on top of them.

'Danke schön,' Robert said.

'Bitte schön,' the waitress said over her shoulder. Patrick leaned over in his seat to watch her go. The woman at the neighbouring table coughed, lightly but distinctly, and waved her hand at the smoke from their cigarettes.

'There were stories about him when he was younger,' Robert said, holding his cigarette as far away from the woman as he could, on the opposite side of the table. 'Heroin, things like that.'

'These seem like silly fantasies to me,' Patrick said. 'Teenage stuff. I bet he was into knives when he was a kid. Throwing stars. You know those kids?'

Robert wasn't sure what Patrick meant but he nodded anyway.

Patrick turned his cigarette in the ashtray, shaping the tip, oblivious to the smoke snaking towards the couple beside them. 'I did like the setting, though. Those campgrounds by the sea. It was eerie.'

'I went there,' Robert said.

'Where?'

'To Blanes.'

'Where is it?'

'Catalonia. Up the coast from Barcelona. It's where he lived.'

'You met him?'

'No,' Robert smiled. 'This was a few years after he died. Just before I met Karijn. I took a train all the way down there and stayed for a few days. It was a kind of pilgrimage.'

'Pilgrimage?' Patrick said. 'He's only a writer, you know. Not a fucking saint.' He shook his head in amused contempt: 'Pilgrimage,' he said again.

'I'm glad I went,' Robert said. He wasn't going to be embarrassed by Patrick. He didn't care what he thought.

Patrick's smile seeped away as he crushed out his cigarette. 'What's it like?'

'Quiet. Small. There's a harbour, big beaches. It must get busy in the summer, but I was there in February. It was grey and wet and cold. It felt like somewhere you could disappear to, which I suppose is what he wanted. He got a lot of work done there, anyway.'

'Did you go to his house?' Patrick was smiling again.

'I stood outside it,' Robert said and laughed, feeling foolish despite his determination not to.

'What's it like?'

'It's just a building. Not old, not new. It's in this narrow little passageway.'

Something smashed and Robert saw Patrick start, his eyes panicked as he looked around the courtyard. Robert turned and saw, at a table on its opposite side, a man looking down at the shattered remains of a bottle of water on the flagstones. The waitress, who had just appeared at their table again, slid their plates in front of them and hurried over, waving her hand and speaking sharply to the man as he leaned down, telling him not to touch the glass.

Patrick looked at the grapefruit-sized sphere on his plate. 'No shit,' he said, 'that is a very big ball of meat.' Taking up his knife and fork he eagerly cut into it. 'Listen,' he said around a mouthful, 'I do seriously want to say thank you for saving me the other night.'

Robert waved Patrick's words away. 'It was nothing, forget about it.'

'It's not nothing. I was being a cunt and I deserved to get spread all over that pavement, but I didn't, and that was down to you.'

'Karijn more than me, I think.'

Patrick looked blank.

'My wife. The one who talked down the guy you were fighting with?'

'Right, of course. Sorry,' Patrick said. 'And thanks for saying "fighting". I think it was a bit more one-sided than that.'

'What was it about, anyway?'

'Stupid crap, you spilled my beer, fuck you et cetera.' Patrick lifted his glass. 'Anyway, cheers.'

'Cheers,' Robert said. They clashed glasses and took deep draughts of beer.

Putting his glass down, Patrick winced and brought his hand to his mouth.

'Sore?' Robert said.

'I'm making it seem worse than it is. I just forget and then . . .'

Robert leaned back in his chair. The evening was warm and the courtyard was bathed in candlelight. He took a long sip of beer and enjoyed the blur of conversation filling the air around him. He was relieved that Patrick was less of a liability than he had expected. He also realised with some surprise that he was enjoying himself. They spoke about London, an article Patrick had read about a Mexican drug lord, and what Patrick made of Berlin, a city that he said could feel overpoweringly bleak. 'I get like that sometimes,' Robert said. 'You should go to the lakes. Wannsee, Müggelsee. They're good places to let some light in. Get your head straight.'

They drank more beer with their food and when the waitress cleared their plates and Patrick suggested a nightcap, Robert found he wanted to stay.

'Two whiskeys,' Patrick said. 'Any preference?'

'Jameson, bitte, and an espresso,' Robert said, hoping the coffee would help straighten him out a bit. He felt drunk.

'Two espressos, two large Jameson,' Patrick said. 'Cheers. Danke.' They sat in silence for a few moments.

'What made you choose Berlin?' Robert said.

'I don't know. Heard good things, I guess.'

'Have you got friends here?'

'Do you like football?' Patrick said.

'Yeah. Don't get to watch much since the kids, though.'

'Who's your team?'

'Chelsea.'

Patrick smiled. 'Another coincidence,' he said as the waitress leaned over and moved their drinks from her tray to the table.

Robert raised his glass. 'To unnerving parallels,' he said. Patrick raised his in reply and they both sipped, exhaled and settled back in their chairs with a synchronicity that made Robert laugh.

'What?' Patrick said with a puzzled smile.

'Nothing. You were telling me why you moved over here.'

Patrick's smile fell away. 'I don't think I was.'

'What happened?'

'What do you mean, what happened?'

Robert had noticed Patrick's evasiveness, but he could also sense there was something he wanted to say, something that had remained at the edge of their conversation all evening. 'You tell me,' he said. 'I feel like you ending up here wasn't, maybe, entirely planned.'

Patrick looked away and looked back at Robert. He laughed and dipped his head, as if impressed. He shifted in his chair and swirled the whiskey in his glass. This time the hesitation gave Robert the sense Patrick was deciding which version of a story to tell. He made himself remain still and silent. At a party a therapist had once told him that if he really wanted to get someone to speak, he should keep his mouth shut.

'I was working for this guy called Sergei,' Patrick said. 'Sergei Vanyashin. Heard of him?'

'The name's kind of familiar,' Robert said.

'He was a guy who made a lot of money when the Soviet Union collapsed. Hundreds of millions, maybe billions.' He sipped his whiskey. 'Somewhere along the way he pissed off Putin, so he had to get out of Russia.'

'Like Berezovsky?' Robert said.

'Yeah, a lot like him. Sergei fled, went to Spain for a bit, then turned up in London. He got good advice, so he knew which politicians to pay off, which donations to make. He claimed asylum, bought some houses, put his kids in school. He'd already been here – there – quite a few years by the time I met him.'

'How did you meet him?'

'He wanted someone to ghost his memoirs.'

'And that's what you do?'

'I've done it a couple of times. I wrote Albie Cooper's book.'

'No way! I've heard great things.' The book had been a big seller a few years earlier, Robert remembered. It had a reputation for being unusually insightful and skilfully written for a footballer's autobiography.

'I had a lot of offers after that – other footballers, an Olympic rower, some TV presenters. Then one of Vanyashin's people got in touch and said he wanted to meet me.'

'They'd read your book?'

'No idea. I suppose so.'

Robert didn't know if it was the alcohol or the after-effects of the beating, but Patrick had become somnolent. He was gazing into his whiskey, apparently unaware of his surroundings. 'What made you say yes?' Robert said more loudly than he needed to, hoping to rouse the other man.

'I almost didn't,' Patrick said, refocusing on Robert. 'I'd never heard of him, but I did some googling – and fuck me,' he laughed. 'I'd never met anyone who lived like that. I mean, Cooper was on two hundred grand a week, more, but this was something else: houses around the world, yachts, helicopters, jets. It was unreal.'

'I imagine it paid well,' Robert said, thinking of the advance he got for his story collection.

'Extremely well,' Patrick said. He tipped his head back to swallow the last of his whiskey. 'Another?'

Robert placed a hand over his glass.

'For fuck's sake, Robert, I'm thanking you, remember?' Patrick put his hand up and looked around for the waitress. 'Have one more drink with me, then I'll let you' – he flicked his fingers towards the door leading back into the restaurant – 'escape.'

Robert saw something in Patrick's eyes that suggested

it would be more complicated to say no, and he still wanted an answer to why Patrick had ended up in Berlin. 'OK,' he said, 'one for the road.'

'Waitress!' Patrick shouted, so loudly that the man and woman at the neighbouring table both jumped, the man's dessert fork clattering onto his plate.

The waitress, taking an order on the other side of the courtyard, flipped her notebook closed and stalked over. Robert wanted to apologise to her but remained silent. 'Was?' she said, looking down at them with disdain.

Patrick tapped the rim of his glass. 'Zwei, danke.' She turned on her heel and went back inside. 'What were we talking about?' Patrick said.

'You were telling me how you made your fortune writing this oligarch's memoirs.'

'My fortune, yeah. Well, it fell apart.'

'Why?'

'Vanyashin died. Last year.'

'How?'

'The inquest said suicide,' Patrick said. 'Just announced it, in fact. The coroner gave his verdict last week.'

'You're . . . what, you don't think that's what happened?'

The waitress slammed the whiskey glasses down on the table with a crack; both men flinched. She pulled a leather folder from her apron pocket and tossed that down beside the glasses. Patrick laughed as she walked away. 'I guess these really are nightcaps, then,' he said, tipping his glass towards Robert.

Robert sipped his drink. He hadn't drunk so much in a long time. 'So, no book then?' he said.

'No book.' Patrick rubbed his face. He looked tired. 'Just a lot of trouble.'

'What trouble?'

Patrick looked around the courtyard, which made Robert look around in turn. Their elderly neighbours had left. Only a few people remained at the other tables. Couples mostly, although in the far corner a man sat alone, a beer and a bowl of fries on the table and his phone held up in front of his face. Patrick leaned forward. 'The sort of trouble,' he said, whispering now, 'that it's best for me not to talk about, and for you not to know about.' He brought his index finger to his lips.

Perhaps it was the outlandishness of what he was saying, but Patrick seemed far drunker than he had a few minutes before. 'You sound a bit paranoid, mate,' Robert said, and smiled to make it clear he was teasing.

Patrick nodded, as if he had been expecting Robert to say that. 'It's real,' he said.

'What's real?'

'I know,' he said, stabbing the table and lowering his voice so much that Robert had to lean in to hear what he was saying. Again Patrick stabbed the table with his finger. 'I know Sergei Vanyashin didn't fucking kill himself, and I know that whoever killed him' – he moved his finger left to right, as if the killer might be sitting at one of the neighbouring tables – 'is looking for me, too.' His eyes, fixed on Robert's, were held widely open, as if his own words amazed him.

'Did you tell the police that?' Robert said.

Patrick sat back and looked down at the tablecloth. He brushed some crumbs onto the ground. 'They interviewed me. I told them I hadn't ever heard Sergei talk about suicide, or act like someone who was suicidal, but I wouldn't say anything more than that.'

'Why not?'

'Why not? What about Badri Patarkatsishvili? Or Perepilichnyy? Or Berezovsky? All dead in the space of a few years; all connected. They all knew each other. With Litvinenko the government might actually point a finger at the Kremlin, because how can you ignore a river of polonium running through London? But even then, it's taken the home secretary eight years to agree to an inquiry. Eight years. And most of the evidence is classified, and it'll stay that way.'

Robert recognised Berezovsky and Litvinenko's names, but not the others. He wanted to ask who they were, but Patrick wasn't stopping. His voice was louder now, his previous caution seemingly forgotten.

'They don't want Russia in the dock,' he said, 'there's too much money to be made. Even after Putin went into Crimea nothing happened. It took a missile bringing down a fucking airliner for Cameron to start talking about sanctions that actually mean anything. It's a fucking embarrassment. Sergei didn't get protection, and I won't either.'

Was Patrick a hunted man? This sounded like bullshit to Robert. 'So where—' he began, but Patrick motioned for him to lower his voice, his caution restored as suddenly as it had been abandoned. It seemed ludicrous, but Robert decided to play along. 'So,' he said quietly. 'Where does this leave you?'

'Right now, here. I don't know what to do. I don't know where to go. But I wasn't going to stay at home waiting for a social call from the SVR.'

'Is that like the FSB?'

'FSB's internal. SVR's overseas,' Patrick said. 'Like MI5 and MI6. And there's the GRU as well. Military. Fuck knows which ones caught up with Sergei. I hope I never know.' He swallowed the last of his whiskey. His eyes flickered from the table to Robert to the courtyard beyond, never settling.

'Why would they come looking for you?' Robert said, trying to sound more curious than disbelieving.

'The fucking book,' Patrick hissed. 'We were nearly two years into the book. He told me –' he lowered his voice further still and hunched closer to the table's surface – 'he told me things you don't want to hear about people it's wiser not to piss off.'

Robert smiled.

'What's so fucking funny?' Patrick said, his eyes narrowing in anger, making Robert wonder if the night they first met was every night for Patrick. He didn't want to be his next opponent.

'I'm on your side, OK?' Robert said, lifting his hands as if surrendering. 'I helped you out, remember?'

Patrick grimaced and rubbed his hand across his face. 'Sorry, I'm sorry. I don't know how to talk about this stuff. I know it sounds mental. I should shut up.'

'No. If you want someone to talk to, I'm here.' Robert surprised himself with these words, but he wasn't sure Patrick had heard him; he nodded but seemed distracted.

'I've kept you here long enough,' Patrick said. 'We should get going.' He pulled out his wallet and Robert did the same. 'Put that away,' Patrick said. 'No arguing.'

'Thank you,' Robert said. Standing reminded him how much he had drunk. He weaved a little as they walked to the top of Sophienstrasse. 'Which way are you?' he said. Patrick pointed up the street. 'That's me,' Robert said, pointing in the opposite direction.

Patrick held out his hand. 'Thank you again, Robert.'

'You're welcome. Thanks for dinner. And all the booze.'

Patrick smiled. 'We'll sleep well tonight.'

Robert began to turn away then paused. 'How did he do it?' he said. 'How did he die?'

'It appears he went for a run and hanged himself from an old English oak. Poetic, isn't it?' Patrick gave a small, grim smile and raised a hand in farewell.

Robert watched him walk away. It hadn't been the evening he expected. He passed a shoe shop with a single pair of men's loafers in the window, set on a plinth with a spotlight trained on them. It wasn't impossible that

Patrick's story was true, he supposed, but it seemed so unlikely. He felt as if he were being played, like he had spent the evening walking into some kind of trap. But Patrick hadn't asked him for anything. He was nearly at Hackescher Markt station when he realised that if Patrick lived in Neukölln he had gone in completely the wrong direction. Slumped on a train seat, his head beginning to throb, Robert supposed it didn't really matter whether Patrick was telling the truth or not, because he was never going to see him again.

Robert woke to the loud chatter of the girls in the bathroom. Karijn's responses were indistinct: deeper, calm. He reached for his phone. It was a quarter to seven. She would be leaving for work soon. His hangover was concentrated in his left eye, which felt like it might start bleeding. He lifted his head, felt the room lurch, and sank back down onto the bed.

He heard the enfilade of Sonja and Nora's feet, then their bodies crashed against his. 'Pappa! Pappa! Wake up!'

'You have to make me breakfast,' Nora said in a sorrowful voice intended to provoke Robert's sympathy. When he didn't reply, she pushed rigid fingers into his cheek.

'All right all right all right,' he said, batting her hand away. 'Did you guys have any dreams last night?' A conversation meant he could remain lying down for a few seconds more.

'No,' Sonja said. 'Give me Saltoos now.'

'How about you, Nora? You always dream.' Robert opened an eye to see Nora nodding. 'What did you dream about?'

'The monster was in my room,' she said.

'You dreamed about that naughty old monster again? What colour was he this time?'

'Red,' she said, smiling as if she was sharing a secret with him.

'Did he try and eat you?'

Nora nodded. 'He wanted to eat me all up!' she said, bringing her hands to her mouth.

'You know monsters are just pretend, don't you? No one's going to eat you up. Not while I'm around.'

'Pappa,' Sonja moaned, pushing and pulling Robert's shoulder. 'Saltoos!'

'Don't whine, älskling,' Robert said irritably. 'First we brush teeth.'

At this Nora broke down into sobs, which were mostly faked, and Sonja tried to claim she had already brushed her teeth with Karijn. 'Ka!' Robert shouted.

'What?'

'Did they brush their teeth?'

'Nej,' she called. 'Have a good day, everyone!'

The door slammed. Robert took a breath. Every morning he vowed not to lose his temper with the kids, but he usually failed; some sticking point – about brushing their teeth or wearing a particular pair of shoes – would generate enough friction for his impatience to boil into anger. He felt pathetic about screaming at his children, but inside those moments, beyond the immediate annoyance of being disobeyed, his inability to write became their fault, and he was convinced that if they listened, if they behaved, if he got them out of the apartment at a quarter to eight instead of ten past, his day would be richly productive and not a waste of false starts and bad ideas.

That morning, the process of getting out of the door went smoothly. As they walked to the Kita, the girls holding Robert's hands, he wondered if his hangover was stifling his temper, his slowed thought process giving him a longer fuse. Or perhaps it was that he was only semi-present, part of him still turning over what Patrick had told him the night before. It was an intriguing story, even if Robert didn't believe all of it. It felt like it could be something.

Back at the apartment he spent most of the day online, searching news stories and articles. Reading about the death of Sergei Vanyashin, a few details of the incident came back to him. As Patrick said, Vanyashin had been found hanging from an oak in the woods outside his Buckinghamshire estate nearly a year ago. Robert saw a photograph: a bare tree with a carpet of dark, dead leaves around it. There was a ribbon of red-and-white police tape running across the picture, twisted so the repeating words POLICE INNER CORDON were upside down. Beyond the tape, a white canvas tent was pitched at one side of the tree. Vanyashin's body had been removed, but Robert assumed the branch he used was the lowest one, long and thick and maybe three metres above the ground. He used a belt, the news report said. Robert couldn't work out the logistics of it, especially given the shape Vanyashin was in around the time of his death, but perhaps he was more athletic than the short, stocky man in the newspaper pictures appeared to be.

The obituaries described him as someone who came from nothing; a failed theatre director who discovered a talent for making deals in the chaotic period when seventy years of communism were swapped for instant free-market capitalism. In 1987 he was driving a cab in Moscow. Ten years later he had a property empire, one of Russia's biggest independent radio stations and a small but apparently well-respected newspaper. Following link after link, the tabs on his browser growing thinner with each click, Robert toured the disordered and bloody landscape of Yeltsin and Putin's Russia. He read about how the oligarchs had written their own rules during Yeltsin's presidency, and how, when Putin came to power and demanded their loyalty, most gave it to him. Those who didn't were either imprisoned or exiled. Some were dead now, including Vanyashin. A few months before him Boris Berezovsky was found, also hanged, in the bathroom of an Ascot mansion. A year earlier another Russian, Alexander Perepilichnyy – Robert remembered Patrick mentioning the name – had collapsed while jogging, and there were numerous other whistleblowers and critics who seemed to have been made to pay for their actions: Alexander Litvinenko, poisoned with radioactive tea while his alleged murderer was given immunity to prosecution by being made a member of parliament; several journalists, including Anna Politkovskaya, who was shot dead outside her apartment; the opposition leader Alexei Navalny, threatened and repeatedly arrested; Mikhail Khodorkovsky, who was the richest man in Russia when he was thrown in prison a decade before. Looking at these half-familiar events in sequence, a connected narrative running from the end of the Soviet system to now – the wars in Chechnya; Putin's rise; the apartment block bombings; the sieges at the Moscow theatre and in Beslan; the dismantling of Yukos; Litvinenko's killing; the invasion of Georgia and the current conflict in Ukraine – Robert saw modern Russia as an extreme case of state-masterminded corruption and violence. If Patrick's story about being on the run was a fantasy, he had chosen a credible enough villain.

Robert thought about the way Patrick had acted when he first met him in the bookshop, and his nervousness as he scanned the restaurant courtyard the night before. He could do something with that hunted quality: the man on the run who doesn't know if he can trust his surroundings, waiting for a knock at the door. He stretched, fists clenched and arms held straight up, as if in triumph. 'You're mine, you paranoid bastard,' he said, and laughed. He looked at his phone. It was time to get the kids.

The next day, Robert's agent emailed with news of a radio commission for a short story. The money's terrible, but it's a good opportunity.

Hey Sally, Robert wrote back, finally a chance to remind people I exist. He tried rewriting the line several times to purge it of self-pity. That was harder than it should have been because, he eventually realised, he wanted to be pitied. Knowing this only made him feel worse.

The turnaround time was tight: three weeks, which meant he must be a substitute for someone who had dropped out. He didn't care, though. As it happened, he had a story he had drafted a couple of months earlier and put away. He thought three weeks might be enough time to make something decent of it. It was based on something he had heard at a dinner party. An Australian woman had told him about a menacing encounter she had with an American man when she had lived in Vietnam. The man turned out to be a secret service agent. Robert had been intrigued and when he next saw Angelique, the host, outside the Kita, he asked for the woman's number. 'Go for your life,' the woman had said when he told her he wanted to write a story based on what she had told him. 'Just remember me when you're famous.' He had emailed her a draft, mentioning that she would notice significant differences from her version. It wasn't like that at all, she replied a few days later, and explained point by point what Robert had got wrong. He never replied. He had only sent it to her as a courtesy; as far as he was concerned the story had become his the moment she told him it.

There was a postscript attached to Sally's next email: What news of the novel?

He wrote a long, despairing response describing all the wrong turnings he'd made, then deleted it. Things are starting to come together, he wrote, and sent it.

When he told Karijn she studied him silently for a second or two, then smiled. 'This is good, Rob!' They were sitting on the couch, both with their laptops open, half-watching *The Walking Dead* on the TV. She sat up, put her laptop on the coffee table and turned to face him. 'Are you excited?'

'Yes . . . kind of. As long as the commissioning editor doesn't think it's shit.'

Karijn clutched his hand. 'Rob, did you write a book?'

'You know I did.'

'I know you did,' she said, nodding. 'But do you know that?'

'It's not that I don't know it, but it feels like I need to start from scratch.'

'When I get a new piece in the workshop,' Karijn said, 'I only know if I've got the skills to do the job when I get inside it and begin to strip it down. But once you're inside it, you're inside it, and you start developing the skills you need to get back out. This job is a good thing to have. You can do it. You value your damage too much. You shouldn't.'

'I don't value it.'

'Value it, respect it, live in fear of it, whatever,' she said. She squeezed his hand. 'You need to ignore it.' She leaned against him and looked at the TV. A woman thrust a sword through a zombie's jaw and out the back of its head. 'I think this is really good timing. You could work on the story at the summerhouse.'

'We're not going for another two months. I've only got three weeks.'

'I mean now. We need to fix the water before winter. It's too much to ask Lars to take care of it.'

Their summerhouse in Sweden drew its water from a well. The week before last their neighbour, who kept an eye on the place for them, had called Karijn and told her that the pump had stopped working.

'What do you think?' Karijn said.

On the screen a boy stared wide-eyed as rotting fingers curled around a doorframe. Even with a plumber banging around, Robert knew four or five days there, with no kids, would be the equivalent of three or four weeks in Berlin. 'Let's do it,' he said. The boy ran, the door collapsed and a herd of zombies staggered into the room.

Robert and Karijn had bought a house in Hackney when they could just afford to do so and sold when its rise in value made a different kind of life possible. Robert would have been happy to stay, but Karijn had been eager to escape the city's polluted air since Sonja was born. A year before selling up, when Robert was still earning an advertising salary, they bought the summerhouse. For a while they talked about living there year-round but inner London to rural Sweden seemed like too extreme a change, so in the spring of 2012, with the London house sold, they moved to Berlin because it was cheaper, greener and less crowded. Robert quit advertising and earned some money from book reviewing and teaching workshops for an English-language creative writing school, but the majority of his time was supposed to be spent writing the novel – time that, for most of the past two years, he had squandered.

The move had been best for Karijn, who had hated the HR job she had in London while she was studying part-time for her upholstery qualification. When Robert had sold his book, he knew she had hidden the extent of her unhappiness in order not to taint his success. Now the situation was reversed and, dispirited as Robert was about his own situation, he was glad she was happier. The workshop she had joined had a good reputation, and she was busy enough to be generating a real income – too busy, certainly, to take any time off before the trip to Sweden they had booked for the end of November.

The house, which they visited two or three times a year, stood on the shore of Viaredssjön, across the water from the village where Karijn had grown up. She had no family there any more. Her father had died when she was a teenager, her sister lived in Stockholm and her mother had left the area a few years ago, moving back to the south of the country where she had been born. Karijn didn't have much contact with either of them, and aside from Lars they had little to do with anyone else at the lake. Parts of its shore were very built up and in the summer the water was busy with boats. In the winter, when the lake froze, there was skating, hockey, ice fishing, and people crossing it on kick-sleds or strolling across its surface beneath the low sun. But while all this activity could be seen from the summer-house, it mostly took place far in the distance. The lake was long and thin and the house was at its most remote corner. Other than by boat, it was accessible only by a twisting, unmetalled road that branched off the highway. In winter its isolation only grew, with the forested hillside at its back casting it in deep shadow for much of each short day.

Robert flew to Landvetter and picked up a hire car at the airport. He liked the drive to the summerhouse, Route 40 cutting through pine forest, and the smaller highway to Borås winding past meadows and lumber-yards and beneath dark granite bluffs. It was midday and the sky was a clear high blue. Robert had the rest of the day to himself. The plumber was coming with the new pump the next morning. He had allowed four days for the job, probably double what was necessary, just in case. He would fly home on Saturday.

Off the highway the road was muddy in its lower reaches – evidence of recent rain – and when Robert brushed past the leaves of the birch trees overhanging the drive he triggered a miniature shower of chill droplets. He was glad of the rain: the summer had been unusually dry. When they were last at the house the lake had sunk low, the lawn had browned, and the underbrush growing up in the spinney of trees that screened it from the road became brittle. On the infrequent occasions that a car drove past, slow-moving clouds of dust had rolled across the lawn like smoke.

Robert gazed across the road into the trees. Even in the light of early afternoon the forest was dark beyond its fringes. Turning away, he followed the flagstone path to the covered porch. He put his bag down beside the front door but didn't open it. Instead he stepped onto the lawn and skirted the house. The ground sloped towards the water, and on the lake-facing side he climbed the steps to the stone terrace that extended from the house. He cupped his hands to the picture window and peered into the living room, and the kitchen beyond it. Empty and still. Glancing down, he noticed some rot on the window frame. He pressed it with his finger to see how bad it was, the wood crumbling at his touch. 'Shit,' he muttered. He turned to face the lake. Across the water, beneath the thickly forested hillside, the sun flashed off cars as they sped along the road he had been on twenty minutes before. On the track that ran alongside the road he saw a freight train heading inland from Gothenburg. When the wind was northerly it carried the noise of traffic to the house, but today it was blowing offshore, coming through the forest strongly enough to pinch the blue lake water into small, sharp caps. Descending from the terrace, he crossed the strand of lawn that ran between the house and the water and walked onto the stone pier that jutted a few metres into the lake. They had a pier but no boat. The plan was to get one next spring, but he suspected that when the time came there would be other things they needed the money for more urgently. Down here the breeze was fresh and growing stronger. A gust flung drops of lake water into his face. Gripped by a sudden urge, he started undressing. When he was down to his boxer shorts, rubbing his arms – the sun was bright but the temperature was around eleven degrees, above average but not at all warm – he backed up to where the pier met the grass, then ran its length and threw himself inelegantly into the water. His breath came in shallow gasps. Throwing his head back he felt the frigid water clutch his skull. He yelled wordlessly, the violent sound echoing back from the shore. His body sparked with pleasure. He went onto his back and kicked his legs. The blank windows of the house stared down at him.

Robert swam back towards the pier. Another gust cut across the lake as he hauled himself out and he shivered as he made his way back around the house, eager to get dry. He brushed off his feet, opened the door and hurried to the bathroom, feeling the empty stillness of the house. No towels. He went into his and Karijn's bedroom and took one from the wardrobe. He dried himself vigorously, getting the warmth back into his chilled limbs.

With the towel around his waist, Robert opened the sliding door that led from the living room onto the terrace and jogged down to the pier to fetch his clothes. A cloud covered the sun and the lake's blue turned greenish-grey. He got dressed on the terrace, noting how loose and uneven some of the flagstones had become. The gaps between them were filled with yellow moss. He walked back through the house and out onto the driveway. From the boot of the car he pulled the groceries he had bought at an ICA just outside the airport. Unpacking the bags in the kitchen – pasta, tuna, hard bread, butter, tomatoes, some bags of salad and a six-pack of the low-strength beers that were the only alcohol available in the supermarket – the simplicity of what he had bought made him realise again just how much time to work he was going to have over the next few days. There was nothing to prevent him starting right away.

Four hours later, the sky over the lake slashed violet and red, Robert hadn't written a word. He was lying on the couch beside the picture window, most of the way through a book he had wanted to read for several months. It was a novel by a woman who had written about a strange real-life encounter with an ex-lover, and a sequence of subsequent conversations she had about it with her family and friends. She made it clear in the text where she departed from actual events and where she returned to them, but did so in a way that made everything – the declared fiction as well as the declared fact – feel much more real and consequential than a conventional novel. With the book splayed on his chest, Robert gazed at the lurid streaks in the sky. He saw a ghostwriter hired by an oligarch, a sudden death, a meeting in Berlin. He could sense how the book should feel, but without being able to hold it at the centre of his thought. It was like a flame guttering in a breeze, never still long enough for its precise shape to be captured.

He stood, shards of hard bread falling from his chest to the floor. As he stretched he moaned, the sound of it incredibly loud in the silent house. He looked out over the darkening water. The wind had died during the afternoon and the lake was smooth, reflecting the last of the light. Shadows crowded thickly in the garden and spread from the corners of the room. He saw in silhouette the nearest of several islands that dotted the lake: small, wooded, uninhabited. He had borrowed Lars's boat and visited it once, but the trip had been a disappointment. When he stepped ashore all he found was scrub and pine trees, and when he trod across the soft, needle-strewn ground, he felt all the mystery the island had held melting away. But then he looked back at the house and saw Karijn step onto the terrace. She stood still for a moment, turned her head as if someone had called to her and went back inside the house. He had felt then the eerie thrill of secret watching. He had planned to tell her about it, but when he got back he found he didn't want to. It was as if the secret wanted to be kept. Now the trees on the island were clotted into a black mass. He thought of someone watching from beneath them, as he once had. He thought of the runner staring up at him on his balcony. It was six thirty. Time to call home.

The plumber arrived the next day just after ten. He was tall, broad-shouldered and a little overweight, his blond hair shaved almost to a skinhead. 'Jag heter Jan,' he said when Robert opened the door.

'Jag heter Robert,' Robert replied. 'Kan du prata engelska?'

'Yes, of course,' Jan said.

Robert's Swedish was little better than his German. He had taken some lessons, but it hadn't stuck. Being here alone, without Karijn, made him feel his inability much more keenly. At the supermarket that morning, picking up a couple of things he had forgotten the day before, he had fumbled at the checkout as the teenage girl serving him smiled and spoke a bright, incomprehensible stream of words. 'Jag inte—' he stammered, before she switched to English and asked him if he wanted help bagging his groceries.

Robert took Jan down to the basement and flicked on the light. The basement's murkiness was intensified by the cheap wood panelling on the walls, which the fluorescent light soured to a dirty yellow. Karijn wanted to make the basement a playroom for the girls, but at the moment the main area was bare except for a couple of beanbags on the concrete floor and a stack of plastic storage tubs. 'Through here,' Robert said, leading Jan to the utility room. The pump stood below an unfinished wooden counter, riveted to the linoleum floor. It was an emerald-green metal tube, a metre tall, spotted in places with rust. Several rubber hoses ran from it. Jan kneeled and tugged at the hoses. He tapped the side of the tall cupboard to his right. 'Varmvatten behållaren?' he said.

'Engelska?' said Robert.

'Förlåt. Your hot water tank is in here?'

'Yes,' Robert said, opening the cupboard door. He stepped back, leaned against the tumble dryer that stood against the opposite wall and watched Jan continue his inspection of the pump.

'How deep is your well?' Jan said.

'Eighty metres, I think.'

'How far from the house?'

'It's on the lawn, by the driveway. Ten metres?'

Jan sniffed. He stood, sniffed again, hawked loudly and swallowed. 'I'll get my tools,' he said. 'You're not going to have water for as long as this takes. It's OK?'

'How long will it take?'

'If the whole pump needs replacing, the rest of today and most of tomorrow.'

Robert nodded. 'That's fine. I've got bottled water. I can bathe in the lake.'

'The natural way,' Jan said gravely. 'You're lucky.'

'Until you give me the bill,' Robert said.

'Bill?'

'The, ah, räkning?' Robert was pleased to remember the word.

'Räkningen, yes,' Jan said, patting Robert on the shoulder as he passed him. 'It will be very large.'

Robert went back upstairs and walked out onto the terrace. His notebook lay on the table, beneath it the printed pages of his story. He had come outside that morning in the dawn light, his cup of coffee steaming in the cool air. As he had read over his work he looked up occasionally to see the lake turning from black to grey to green, the trees' shadows shrinking and turning on the lawn. He was relieved he hadn't remembered the story as being better than it was. It needed a revision, but not a rewrite. He relished the prospect of a few days' work with an actual outcome at the end of it, rather than the days and weeks and months he had spent chasing ideas for a novel without getting anywhere. Beyond a daily Skype call, he could think only of the work. He told himself that being away from Karijn and the kids wasn't something to feel guilty about; it wasn't as if he had been lying the night before when, over a lagging, pixelated connection, he said how much he was missing them. The girls' faces had been thrust close to the camera while

Karijn stood over them. The phone must have been lying on the kitchen table; it gave him the impression that he was in a pit and they were peering down at him from its edge. The conversation was repetitive and broken up, one of those almost mindless exchanges that used to frustrate him before he came to consider them more as ritual than anything else. The occasional freezing of the image and delayed responses were all part of it, as certain phrases – 'You're frozen; you're gone . . . can you hear me now? Can you hear me now?' – became refrains slotted between bursts of improvised speech. What they were saying didn't matter; they might just as well have each repeated, 'I'm here, and I love you,' for the duration of the call.

After Jan had driven off to get lunch Robert made a sandwich, packed a bottle of water and his notebook in a rucksack, walked up the drive, crossed the empty road and entered the forest. The ground was hilly and pathless, covered in a green moss so thick that it closed over his feet with each step. A light rain began, ticking against the hood of his waterproof. He walked beneath tall, straight pines that stood at wide intervals from one another. Their lower branches were short spikes, their upper ones long and thick with needles, forming a canopy that turned the daylight murky green. Robert descended into a swale, at the lowest point of which enough water welled from the moss to soak through the uppers of his trainers. 'Shit,' he said, the word evaporating in the forest's stillness. He tried hopping between rocks to avoid the waterlogged ground. The rain grew heavier and colder. He wouldn't be having his lunch in the forest, or writing sat against a tree as he had intended, but he still wanted to press on further. If he turned back now it would feel like defeat. He climbed a steep slope, having to grasp at the ground several times and muddying his knees. Where the ground levelled he turned and in the distance, through the trees, he saw the lake lying grey under the rain. He realised that at that moment he was probably the only person in the forest. Solitude this total had been an addiction for him once. Ten years before, after an ugly breakup, he had seen less and less of his friends and eventually stopped going out at all. He realised then that being alone meant never having to say how he was, what he wanted, what he was thinking or doing. It was freedom from the self. Only when he was hired by the start-up where Karijn was working did he feel any desire to connect with someone again. It came on unstoppably, like a craving. The first time she came to his flat he immediately saw what a cramped, dirty grave of a place it had become.

The rain intensified. His jeans were heavy with water. He chose another route back to the house, one that took him out of the forest and onto one of the logging roads. To his left was a stripped hillside, the ground studded with tree stumps. A bulldozer stood in the middle of a clearing, slightly angled against a hillock as if its driver had climbed down from it just a moment before, but it seemed that no one was working today. He passed stacks of long, sodden logs and skirted puddles filled with water the colour of milky coffee, treading carefully on the slick, muddy ground. The cold sat deep within his soaked arms and thighs. Why had he continued on so far? He had somehow forgotten that there was no water at the house. He could boil mineral water and make a footbath from a plastic tub, he supposed. He laughed. Karijn would laugh at him, too. He heard the sound of an engine and looked behind him as a white van bounced down the track. He stepped onto the verge. The way the light struck the van's windows made it impossible to see inside the cab. For a moment he considered flagging it down and getting a lift, but it had already passed him. It rounded a corner up ahead and the noise of its engine faded, leaving only the hiss and spatter of the rain.

It rained for the rest of the afternoon, crackling on the roof, running in fringes from the eaves and driving a smoky mist up from the surface of the lake. After changing into dry clothes, Robert lay on the couch reading the Albie Cooper autobiography Patrick had written. By four thirty, Jan was satisfied that the faulty pump was the only thing wrong with the system. He said he would be back the next day with a replacement and that the job would cost twenty-five thousand kronor. Robert winced. 'But your water regulator still works,' Jan said. 'That's good. It would have been more otherwise. The "bill",' he added, smiling for the first time.

'Great news,' Robert said, unable to smile back.

That evening, after he had Skyped home to say goodnight to the girls and updated Karijn on the work – she groaned at the cost – Robert took Lars a bottle of Ardbeg to thank him for keeping an eye on the house. He brought one every visit; it was the only kind of payment Lars would accept. Robert used a torch to light his way, as there were no streetlights out here and the hilly road was crumbling and potholed. The potholes were filled with water from that afternoon's downpour and the rain-dark stones embedded in the road shone like birds' eyes in his torch beam. The wet air made the night feel especially cold and Robert pulled up the hood of his jacket as he walked. As if taunting him, the water that dripped through the tree branches sounded like the snap of a fire.

Lars was eighty and had lived in Borås for most of his life. When he and his wife retired from Ericsson, where they both worked as engineers, they had moved out here to a cottage on a bluff overlooking the lake. As the road rose steeply in the final climb before Lars's house, Robert remembered the way the old man had appeared in their driveway when he, Karijn and Sonja, just two then, were moving in. Almost immediately he had offered to keep an eye on the place for them when they weren't around, and Robert had written him off as a busybody they would never be rid of. Instead he had become invaluable and whenever a trip was imminent Robert looked forward to visiting him.

Lars's wife had died a couple of years before Robert and Karijn bought the summerhouse, and the old man told Robert that his children, one of whom lived in Stockholm and the other in Copenhagen, wanted him to give up the cottage and move into a home. 'I'll leave here in a box,' he told Robert most times he saw him. But although Robert wanted to keep Lars as a neighbour, he could see what the man's children were talking about; he was trim and in apparent good health, but he might be better off somewhere less isolated.

'Why? I'm not lonely,' Lars said as they sat in his living room, the low lamplight reflected in the large, black windows facing the lake. 'I have my music, I have the water, the forest. Should I trade all this for bingo? Fuck off, Robert.'

'You have a point,' Robert said, draining his glass and feeling the whisky's heat soak through him. He had waited until the end of the evening to bring the matter up. 'Just tell me if there's ever anything we can do to repay you, or just –' he raised his voice as Lars waved away his offer – 'just do for you, as neighbours.'

'Fine, fine,' Lars said. 'I like life alone, is that unreasonable? When I tell the boys that, they think it means I never loved their mother. Come on, I'll take you home in the boat.'

Robert often saw Lars's little motorboat out on the lake, but its mooring, a jetty that lay at the foot of a precipitous set of steps hewn from the bluff, was probably what made him most anxious about Lars's situation. As much as he liked the idea of cutting across the black water to his house – a three-minute journey versus a fifteen-minute walk – he didn't want Lars climbing those stairs in the dark when he returned. 'I feel like stretching my legs,' he said.

'Then I'll come with you.' Robert began to protest, but Lars spoke over him. 'My doctor insists. It's for my circulation, and I haven't been out today.'

They put on their jackets and scarves. It was a clear, cold night and the temperature was dropping. By the light of their torches they walked along the road, to the left the dark wall of the forest and to the right the lake, silvered by the distant half-moon. There was no wind; the water lapped softly against the shore. Maybe Lars had it right, Robert thought. It would be something to live here all year round.

'That is good whisky,' Lars said after they had walked in friendly silence for some time. A little way off, Robert saw the lamppost at the top of his driveway. 'Did I tell you I worked in Scotland once?' Lars said.

'Only every time I see you.'

Lars's laughter broke down into a cough. 'I used to have new things to say every day, can you imagine?' Robert's foot struck a pebble that rattled away down the road. An owl's hoot came from the forest. 'I could have taken care of the pump, you know,' Lars said.

Was he offended? Robert wasn't sure and was too tired to try and find out. 'I wanted to come out here, Lars. I need the time to write.' They stopped at the top of Robert's driveway, in the lamppost's bright white pool.

'How is it, to write?'

'Most days it's like driving nails into your eyes.'

Lars laughed. 'And the good days?'

'When I have a good one I'll let you know. Here it's special, though. Peaceful.'

'Yes,' Lars said with a sigh. 'Here no ill can abide.'

'What's that from?' Robert said.

Lars smiled and grasped Robert's shoulder. 'Thank you for the whisky, and the walk.' He turned and went back the way they had come. Robert watched him go, his torch beam like a hound now close to his feet, now bounding along the path ahead of him.

Jan came at nine the next day with the new pump. Around eleven Robert shouted down to him that there was coffee and he came and drank it on the patio where Robert was working. The breeze blowing in off the lake made the day even cooler, but Robert preferred to wear a jumper and scarf rather than go indoors. 'Have a biscuit,' he said, pointing at a plate on the table beside him. Jan took one, put the whole thing in his mouth and chewed purposefully as he looked out over the lake. 'How's it going?' Robert asked.

'Good,' Jan said, in a tone that made it difficult to continue the conversation.

Robert tried to work, but Jan's silence was the kind that emanated, colonising the air. He put the pages he had been working on underneath his coffee cup so they wouldn't blow away. 'How's business?' he said. 'Are you busy?'

'Always,' Jan said.

'Is it just around Borås you work, or do you go further afield?'

Jan took a sip of coffee. He put his hand over his eyes and rubbed it up and down. When he took his hand away he blinked a few times, as if the grey day were painfully bright. 'Around,' he said eventually.

'That's OK,' Robert said. 'We don't have to talk.' He returned to his work, but while Jan remained sitting on the patio looking at the lake he found himself reading the same lines over and over without being able to make sense of them. He began to write a note but couldn't get the words to form. He remembered a memoir he had read in which a novelist took an assignment as a war reporter. He felt so self-conscious about his lack of experience that when his handlers took him to the aftermath of a bombing at a market he could only stand in the carnage with his notebook and write things like *They are looking at me so I am writing in my notebook*. Eventually Jan stood, stretched and went back inside the house.

An hour later he came outside again to tell Robert he was going home for lunch. As Robert ate a sandwich, watching islands of shadow cast by clouds on the surface of the lake, he thought about what Patrick had told him that night at the restaurant. He picked up his pencil and began to note down what he remembered of the conversation. He heard Patrick's voice, urgent and low, telling him about Vanyashin. He remembered the way Patrick had looked around as if expecting to see Russian agents closing in, poised to strike.

Around three thirty, an hour after he had returned from lunch, Jan came outside and stood beside the table, his arms crossed over his chest. 'Is anything wrong?' Robert said.

Jan exhaled heavily through his nostrils. 'I need a part,' he said.

Robert waited, unsure of what was required of him.

'I thought I would finish now,' Jan said. 'But I need a part.'

'OK, so, tomorrow?'

'Not tomorrow. Friday. It's not so easy to get this part. It's . . .' and then he said something in Swedish that Robert didn't understand. 'It should have been with the pump, but it is missing.' He said it as if someone had died.

Robert told Karijn about it that night over Skype, mimicking the plumber's moroseness. He had spoken to the girls earlier and called back after they were asleep. 'You people,' he said over her laughter, 'you take solemnity to a whole other level.' He was sitting outside wrapped in a blanket, the brightness of his laptop screen deepening the darkness around him. In the distance he saw beads of light, white and red, move along the highway.

'We miss you,' Karijn said.

'I miss you guys.'

'Are you getting a lot done?'

'I've pretty much finished the story. Actually I've been kicking something else around.'

'What's that?' She was sitting at the dining table in the living room with her chin on her fists. Her glasses were pushed up onto her forehead, holding back the mass of her hair.

'Remember the guy you saved, the one I went to dinner with?'

'The bullshit artist,' she said.

'Yeah, the writer.'

'Bullshit artist. That's what you called him. But you liked him, didn't you?'

'I don't know about liked. But who turned out to be not a total nightmare, yes.'

'No,' she said, stretching the word teasingly. 'I know you, Robert Prowe. You liked him. You thought he was cool in some weird guy writer way.'

A cracking sound came from the darkness, near the water's edge. Robert tilted the laptop's screen down to get the glare out of his eyes, but he couldn't see anything.

'Rob? What is it?'

'I heard something. I don't think it's an elk, thank god.' Early one morning, not long after they bought the house, they had woken to see one tramping slowly across the lawn and nosing at the flowerbeds. Awed by its size, they watched it from their bedroom window as it grazed, then moved off into the mist. 'Anyway,' he said, raising the screen, but Karijn's face had frozen and distended, her jaw multiplying into a flood of overlapping squares. He drummed his fingers on the table, waiting for reconnection.

'—hear me now?' Karijn's voice returned a few seconds before the image unfroze.

'OK, fast, before I lose you again,' Robert said. 'I don't know how much of what Patrick told me is bollocks, but it's given me an idea.'

'So you're going to see him again?'

Robert paused. 'I don't think – I wasn't planning on it. You think I should?'

'If it's his story you want.'

'Maybe,' he said, 'but it's what I'm supposed to be able to do, isn't it: make stuff up.'

'But you want to write about stuff that happened to him, right?'

'Stuff he claims happened to him, yeah.'

Karijn rubbed her eye. 'I'm tired, Rob. The girls were shits tonight.'

'Sorry.'

'Maybe I'm not understanding something,' she said. 'You want to use this person's—'

'Patrick.'

'This Patrick person's own experience, that he shared with you, for the basis of a story.'

'A novel, yes.'

'You have to tell him, Rob. Of course you do. What are you thinking?'

Robert felt a heat and heaviness behind his eyes, a heaviness that almost pulled his head down onto the table. He felt it whenever Karijn spoke to him like this. The cracking came again, followed by the sound of something entering the water. He peered into the darkness, the interruption giving his anger time to recede. 'You're right,' was all he said. 'I'll talk to him.'

She nodded. 'You'll feel better for it, I promise.' She yawned. 'Holy shit, I'm tired. I have to go to bed.'

Her yawn triggered his. He blew a kiss and they ended the call. He stood and stretched and yawned again. He could feel the presence of the lake and hear the gulp of water against the pier, but all he could see of it was occasional flashes from a wavelet catching a distant car's headlights or, away to the east, the house lights that sent jagged white lines across its shifting surface. He turned and looked into the house, dark except for a single light above the kitchen counter. He felt exposed for a moment, too visible, as if he were being watched. He laughed at the childishness of his fear. 'Lonely, so lonely,' he called into the night. 'I am best so!' Instead of going inside he sat down at the table again and opened his email. I've been thinking about what you told me at dinner, he wrote. I think you've got a fascinating story to tell. If you're interested, I'd really like to talk more. He read what he had written. He deleted it all and wrote: This might be presumptuous, but I was thinking maybe you don't know so many people in the city and could use a friend? Let me know if you want to meet up. Or tell me to fuck off if you don't!

The next morning Robert was outside working before it was fully light, still in his pyjamas but wearing a coat, scarf and hat over them. He wrote the story out again one last time, from beginning to end, making corrections and additions as he went. When he was finished, he closed his notebook, stood and stretched, took off his coat, pulled off his sweater and T-shirt, dropped his pyjama trousers and walked down to the pier. The sun had risen but the day was gloomy. An ashy fog hung over the lake. His skin shrank into goosebumps against the sharp edge of the air. He strode to the end of the pier and kept walking, plunged into the cold, dark water, kicked up towards the surface. He broke through and gasped at the shock of it, his mind crystalline, and for a few pristine moments – too few – it was as if he didn't exist at all.

The sun was out in Berlin and when Robert called from Schönefeld Karijn told him they were getting ready to go to Mauerpark to meet Heidi and her daughter. He dropped his bag off at the apartment and walked over, enjoying the still-warm air.

'Pappa!' Nora yelled as she ran across the playground. They had spent days, maybe weeks, here, first on the swings, then on the climbing frame, and more recently around the large wooden pirates' galleon that sailed on a sea of green poured rubber. There was a vast sandpit, too: an abandoned excavation in which old scooters, broken action figures and plastic tools lay scattered and half buried.

Sonja called from the swings, 'Annie's here, Pappa, look!' Sonja venerated Heidi's daughter, who was eighteen months older than her. Sonja squealed as Annie gave her an energetic push. Robert saw Karijn and Heidi chatting a few metres from the swings. Heidi was one of the friends Robert had made in Berlin's clubs, the oddness of which still struck him from time to time; their lives were so different now. The women waved as he approached.

'It's good to see you,' Karijn said, hugging him tightly.

Heidi hugged him too. 'We're so old, Robert,' she said. 'I was just telling Karijn. I feel like a fucking grandmother.'

'You're not even forty,' Robert said.

She gasped with disgust. 'It's over. My children have destroyed me.'

For Heidi, something was always ending. Robert could remember the end of her twenties, an apocalyptic event to which several weekend-long sessions were dedicated; and her first pregnancy, throughout which she predicted she would never go out again and would be forgotten by all her friends. Now he never saw her without hearing at least one reference to the approach of her forties. In her opinion Berlin, too, was continually on the brink of change it would never recover from. When he and Karijn had decided to make the move and were choosing a neighbourhood, he told her how much he had enjoyed walking around Kollwitzkiez. She laughed bitterly. 'Prenzlberg used to be my place,' she said, jabbing her chest with her finger. 'Now it's Little Swabia. They want Berlin, but Berlin is too dirty for them, too crazy, so "quiet please, pick up your trash, please." They should fuck off back to Augsburg.'

Robert had laughed, but he regretted being part of the same process that drew affluent southerners north and made neighbourhoods increasingly sedate: just another newcomer who didn't want three-day parties in his basement. Like a lot of people who had arrived in Berlin since the millennium, he wanted the city he had first loved to continue existing, but not in his Kiez. In Mauerpark it was the same: he liked seeing clubbers sprawled in wasted constellations across the grass, but didn't want their weed smoke drifting over the rainbow-painted fence into the kids' playground.

'Where's Otto?' he asked Heidi.

'Frank took him to handball practice. He's trying to make someone in the family like it.'

'Mama!' Annie called. She was beside the fence in the back corner of the playground, where it met a crumbling brick wall. She was waving her hand urgently, an excited smile on her face. 'Ich komme,' Heidi called.

Sonja ran past and Robert knelt down and caught her with an outstretched arm. 'Did you miss Pappa?' he said, hugging her tightly as she squirmed to escape his grasp.

'Let me go,' Sonja shouted.

'You didn't miss me?' Robert said in mock outrage, digging his fingers into the flesh between her ribs and hip.

'Let. Me. Go!' Sonja wailed into his ear.

'Jesus!' he said, pulling his arm away. Released, Sonja ran off towards Annie. 'Fuck's sake,' he said.

'Robert.' Karijn put her hand on his shoulder.

'They're sick of me already.'

'Don't be like that.'

'It was a joke,' he said, but his voice was flat and unconvincing. He felt exhausted. The playground was filled with harsh screams. He thought of the measured beat of the rain falling in the forest. 'They'll miss me when I'm gone,' he said with false brightness. 'When they have only my complete works to remember me by.'

'It sounds like those are growing by the day,' Karijn said.

'Not that anyone cares.'

'I care.'

'Thanks, älskling, I know you do. But I need people who aren't married to me to care, too.'

'You need the person who's married to you to not feel like she's raising three children,' Karijn said, her voice strained. 'Write, don't write, but leave us out of the pity party. Can you do that? Can you be with us a little bit before you tell me, yet again, that your life is a disaster?'

'OK,' he said. He tried to say something more but couldn't. Instead he nodded to where Heidi and the girls were huddled by the wall. 'What have they found?' They walked over together. 'How are things at the workshop?' he said.

'Good. Uti's subcontracting me to work for some of her clients. It's super-busy. But I,' she said, turning to look at him, 'am taking it in my stride.' She stuck out her tongue.

'Point taken,' he said. He stopped and looked down. His daughters, Annie and Heidi were all speaking quietly to one another. 'What did you guys find?' he said.

Heidi stood, revealing a long, rigid bar of fur from which curled four shockingly pink feet. 'Dead rat,' she said.

Patrick replied that evening. Robert was slumped on the couch trying to read, white noise playing in his headphones, but he kept getting distracted by the moody German TV show Karijn was watching. It had something to do with time travel, or different dimensions. The characters kept meeting alternate versions of themselves, and spent most of the time looking baffled. He felt a vibration from his phone, which lay face down on the couch beside him. He saw light seeping from its edges. He picked it up and squinted at the too-bright screen, thumbing it dimmer as he read.

Meeting up sounds good. Out of the city until next week. Tuesday? I'll think of somewhere.

'He wants to meet,' Robert said, struggling up and holding his phone towards Karijn. She pushed his hand away and looked down her nose at the screen – in the past year she had become longsighted and it still surprised him when she pushed anything he showed her an arm's length away.

'You look like a scandalised great-aunt,' Robert said.

'I'm sure that would be funny if I understood what you meant,' she murmured, her attention on the email. 'Ah! Your weirdo crush. That's good.'

Robert hit reply. Great. Till next week.

By Wednesday morning Robert had the radio commission ready to send to Sally. After that the week passed slowly. The weather grew colder. Other than prepare for a one-day workshop he was running that Saturday, he had little to do. He would have liked to cancel – he found workshops draining, and it was becoming increasingly difficult for him to provide the required level of positivity about anyone wanting to write anything – but he couldn't say no to the money. He was grateful that rent control meant they still paid six hundred euro a month for their apartment, the same as it had been in 2012, and for now Karijn was making enough to keep them afloat. But they had the mortgage on the summerhouse too, and Robert knew if things didn't change soon, he would need to find another source of income. In London he had worked as a copywriter for nearly a decade. He didn't want to go back to it, but he would have to if he didn't deliver the novel.

Robert took a walk when the workshop broke for lunch. He wanted a pack of cigarettes. The venue, an airless basement function room, was in Charlottenburg, just off the Ku'damm. He was coming out of a Späti when he saw Patrick across the street, disappearing behind the swollen trunk of an old plane tree. When he re-emerged Robert called to him, but Patrick kept on walking. Robert followed him towards Ku'damm, walking fast to catch up. But as he closed the gap he remembered Patrick had said he was out of the city till next week. So what was he doing here? Patrick's head was down as he hurried along, his hands stuffed into the pockets of his black bomber jacket.

His plans might have changed, but Robert was suddenly convinced the other man had lied to him. As he followed him he felt the same strange, exquisite thrill he had felt as a child during games of hide and seek – simultaneously enjoying and dreading the thought that he might at any moment, were Patrick only to turn around, be caught. He moved faster as Patrick turned onto Ku'damm – for those few seconds when he was out of sight Robert felt panic rise in him. He turned onto a pavement crowded with shoppers; he scanned desperately before he saw Patrick some way down the street. Robert ran a little, closing the gap to a few metres. When Patrick stopped to wait at a crossing, Robert ducked under the awning of a grocery store and watched him from there. Part of him wanted Patrick to turn around and see him, to dispel the tension that had been building in him since he began his pursuit. At the same time Patrick's obliviousness made Robert feel charged with potency, as if he had the other man under his control. By the time the lights changed a crowd had assembled at the crossing. Robert saw Patrick's head bobbing within it, but the lights had changed again before he reached the kerbside and a bus rolled past and blocked his view. He stepped into the road and a scooter's sharp horn blast sent him stumbling back onto the pavement. When the light next turned green he ran across the street and looked first left, then right, but Patrick had gone.

On Monday night another email arrived: Soviet War Memorial Treptower Park 10 am. Please come alone. 'Fuck's sake,' Robert breathed. He didn't know if he could keep a straight face if Patrick persisted with this le Carré stuff. He didn't know whether he should meet him at all.

But on Tuesday morning, the sun a white spot in a grey plain of cloud, Robert walked to Schönhauser Allee and rode the S-Bahn to Treptower Park. On the train he checked the batteries on his voice recorder. He wanted to record Patrick, if he was able to do it surreptitiously. After a couple of stops a homeless man banged through the connecting doors into Robert's carriage. He was selling *Motz*. He gave a short speech and moved through the carriage, bowing slightly in front of each passenger to show them the magazine. The gesture struck Robert as courtly. Most of the passengers ignored him. 'Nein, Entschuldigung,' Robert said when the man bowed before him. He moved on without a word and stepped off the train at the next stop.

Standing before three paths on the cobbled ground outside Treptower Park station, Robert chose the middle way. It wouldn't take him directly to the memorial, but he was twenty minutes early. As he strolled past soaring birches and stands of oak and ash, he wondered why he had never visited the park before. Away to his left was the Spree. Ahead of him, through the trees, an almost deserted field of grass stretched into the distance.

He passed a concrete block with a blue-tiled porch: 'Figurentheater', the sign read. A billboard posted on the outside of the building showed a wood in silhouette, a number of troll-like figures marching through it. The path curved, leading him to a long, straight road busy with traffic. The road was lined with large plane trees, their trunks as pale as eucalyptuses. Across the road Robert saw the monumental stone arch that marked the entrance to the war memorial.

He passed a statue of a woman with her head bowed, a fist clutched to her chest. Behind her stood a line of thin, solemn poplars, like mourners at a grave. A crow cawed as it launched itself from one of the trees. The path began to climb. Fringed with weeping birches, their dangling branches brushing its stone slabs, the path ended between two huge, angular structures carved from red granite. They looked like angels' wings, or the leaves of an enormous gate. They opened onto a platform that looked down on the main body of the memorial: a paved rectangle the size of a football pitch containing a series of immaculate square lawns. At the far end of the lawns a grand flight of steps rose to the feet of a gigantic Soviet soldier. In one arm he carried a child, and in the other a broadsword.

Two women sat cross-legged on the platform's parapet. They glanced briefly at Robert as he passed. He heard one of them say, 'I said I wouldn't tell you, even if I knew.' Her accent was American.

'And what did she say?' her friend said, pulling a sucked hank of hair from her mouth.

Along both sides of the central lawns ran lines of engraved white stone blocks. Benches stood adjacent to several of these blocks. On one of them a man sat smoking. Patrick. As Robert descended the steps from the platform the long, low note of a train horn came from somewhere beyond the trees. A man ambled past, his dog running on ahead. There was no one else around.

Robert had to give Patrick credit for his choice of location. If he wanted to play at being a spy, or whatever this game was, then Treptower Park was a good place to do it. Patrick stared at Robert as he approached. He blew out a cloud of smoke, which seeped up into the branches of the linden tree that overhung the bench. 'Good morning,' Robert called, but Patrick only glanced in the direction from which he'd come and took another drag of his cigarette. Robert looked at the stone block beside him. It bore an engraving of a staggered rank of Soviet infantrymen, their rifles held at hip height, Lenin's profile in the sky above them. 'It's like a comic strip,' he said, sitting down on the bench beside Patrick.

'It's a sarcophagus,' Patrick said. 'There are five thousand Red Army soldiers buried here.'

Patrick's speech was barely inflected. Robert couldn't tell if he was angry or miserable. 'Incredible,' he said, trying to sound as if he meant it. 'I think I might have read that somewhere. You've been away?'

Patrick grunted.

'When did you get back?'

'Last night.'

Robert thought about telling Patrick he had seen him three days ago. He wanted to see what his reaction would be. But he enjoyed the feeling of secretly knowing more than the other man realised.

'There's a quote from Stalin carved into every sarcophagus,' Patrick said, tossing his cigarette butt on the floor and watching as the last few wisps of smoke rose from it. 'Did you read about that, too?'

Robert didn't know why Patrick was so testy. This was a different man to the one he had met a few weeks earlier. Instead of replying he took his tobacco from his pocket and began rolling a cigarette. When he lit it, Patrick finally spoke.

'Someone I know who's spent a lot of time in Russia says they're still working through Stalin.' He lit another cigarette. 'He says most of Russian history for the last hundred years has been either a myth or a lie. If anything doesn't fit they just make up a new story. The difference with Putin is he doesn't bother to pretend that he isn't making it up. So one man's found hanging from a tree, another gets poisoned, a passenger jet gets blown out of the sky – it doesn't matter what it is, it all gets sucked into the story. Invading Russian soldiers are "little green men" of unknown origin, assassins are sightseers, journalists are enemies of the state. "Make-believe on a national scale," is what my friend calls it. No verifiable truth, just rival versions of reality.'

'What happened to Vanyashin, to you . . . it must be really hard,' Robert said.

Patrick blew on the tip of his cigarette, the ember flaring. 'Why do you care?' he said.

The dog walker had gone. So had the women on the parapet. Robert and Patrick were alone, the cloud thick and still above them. The air was cool. For the first time that year, Robert felt the turn towards autumn. He hunched into his coat and shifted closer to Patrick. 'I just thought you might want to talk about it,' he said. 'If I'd been through that I'd be a mess. It's rough, really rough. But like I said, if I'm overstepping—'

'I appreciate the offer,' Patrick said. 'I do. But I feel like maybe the wisest thing would be not to talk about it at all. I shouldn't have told you anything in the first place.' He threw his cigarette on the ground, where it landed close to the previous one.

'Too late for that,' Robert said, smiling. He couldn't decide if Patrick's unwillingness to talk made it more or less likely that his story was a fabrication. Had he lied to make himself seem more interesting, and wanted to back out now he was being called on it? 'Look, I get it,' Robert said. 'I just keep thinking of something Karijn tells me.'

'Your wife,' Patrick said distractedly, straightening up on the bench. It seemed like he was about to leave.

Robert put a hand on Patrick's arm. 'Hear me out,' he said. 'When I get really stressed, which is often, she always has to remind me to talk about what's going on. I never want to, but she makes me. And it doesn't make things go away, but it' – he described a sphere with his hands – 'it gives it a shape, you know? And if it's got a shape, if it's no longer some amorphous mass, then it turns out I can deal with it better.'

Patrick studied the paved ground at his feet. Robert felt certain that this was the end. He was surprised by how desperate he felt at the prospect. Patrick looked up as if waking. 'It's cold,' he said. 'Let's get a coffee.'

'Tell me again how Vanyashin found you.'

'Through a guy called Tom Allan. An old university mate.'

'That isn't what you said before.'

'I didn't know if I could trust you before.'

'You don't know now,' Robert said, and smiled.

'All right. Hadn't decided to trust you.'

They were sitting across from one another in a leatherette booth in a cafe just outside the park. It was fitted out like an American diner. A doo-wop record was playing on a pink-and-yellow Wurlitzer.

'So, who's Tom?'

'A wild bastard. Welsh dad, Russian mum. A good guy

to know; smart. After uni he went to Russia and got a job in TV. He wanted to make documentaries. He stayed a long time, more than ten years. When he was back we'd meet up and he'd tell me all about how messed up it was.'

'What was messed up?'

'The whole fucking country. He was filming interviews with gangsters and billionaires and prostitutes. Reality TV stuff. They loved him because he was from the West and they all wanted to make TV like the West did it, so he was the golden boy.'

'Why did he come back?'

Patrick flicked a packet of sugar against his fingers. 'He got frustrated. He was there for the end of Yeltsin and the first few years of Putin. He got more and more interested in corruption, those types of story, but his bosses kept pulling the plug on him. He tried doing stuff on terrorism and it was the same. You know, he was actually on his way to Domodedovo airport when it got bombed. You remember that?'

'No.'

'A suicide bombing, three, four years ago. His crew were the first cameras there, but before they could do anything with the footage the FSB confiscated it. For analysis, they said. He never saw it again. After that he was done.'

'How did he know Vanyashin?'

'He made a film about these women who were like professional mistresses – they'd hang out in particular bars and clubs in Moscow looking for "Forbeses". That's what they called millionaires, oligarchs, whatever. Tom met Sergei at one of those places.'

'Shopping for a mistress?'

'I guess. They liked each other, they talked for a long time and then Sergei told Tom, "If anything about me turns up in your programme, I'll break your legs."'

'He was serious?'

'Tom thought so. But Sergei hooked him up with some other people who were happy to talk on camera, and after that they stayed in touch. After Sergei came to London he'd contact Tom – Tom was still in Russia – and ask his advice on this and that.'

'Like who to bribe to get an asylum application granted?'

Patrick looked uncertain for a moment then smiled. 'Well remembered. Yeah, I think Tom did help out with that. And when he came back to the UK Sergei hired him.'

'As what?'

'Fixer, adviser. He was still doing film stuff – promo videos for some of Vanyashin's companies, some documentary shorts that went up on YouTube. Sergei liked surrounding himself with lots of people with different skills. He kept everyone on retainers, so when he needed something they were always available. He would obsess over something for a week or a month, drop it for something else, then come back to it a month later, or a year, whatever. You could do what you liked when he wasn't using you, as long as you were there when he clicked his fingers.'

'Why didn't he get a Russian writer?'

'Well, think about it. He knew the book he wanted to write would have zero chance of getting published in Russia. He wanted it to reach people there, but he knew it could do more damage if he told the story in the West. The Browder stuff was happening, the Magnitsky Act.' Patrick looked at Robert as if his meaning was self-explanatory.

'I don't know what those things are,' Robert said.

'Sergei Magnitsky was an auditor working for this American guy, Bill Browder, who ran a big hedge fund in Russia.' Patrick sounded tired, as if he had hoped he would never have to explain all this again. It gave Robert the odd sense that he was reciting from a script. 'Browder's fund got seized by the government – they do that kind of thing all the time – and Magnitsky got arrested. He was beaten up, fell ill, didn't get the medical attention he needed and died in prison. Browder's been lobbying ever since for the people he says are responsible to be punished. What the Magnitsky Act does is ban any Russian officials who break human rights law from entering the States or using its banking system. It got passed a couple of years ago.'

'They can't use American banks, so what?'

Patrick frowned. 'Because that's what this is all about. Putin's officials take billions out of the economy and run the money through Cyprus or the British Virgin Islands or Panama, then use the cleaned cash to buy up real estate in Knightsbridge or Manhattan. Or here in Mitte,' he said, tapping the Formica table. 'Browder thinks that if you hit these people in their bank accounts, and block their access to their châteaux and penthouses, you're actually going to hurt them.'

'What do you think?'

'I think he's right.'

'And this is what Vanyashin's book is about?'

'No,' Patrick said, shaking his head, 'not – I mean, it might have touched on it, but we never specifically . . .'

Robert watched Patrick struggling to finish his sentence. It was puzzling how uncertain he seemed about what the book contained.

'It's hard to say exactly,' Patrick finally said. 'What he wanted changed from month to month. But yeah, he wanted to call out the government for looting the country. And he absolutely wanted it to hurt the big man.'

'He wasn't worried about what that might mean?'

Patrick smiled. 'The first time I met him he told me, "This book will be a blade, and I want it in Putin's arse right up to the hilt."'

'Where did you meet him?'

'At his house. Three years ago.' He sipped his coffee. 'Almost exactly three years ago. I can't believe it's been that long.'

He had taken the tube to Holland Park Avenue, crossed

the busy road and walked up a steep, narrow side street. The houses he walked past were probably worth millions, but they were terraced and small, more like posh cottages than mansions. He had been expecting something much grander. He passed a van with its cab light on. The uniformed man in the driver's seat stared at Patrick. As Patrick returned his gaze the man reached up and shut off the light, but Patrick could still faintly see his head turn to follow him as he passed. The logo on the side of the van read '1 Security'.

At the top of the hill, where the road took a sharp left, Patrick came to a long wooden gate set into a high, ivy-covered brick wall. Beside the gate stood a short, thickset man dressed in a black suit and thigh-length overcoat.

'Can I help you, sir?' the man said. He sounded French.

'I'm here to see Sergei Vanyashin.'

'Your name, sir?'

'Patrick Unsworth.'

The man spoke Patrick's name into his cuff. After a moment he nodded and motioned Patrick towards a smaller gate set into the wall behind him. The man removed one of his leather gloves and pressed his thumb to a panel mounted on the gatepost. The panel emitted a trill and the gate swung open. 'Enjoy your evening, sir.'

'Thank you,' Patrick said, stepping through the gate onto a gravel driveway that was far larger than anything he had expected: it curved around a circle of lawn, at the centre of which stood a tall plane tree strung with golden lights. The building was more like a manor house than something he expected to find at the top of a narrow London street. Dazzling white lances, thrown from spotlights, striped its exterior. It was Georgian, he thought, with what looked like some more recent additions. His footsteps crunched on the gravel as he made his way towards the large front door, the flickering light from the carriage lamps on either side of it casting golden pools onto its glossy black surface. Before he could knock, the door swung open. In the hallway stood a short, grey-haired man in black trousers and a white jacket, its gold buttons done up to the neck. 'Please come in, sir,' he said, bowing slightly as he spoke.

Patrick stepped across the threshold and stopped, uncertain where to go. A number of doors led off the entrance hall, but all of them were closed. Music thudded from somewhere in the house and he heard the distant sound of many voices. A chandelier cast a bright golden light, but its thick chains threw a web of shadow across the wall, the rug at his feet and the broad, carpeted staircase ahead of him. For a moment Patrick felt a childish urge to leap from one section of light to another, avoiding the channels of darkness.

'Mr Vanyashin has asked that you wait for him in the study,' the man said, opening one of the doors off the hallway. It led to a book-lined room. Spotlights glowed dimly, but the main source of light was a green-hooded lamp on a large desk.

'May I get you a drink, sir? A glass of champagne, perhaps?'

'Thanks,' Patrick said, although he didn't like champagne. The man – the butler, Patrick supposed – closed the door behind him. Too nervous to sit down, Patrick scanned the bookshelves. He saw a mixture of books in Russian and English. There were a lot of classics in modern Penguin editions – Dickens, Kipling, Lawrence, James – their spines mostly unbroken. In a low corner he saw a small selection of well-worn airport novels, their pages swollen from sun and seawater.

Patrick moved to the desk and inspected the books that lay on its leather-inlaid surface. There was a volume of Shakespeare's history plays and some books about Russia. One, *Dawn of the Oligarchs*, was splayed open on the desk. It had a group of Russian dolls on the cover. Patrick recognised Boris Berezovsky and Lenin, but none of the others. He flipped to the index and searched for Vanyashin's name, finding just a single entry, deep in the book. As he turned the pages to find it the door swung open and he dropped the book to the desk, as if he had been caught doing something wrong. The butler had returned, holding a small silver tray on which stood a solitary glass of champagne.

The man crossed the room towards Patrick. 'Mr Vanyashin regrets he has to keep you waiting a short while longer. Would you like anything else? Some food?'

'No,' Patrick said as he took the champagne. 'This is fine, thanks . . . uh—'

'You can call me Ted, sir.'

'Ted. Thanks.'

When Patrick was alone again he picked up *Dawn of the Oligarchs* and searched for the right page. *Others the Kremlin began to turn the screws on included the fertiliser magnate Igor Makarovich and fledgling media tycoon Sergei Vanyashin, whose Moscow Voice radio station had angered officials with its critical – read accurate – reporting of the* Kursk *disaster, and, shortly before he fled the country, the* Nord-Ost *siege.* That was it. He put the book down and picked up another: *The Gallic War* by Caesar. He crossed to a tawny velvet couch, took a gulp of champagne and opened the book at random. Caesar was demanding corn from some people called the Aedui, but one of the tribe's most powerful members didn't want to give it to him. When Caesar found out who it was, Patrick expected him to execute the rebel and seize the corn, but instead he held a series of meetings and solved the problem diplomatically. An editor's footnote, however, explained that the rebel was taken prisoner, formed part of a triumphal parade in Rome several years later, and was eventually 'put to death quietly, away from the public eye, in the typical Roman fashion'. Patrick put down his empty glass on a low table beside the couch. He yawned and stretched. He could sleep on this couch.

It was more comfortable than his bed. It was almost the size of his bed. His phone buzzed, a message from Tom: U here? Before he had time to reply the door opened again. 'Ted!' he cried. The champagne had loosened him up.

'Mr Vanyashin will see you now, if you'll follow me.'

Patrick followed Ted across the entrance hall and down a passageway that ran beneath the staircase. As they passed through a doorway into a thickly carpeted corridor, the dance music he had heard when he first entered the house grew increasingly loud, then became deafening as Ted opened a door into a huge and crowded kitchen. Men and women stood around a large granite island cluttered with bottles, packs of cigarettes and torn shells of champagne foil. There were people of all ages there, although it seemed to Patrick that the men were mostly older and the women younger. They were craning their necks to chatter in each other's ears, or facing one another and shouting over the music. Beyond them lay an open space in which five or six tall, extremely thin women, all wearing short black dresses, were dancing. They looked very young, Patrick thought. Still teenagers, perhaps. The room's far wall was made entirely of glass; ghostlike doubles of the women danced in its depths.

Patrick heard somebody shout his name and saw Tom shouldering his way towards him. He pulled Patrick into a bear hug. The smell of alcohol coming off him was so intense that for a moment Patrick thought it was cologne.

Tom released him, stepped back and turned towards the island. Patrick noticed Ted had disappeared. Tom delicately moved a shot of vodka through the air towards Patrick, his chubby fingers pinching the glass from above. 'I think I'm all right,' Patrick shouted.

'If you're not drinking,' Tom shouted back, 'you're not fucking all right, all right?'

Patrick took the glass, tipped the chill liquid down his throat and shuddered.

'Welcome to Russia!' Tom shouted. He held his arms above his head and thrust his hips from side to side in vague relation to the music. As a new song began a woman beside them, in vest top and hot pants, whooped and pumped her fist in the air.

'Where's Vanyashin?' Patrick said, but Tom ignored him. He had his eyes closed and was mouthing the song's Russian lyrics. Patrick gripped his shoulder. 'Where's Vanyashin?' he said into his ear.

Tom stared at Patrick for a moment as if he was going to ask him who he was, then his gaze sharpened and he barked out a laugh. 'Come on, I'll take you to him.'

Tom ploughed through the press of bodies, tugging Patrick along behind him. Passing the dancefloor Patrick saw that a man in a dark silk shirt, unbuttoned to the navel, had joined the young women and was dancing towards them groin first, his arms held out as if for an embrace, fingers snapping on the beat. One of the women stopped dancing and leaned against a long table covered in platters of food: whole grilled fish, heaped salads, sliced meat and glistening black mounds of caviar. 'Are you hungry?' Tom shouted as he opened a door leading from the kitchen.

Patrick shook his head and followed Tom into a whitewashed passage that felt like a service area rather than part of the main house. Patrick closed the door behind them. As it shut, the noise from the kitchen became almost undetectable.

Tom smiled. 'Soundproofed,' he said. 'Sergei gutted this place and rebuilt it from the ground up. Wait till you see his tent.'

'Tent?' Patrick said, but Tom, walking on ahead, didn't seem to hear. The passageway turned a right angle and ended at a flight of stairs descending to a lower level.

'Before I forget,' Tom said, 'do you still smoke?'

'Yeah, sure,' Patrick said, reaching for his cigarettes.

'Not around Sergei you don't,' Tom said, pushing the pack away. 'He hates it, which is pretty fucking weird for a Russian. He tried a ban, but he knows too many chain-smokers – Berezovsky went apeshit about it. His compromise is that no one smokes within five metres of him.'

'Even Berezovsky?'

'Everyone except Boris Abramovich. Now,' Tom said, beginning to walk down the stairs, 'welcome to the bunker.'

Patrick concentrated on his breathing as he followed

Tom. He had expected a formal meeting, not a labyrinth beneath a house party. At the bottom of the staircase a short passage led to a door. Tom pushed a button and after a moment the door clicked open. They stepped into a vestibule, thickly carpeted and hushed. Patrick saw another closed door ahead of them, beside it a man who, from his suit to his jawline, looked identical to the guard at the front gate. There was a moment's silence, as if no one wanted to speak first.

'Jesus,' Tom sighed wearily. 'Tom Allan and Patrick Unsworth to see Mr Vanyashin,' he said.

'Lift your arms please, Mr Allan,' the man said. He ran his hands along both of Tom's arms then down his trunk. As he crouched to pat down each trouser leg, Tom swivelled around. 'This guy sees me all the time. He saw me half an hour ago, and we still have to go through this bollocks.'

'Mr Unsworth,' the man said and repeated the search. He paused at Patrick's jacket pocket. 'What is this?'

'Dictaphone,' Patrick said. 'Voice recorder.'

The man stepped back and held out his hand. 'Can you remove it, please?'

Patrick took the recorder out of his pocket and gave it to the man.

'It will be returned when you leave,' the man said. He indicated that Patrick should raise his arms again, stepped forward and finished frisking him. 'Thank you, gentlemen,' he said as he stood. He turned and rested his thumb on a pad beside the door. It chirped and the door swung open.

Patrick followed Tom into what appeared to be more a tent than a room. The walls were covered in rust-red fabric, curving strips of which ran from the edges of the room to the centre of the ceiling. He felt as if he were standing inside a miniature big top. The floor was covered in animal hides and at the centre of the room was a circle of low couches on which three men reclined, all of them wearing shirts, suit trousers and velvet slippers. One of them, whose round belly strained against his shirt, was smoking an electronic cigarette. Another, short and bullish, his black hair scraped back to reveal a pronounced widow's peak, stood when he saw Patrick and Tom. His shirt was deep blue, pinstriped and white-cuffed: a banker's shirt. His trousers, clearly tailored, had a silver sheen. 'Patrick?' The man's voice was low and strong. He looked at Tom and smiled. 'Is this the great Patrick Unsworth?' His accent was thick. 'Ahnsvurt,' he said.

'The one and only, Seryozha,' Tom said, waving his hand with a parodic flourish. 'Patrick, this is Sergei Aleksandrovich Vanyashin.'

Patrick stepped forward, stumbling as he caught his foot on the edge of one of the overlapping rugs.

'You've been enjoying my champagne,' Vanyashin said, reaching out to help Patrick regain his balance. 'I'm glad. I don't trust men who don't drink.' He turned and shouted something, a name or a command, Patrick couldn't tell, and a man wearing the same uniform as Ted entered from a side door hidden behind a drape of the red cloth covering the walls. Vanyashin spoke briefly to him in Russian then turned back to Patrick. 'Sit,' he said, waving him towards the couches.

Patrick sat, conscious of the other two men watching him from where they lay. The fat one's eyes crinkled as he dragged on his cigarette, its LED tip lighting up. The other, tall and slim, with a shock of blond hair, gazed at Patrick in a way that reminded him of a cat, evaluating and aloof. Both men looked about Vanyashin's age, which, Patrick had learned from the internet, was fifty-one. Tom threw himself onto a couch. Vanyashin sat back down on his, the only one, Patrick noticed, that was draped with a sheepskin. Vanyashin pointed at the fat man. 'That is Uri,' he said. 'And that is Aleksey.' The men nodded but didn't speak. Vanyashin said something to them in Russian, Uri replied, then Aleksey spoke rapidly, moving his hand backward and forward in time with the pattern of his speech. He chopped a length of air into separate sections, looking intently at Vanyashin as he did so. As the men continued speaking Patrick saw Tom lie back on his couch and close his eyes. He would have liked to do the same but felt he should make a show of interest in what the other men were saying, despite not being able to understand them. Given how loose everyone seemed, he wondered how long ago this party had started.

The waiter returned with a tray holding a bucket filled with ice and four bottles of what Patrick supposed was vodka. Around the bucket stood a cluster of short glasses, clouded with frost, and a heaped bowl of short cucumbers. The waiter placed the tray on a large, low table between the couches, clearing away the plates of half-eaten food and crumpled napkins scattered across it.

As Vanyashin, Uri and Aleksey continued to talk, Patrick looked around the room and realised what it was supposed to be: a Roman tent. The clasps that gathered the fabric against the walls were imperial eagle heads. The couches they lay on, and the tables beside them, had the distinctive curved legs Patrick remembered from the illustrated history books of his childhood. He remembered what he had read earlier about Caesar and the Aedui. He laughed to himself. What the fuck was this? As if Vanyashin had heard him, he broke off his conversation and asked, 'What do you think of my campaign tent?'

Unprepared, Patrick nevertheless began to answer, stammering in the hope the sounds he was making would become words.

'It's a . . .' Vanyashin started and stopped, eyes boring into Patrick as he searched for a word. 'It's a folly, I know this word,' he said, smiling. 'I have a tremendous interest for Caesar. Did you know I directed Shakespeare's play?'

'I didn't know that,' Patrick said, sitting up, supposing the interview had begun.

'Yes, I was a theatre director. I studied. This was in Soviet Union and there was a very high standard. Somehow the education system was still working even when nothing else was. In my production Andropov was Caesar. This was eighty-four, eighty-five so not safe, not a wise thing. When my teachers understood what I was doing, they threw me out.'

'I was reading a book upstairs, about Caesar in Gaul?'

Vanyashin nodded, as if he had been expecting this. He stood, pulled a bottle from the ice and twisted off the cap. 'How can someone not admire a man who was a genius in so many different ways?' He poured and passed a glass to each of them. 'Soldier, politician, administrator. And' – he raised his glass, prompting the others to do the same – 'a great writer, too. Hail Caesar!'

Patrick sipped from his glass, but when he saw the others upend theirs he felt he had no option but to do the same. It was a large measure and he coughed after he swallowed, the taste of the cold, peppery liquid flooding back into his mouth. Tears filled his eyes.

'But a strange thing happened,' Vanyashin said, ignoring Patrick as he coughed again. 'After he defeated Pompey, the moment when Shakespeare begins his play, Caesar's good judgement' – he clicked his fingers – 'disappears. He celebrated his victory over Pompey – a hero of the Republic – in a way that offended the Romans. He appointed his friends to powerful positions, he became more and more a . . . Tom, diktator? Is same word?'

'Da, Seryozha,' Tom said, leaning towards the table to take a cucumber from the bowl, 'diktator is dictator.'

'Dictator,' Vanyashin said, seeming to savour the word. 'Just like Number One in the Kremlin, who has surrounded himself with siloviki and turned his back on his country.' He stood and went around with the bottle, refilling each glass to the brim. 'If I could direct the play now Caesar would be Putin of course, because the question it asks – who should be leader, by what right are they leader – it's perfect, yes?'

'But Medvedev's the president now,' Patrick said, pleased to prove he knew something relevant.

Vanyashin shook his head and pointed the neck of the vodka bottle at Patrick. 'Dimochka has been keeping the seat warm, that's all.' He lifted his glass and shouted: 'To the return of Vladimir Vladimirovich to the presidency, and to each dictator a Brutus!'

Patrick struggled to keep the next glass down. His throat burned. Uri threw his head back and hollered like a cowboy. Aleksey laughed. Patrick sat, rested his elbows on his knees and hung his head. He felt like he'd been punched.

Vanyashin rubbed Patrick's back with, Patrick thought, surprising tenderness. 'But our friend in the Kremlin,' Vanyashin said, 'shares Caesar's faults but possesses none of his talents. Do you know what makes Caesar's writing exceptional, Patrick?' Vanyashin, rubbing Patrick's back vigorously now, didn't wait for a reply. 'His material,' he said, his speech quickening. 'A writer is only as good as his material, you agree? That's why you want to work with me, because my material is best: twenty-four fucking carat material.' Vanyashin stopped rubbing, Patrick's back hot from the friction. He sat down beside Patrick, wrapped his hand around the back of his neck and pulled him close. 'Caesar was an invader,' he said, whispering the words in Patrick's ear. His breath smelled of vodka and beneath it something gamey that Patrick struggled not to flinch away from. 'He took his legionnaires to the edge of the known world, then past it. The oligarchs did the same. We put Russia on a new course and changed the world. The oligarchs were raiders. Generals. True heroes, really. Many came from nothing. I drove a taxi. Not even Lada but Moskvitch! Fucking cardboard car. And now,' he looked around and smiled, his voice growing loud again, 'now we've invaded you. We own your football clubs. We own your newspapers. We live in your best neighbourhoods. You know, my wife goes to Asprey to buy necklace and Russian-speaking girl is there to help her. Specially hired! Harvey Nichols the same. We are here now and we do not go away. People want to know more I think. About us, about Russia, about our friend in the Kremlin and his money. In particular his money, who he takes it from and gives it to. Not kompromat bullshit like he's fucking her, he's fucking him. Not this. Bank accounts. Offshore fortunes. This is what people should know. So, we'll write bestseller and everyone will talk about it.' He clapped Patrick hard on the back. 'What do you say?'

'OK,' Patrick said, dazed from the vodka and the speech.

Vanyashin turned to Uri and Aleksey, a look of confusion on his face. 'OK?' he said. The two men looked at Patrick.

'I mean—' Patrick began, alarmed he had said something offensive, but Vanyashin held up a finger to silence him. He took another bottle from the ice bucket and twisted off the cap.

'In Russia we don't say "OK",' Vanyashin said, filling first his glass then Patrick's. 'In Russia, we shake hands' – he offered his hand to Patrick and Patrick took it – 'and we share a drink. Za vstrechu, Patrick.'

'Za . . .' Patrick began.

'Vstrechu,' Vanyashin said.

'Vistretchu,' Patrick approximated. He closed his eyes and forced the drink down.

Again Vanyashin squeezed Patrick's neck and pulled him close. 'I have a secret that will bring him down,' he whispered. He raised a finger to his lips then leaned away. 'Tom, show Patrick out.'

The security guard returned Patrick's recorder and he and Tom climbed back up the staircase. Grazing the wall, Patrick realised how drunk he was. At the top of the stairs, where the passageway turned, Tom stopped and grasped Patrick's shoulder. 'You all right?' he said.

'Yeah. Pissed.'

'Bit of a freight train, isn't he?'

'A bit,' Patrick said and laughed. He leaned back against the wall and pressed his hands to his face. 'That was a lot of fucking vodka.'

'You'll get used to it. Next time do a couple of lines first, then you can drink like a fish.'

'Sage.'

'Anyway, he likes you. That's all that matters.'

'You think so? I managed to show him I know fuck all about Russian politics.'

'That's just research.'

'The only other thing I did was stare.'

'Like a good ghost,' Tom said. 'If he hadn't approved, you'd know about it.' Tom drew close and lowered his voice. 'Between you and me, Sergei can be a proper cunt sometimes.'

'Show me a billionaire who isn't.'

Tom laughed and punched Patrick's arm, hard enough to deaden it. Patrick felt his last reserves of energy seeping out of him; it took an effort not to fall back and slide down the wall. 'What time is it?' he said.

Tom shot his wrist free of his suit jacket. 'Just after midnight.'

'Nice watch,' Patrick said. It was black and silver, its large face packed with dials.

'It's a Breguet,' Tom said. 'Engine-turned dials.'

'I have no idea what that means, but it sounds impressive.'

'Sergei's a generous man if you're on the team, as I'm sure you'll find out. Come on, let's get a drink.'

'I need to sleep.'

'Don't give me that.'

'I mean it. I'm done.'

Tom held his gaze for a moment without speaking. 'This time, I'll let you go,' he said. 'Next time won't be so easy. I'll get you a cab.'

They made their way back up the passageway. As Tom opened the door to the kitchen the music and voices roared out, like pent-up water suddenly released and rushing to meet them. The improvised dancefloor was crowded now. People danced alone, in pairs, in threes and fours. In the middle of the crowd a man held a champagne bottle aloft as he jumped and a column of froth hung frozen for a moment before raining down on the dancers, some of them crying out in joy and some in protest. Above them a woman stood on the table where the food was arrayed, shuffling to the music and flicking ash from her cigarette onto the caviar, the salads, the fish. A pancake was impaled on the spike of her heel. The glass doors had been thrown open to the night and people danced outside on the floodlit deck, shouting to each other above the music, their breath and the smoke of their cigarettes clouding the cold air.

Assailed by the noise and the movement Patrick staggered into Tom, who threw an arm around his shoulders.

'Don't black out on me, scribe.'

Tom's arm was heavy. Patrick shrugged it off. 'I'm fine,' he said. He just needed to be somewhere quiet. He moved through the dancers and past the kitchen island where heads bobbed over lines of white powder, stark against the black granite. He pushed through a group of people knotted around a man, stripped to the waist, who was chanting something as he did rapid push-ups. At the door he had to turn sideways to move past a couple kissing, the man grinding his hips manically against the woman. He walked back along the corridor to the entrance hall and stopped there, dazed. Voices came from a room off the hallway, opposite the study where he had waited earlier. He looked through the open door and saw two men, one in livery, the other in a sober charcoal suit, lifting a woman in a tight red dress onto a black leather couch. The woman's long legs dangled from it and onto the floor. Her feet were bare. Her head lolled.

Patrick realised that he knew the man in the white jacket. 'Ted,' he said.

'What's going on?' said Tom, emerging from the kitchen corridor.

Ted looked blankly at Patrick. He walked to the door and closed it in his face.

'Come on,' Tom said, pulling his phone out, 'I'll call you a cab.'

'What about an ambulance?' Patrick said.

'Leave it. That was Sergei's doctor in there. He'll handle it.'

'Are you sure? Shouldn't we . . .'

'She probably just needs to sleep it off. Where shall I tell this cab it's going?'

'I don't want a cab,' Patrick said. He was surprised Tom was so unconcerned about the situation.

'It's your shoe leather. Good work tonight.'

'Thanks for the introduction,' Patrick said. 'I appreciate it.'

'What friends are for. If it all works out, that is. If it goes tits up, it was never anything to do with me.'

Patrick smiled, but paused as he opened the front door. 'Check on her, Tom, won't you?'

'Sure, I'll do it right now. But don't worry.'

It was cold. Patrick heard the door close behind him as he stepped onto the drive. From the other side of the house came a muffled beat and the massed tangle of voices; laughter; a bellow of celebration or rage. He walked away, his footsteps on the gravel sounding, he thought, absurdly loud. At the gate, the same guard kept watch. 'Good evening, sir,' the man said, his breath steaming.

'Goodnight,' Patrick said. He set off down the hill, stepping a little heavily in an attempt to walk in a straight line, feeling the guard's eyes on his back. He saw a policeman walking up the centre of the street, a leashed Alsatian a few paces ahead of him. He wondered if he should tell him about the woman, ask him to call an ambulance, but as the man drew near Patrick saw that he wasn't a policeman but a private security guard, a large 1 emblazoned on his stab vest. The man held Patrick's gaze as they approached each other.

'Evening, sir,' the man said, his words sounding more like a challenge than a greeting.

'Evening,' Patrick said.

At the bottom of the hill he saw the tube station was closed for the night. Hunching against the cold, he began walking towards Shepherd's Bush to find a bus home.

The sky above the city was dull as a pebble. Robert had a headache. He made both the girls cry that morning, yelling at them when they ignored his repeated requests to brush their teeth and put their clothes on. Things seemed fine by the time he dropped them at the Kita – his anger and their misery had quickly disappeared once they got out of the apartment – but disgust at his behaviour weighed on him as he walked back down Schönhauser Allee to the Balzac opposite the shopping centre, the counter crowded with people on their way to work buying takeaways.

He found a table, opened his laptop and started reading what he had worked on after his meeting with Patrick. At first he had written down as much of what Patrick had told him as he could remember. Then he wrote it again and rewrote it, adjusting emphases, adding inventions and making deletions. Each pass made it feel more like it was his, but he wanted to talk to Patrick again. He knew that the more he had from him, the better it would be. *How are things?* he wrote in an email. *My kids are driving me crazy and I need some adult conversation. Shall we get breakfast this week?* If Patrick kept talking, he thought, he would keep writing.

He reread the most recent couple of pages, which ended with Patrick leaving Vanyashin's house. He wondered if the Roman tent was too much. As soon as Patrick had told him about Vanyashin's obsession with Caesar he knew he wanted to make more of it. Robert had gone to Saint George's one afternoon and flicked through a copy of *The Gallic War*. Closing the book, he tried an experiment: the page he opened it to would be the page Patrick opened it to. Reading it now he wondered if he should try and find a different passage, but he wanted to respect the process he had decided on. He idly imagined being interviewed about the book and telling this story about it. Refocusing on the screen, he shortened Patrick's exchange with Tom at the front door and gave Patrick the thought of telling the policeman about the unconscious woman. Satisfied, he saved the file on his laptop and to a thumb drive he always used to back up anything important.

He called up the front page of the *Guardian*. Nigel Farage was demanding that HIV-positive immigrants be kept out of Britain. Cunt, Robert whispered, his agitation growing as he read the article. He thought of the day the previous year when he and Karijn had taken the girls to Oranienplatz to see the asylum-seeker camp there. At the entrance to the camp Karijn showed the girls a painted sign: 'kein mensch ist illegal'. 'That means "no person is illegal",' she said. 'Everyone has a right to live in freedom.' It had rained the night before and wooden pallets had been laid across the obliterated grass to make a track.

They walked through a jumble of tents, some with clothes hung to dry over their guy ropes, one with a number of shopping trolleys parked outside it, all filled with bulging plastic bags. In one section of the camp a banner hung between two trees: 'Lampedusa village in Berlin'. Many of the tents had plastic chairs arranged outside them. In front of one, beneath a rickety awning, there were even two faux-leather Chesterfield armchairs angled slightly towards one another, as if they stood in a study and not on the boggy ground of a Berlin square.

A man playing a flute in the doorway of his tent nodded his head and gave a trill when he saw the girls. Others turned away. The camp had become an exhibit of sorts and Robert worried that it was being treated like another stop on the Berlin tourist trail, slotting in between Checkpoint Charlie and Tempelhof, and that they were part of that process just as they were part of the gentrifying wave. While it was the symptom of a modern emergency, OPlatz, as the encampment had become known, also felt like a throwback to an older, more radical Berlin, which was another reason why Robert had wanted the girls to see it. When he explained to Sonja who these people were, and that they didn't have anywhere to live, she looked at him and said, 'Can they come and live in our house?' He knew she didn't know what she was talking about and how easy it was for him to be sentimental about things his daughters said, but he thought it was one of the kindest questions he had ever heard. More kind than he was able to be. He might have bought the refugees a bag of groceries, but he had never offered any of them a bed. Now they and the camp were gone, and Oranienplatz was a normal city square again.

'How was your day?' Karijn asked when she came in.

Robert was sitting at the kitchen table reading a book and drinking a beer. 'Good,' he said. 'How was yoga?'

'A delight,' Karijn said, opening the fridge. She pulled out a bag of carrots and a tub of hummus.

'Chakras sorted?'

'You ought to try it,' she said, taking the peeler out of a drawer. 'It would give you some time away from your troubles.'

'I don't know what I'd be without my troubles,' he said.

Karijn rolled her eyes and bit the end off a carrot.

'Have you spoken to Lars?' Robert said.

Karijn nodded as she chewed. 'He went over yesterday. He said everything's working.'

'All praise the weird plumber.'

'We should think of what we need to sort out before we go. It's only a month away.'

'Yeah,' he said, unable to keep a note of reservation out of his voice.

'Or . . . no? What?'

'No, yeah, we should. It's just this Patrick stuff. Lots to do on it.'

'My god, Rob, you'll have plenty of time to work. Just roast a sausage with us in the forest from time to time, OK?' She put the hummus back in the fridge. 'How's it going with him, anyway?'

'Pretty good.' Karijn sat on his lap and he put his arm around her waist. 'I've got most of what I need, but I want to ask him some more questions.' He drew her more tightly towards him and laid his head against her breast. He felt her heartbeat.

'How is he with you writing about it? Did you have to persuade him?'

He heard her voice twice, a little muffled from above and as a bass vibration through her chest. 'I think he's flattered,' he said, keeping his head pressed against her body. He didn't want to look at her as he spoke. 'To be honest, he loves the sound of his own voice. It's getting him to shut up that's the problem.'

'Maybe invite him for dinner.'

'No,' he said automatically. He hadn't expected her to suggest it.

She laughed. 'Is it such a terrifying thought?'

'No, it's—' Robert tried to think of the most off-putting response. 'I guess it's just that I don't know how much of what he's telling me is genuine. It's a good story, but you remember what he was like the night we met him. I'm worried he might be a bit, I don't know, unpredictable.'

Karijn pulled away and looked at him. 'You don't think he's actually dangerous, do you?'

Robert drew in a deep breath, as if evaluating. 'I'd say probably not,' he said slowly. 'But I'd want to be certain before I invited him into our home.'

Karijn ran her hand into Robert's hair and tilted his head up. She looked directly into his eyes. 'If you ever feel like you're unsafe, you get away from him, OK? Don't try and be brave.'

'Definitely,' he said.

'Promise.'

'I promise.'

It was more than a week before Robert saw Patrick again, and then only after two cancellations. One came at 3 a.m., the text reading only: Can't do tomorrow, and another after Robert had already been waiting for an hour at a cafe in Wedding. So he felt relieved when he saw Patrick walking down the tree-lined street in Charlottenburg. The place Patrick had chosen was in a Kiez Robert had never visited before, so he had taken the opportunity to get off the S-Bahn a couple of stops early and have a look around. The last few days had been cold enough for him to get his winter jacket out of the wardrobe; the plane trees lining the street were finally losing their leaves. The morning was bright and mild, though, so Robert had chosen to sit at one of the cafe's pavement tables, the chairs around which were draped with tartan blankets. 'It's good to see you,' he said as Patrick approached.

Patrick glanced at the other people seated outside, then turned and looked back down the street in the direction he had come. 'Let's go inside,' he said.

Robert smiled. 'It's November and the sun's shining,' he said. 'Wait till you've lived through a Berlin winter. You'll never sit inside when the sun's shining.'

'Let's go inside,' Patrick repeated.

Robert sighed, but picked up his bag and coffee. He followed Patrick to the table furthest from the door, beside a corridor that led to the toilet.

Patrick ordered a cappuccino. 'I'm sorry about not turning up the other day,' he said. 'I was being followed.'

'Are you serious?'

'Serious,' Patrick said

Robert resisted the urge he felt to laugh. 'What did you do?' he said, sounding as concerned as he could. He studied Patrick closely as he answered.

'I wandered. I wasn't going to bring them to where you were. I took a couple of trains, got on a tram. Eventually I lost them.'

'You lost them,' Robert said. 'Impressive! I mean, they must be pretty expert at tailing people, right?' He worried he had gone too far, that Patrick would detect sarcasm in his voice, but the other man only shrugged in modest acceptance of the compliment.

The waiter set Patrick's coffee down. 'Danke,' Patrick said. 'You mentioned your kids were doing your head in. Has it got any better?'

'They're fine,' Robert said. 'But I'm incredibly glad you're not them, or a parent. It gets a bit suffocating sometimes, all the kid stuff.'

The bell attached to the cafe's door rang and Patrick's eyes snapped towards it. Robert turned and saw a mother with a pram trying to negotiate the narrow opening. The waiter went over to help her. Robert saw the tension in Patrick's body. 'It's OK,' he said. 'It's all right.'

Patrick forced a laugh. 'Yeah,' he said. 'Sorry.'

'What happened after that first meeting with Vanyashin?' Robert asked lightly. 'Did you start on the book straight away?'

Patrick didn't answer. He tore open a tube of sugar and slowly tilted it above the foam of his coffee. The golden grains briefly hissed as they slid from the tube. 'Maybe it's better we don't talk about that stuff,' he said.

'Hey, absolutely,' Robert said. 'Sorry for asking. I just find it fascinating. How do you go from meeting someone to writing a book about their life?'

'Trade secret,' Patrick said. He smiled. 'It's always different, to be honest. But with Sergei it was . . . challenging.'

'Oh yeah?'

'Yeah, but I didn't know how challenging at first. In fact, it started off really well. The day after I went to his place Tom called and said I had the job if I wanted it. Then he told me the fee.'

'How much?'

'Put it this way: I wanted the job.'

'Fuck that, tell me.'

Patrick hesitated for a moment. 'Three-fifty, plus expenses.'

'Jesus Christ.'

Patrick took a sip of coffee and placed the cup carefully back on its saucer. 'Fifty grand was in my account later that day.'

'Then what?'

'For a long time, nothing. I was waiting for a meeting, a schedule of interviews, whatever. I still didn't know what I was going to be writing, a memoir, a manifesto . . . I'd call Tom and he'd say, "It's on the list," or, "Sergei's Sergei," that kind of thing. I got the sense it was a pretty chaotic set-up.'

'Fifty grand and nothing to do. Sounds amazing.'

'Yeah, well, I figured I needed to be ready when he said jump. I read up on Russia, the oligarchs, Putin. Tom sent stuff through sometimes, links and things, "Sergei wants you to see this," but it was all more or less random until three or four months after I met him.'

'We're in 2012 now?'

'Yeah; February or March. A courier came to my flat. He gave me a flash drive with hundreds of files on it.'

'What kind of files?'

'Financial stuff: spreadsheets, bank account details, lists of transactions. PDFs of what looked like contracts. But most of it was in Russian so I couldn't really tell.'

'What was it all for?'

'That's what I asked Tom. He said it was for the book. I said, "You want an accountant working on this, not a ghostwriter." He told me I'd know more about it when I needed to, and that was the last I heard for another couple of months. Then he called and told me to pack for a weekend in the country, because Sergei wanted to get going with it.'

'Did you feel ready?'

Patrick rotated his neck, like he was working out a knot. 'I'd done a lot of prep by then, but yeah, I was nervous. Tom called late on a Thursday and told me I'd be going to Vanyashin's estate on the Saturday morning. I didn't even ask where it was. I spent Friday going over my notes and thinking about what I wanted to ask him. I had a whole list of questions.'

'What kind of questions?'

Patrick laughed and shook his head but didn't say anything. Robert couldn't decide what these pauses meant; was Patrick buying time to manufacture an answer, or was he choosing what to include and what to omit?

'I know what I would have asked him,' Robert said, trying a different tack.

'What?'

'I would have asked him if he regretted going up against Putin. If exile was a price worth paying for sticking to his principles.'

'Sergei's principles were complicated,' Patrick said. 'But

it's not a bad question.' He laughed. 'Smarter than what I wanted to ask.'

'Go on, what?'

'The first question on my list was, "How much are you worth?"'

Robert snorted. 'Once you're into the billions I wouldn't say it matters so much, would you?'

'Spoken like a broke writer,' Patrick said. 'Before I started digging into it I'd have said the same: really fucking rich is really fucking rich. I had a sense of the oligarchs' – he twitched his fingers in the air around the words – 'as this undifferentiated lump, but when you look closer at all the conflicts and alliances between them, you realise the differences in their bank balances really matter. I already knew a lot about Abramovich, of course, he'd been on the radar ever since he bought Chelsea. And most people knew who Berezovsky was after Litvinenko was killed, if not before. But I was learning about people I'd never heard of, or whose names I knew but nothing else. People who owned entire oil companies, banks, TV stations: Khodorkovsky, Aven, Fridman, Deripaska.' Patrick was speaking increasingly quickly, as if now he had started talking about this he wouldn't be able to stop. 'Vanyashin was fabulously rich, obviously,' he said, 'but he wasn't in the same league as those guys. Maybe his wealth was in the hundreds of millions rather than the billions, I don't know. That's what the Rich List said, but those numbers are estimates at best – sometimes just guesses.

A lot of his money was hidden offshore in this maze of shell companies. The scale of that, the architecture of it, didn't come out until after he was dead. There are probably lawyers still trying to untangle it all.' Patrick lifted his coffee cup and spooned the dregs of foam from it. 'I didn't know if he was going to answer any of my questions,' he said. 'For all I knew he just wanted to dictate speeches to me – maybe get me to tart up the language a bit. But it mattered for the kind of book I wanted to write, because I needed to know who this guy really was. Look at Berezovsky. He was tight with Yeltsin, he led the group that chose his successor – and Putin was a nothing guy back then. When those two fell out over the *Kursk* and Chechnya, and then the Litvinenko stuff, it was news around the world. But if Vanyashin attacked Putin, what would the response be? Would people care? Would Putin even care? I didn't know.'

Robert signalled to the waiter. 'You want another coffee?' he said. Patrick nodded. 'Zwei Kaffee, bitte.' The waiter nodded as he took away their empty cups. Robert leaned forward. 'What about that secret Vanyashin told you about. That would bring Putin down. Was that true?'

Patrick frowned. 'He said he had something that would hurt him. But this is exactly what I mean: all I was going on was what he told me. This guy had been exiled and stripped of his businesses. The ability he'd had to broadcast and influence opinion in Russia was gone. Yeah, he was rich; rich enough to have a massive house in Holland

Park and another one out in the country he could fly me to in his helicopter, but maybe in the grand scheme he was just as irrelevant as when he was a Moscow cabbie. Maybe he was a fantasist, you know?'

'For three hundred and fifty grand would you have cared if he was?'

Patrick didn't return Robert's smile. He was slumped in his seat now, his face slack. 'It would have been much better if he had been,' he said. The energy with which he had been speaking a moment before had seemingly drained away. But then, as he stared past Robert, his eyes narrowed. He sat up in his chair. 'We need to go,' he said, quietly but urgently. 'Now.'

'What? Why?'

'There's a man – don't turn around,' Patrick said, as Robert began to. 'Let's go.'

'Is this a joke?' Robert said.

'Let's fucking go.'

'Zahlen, bitte,' Robert called and took out his wallet. He felt annoyed, as if they were playing a game and now Patrick was taking things too far. 'Let me get this,' he said, but Patrick ignored him. Robert turned to look behind him. At a table beside the door he saw a man eating a pastry. He looked like he was in his mid-forties, with a broad chest and a weightlifter's sloping shoulders. He wore a black hooded jumper and jeans. His hair was brown and functionally cropped, which, combined with the hood, gave him a monklike appearance. His eyes caught Robert's for a moment and flicked away. The waiter put the bill on the table. Robert left a ten-euro note, stood up and swung his bag onto his back. Patrick walked across the cafe with his head down. The glass pane rattled and the bell clanged as he yanked open the door. Robert followed, glancing again at the man as he passed him and again, for an instant, their eyes met. The man's were the pale blue of a gas flame. 'Zahlen, bitte,' Robert heard him say as he went through the door. It doesn't mean anything, he told himself.

Patrick was already some way ahead, trotting along the street. 'Patrick, wait,' Robert called. 'This is ridiculous, isn't it?'

'Has he left yet?' Patrick shouted, refusing to slow or turn.

Robert looked back and saw the man step out of the cafe and turn his face up to the sun. He put on a pair of sunglasses and began walking in their direction. 'He's coming this way,' Robert said, jogging to catch up with Patrick. 'But come on, listen,' he said as he fell into step with him. 'If someone was following you, don't you think they'd be a bit more subtle about it?'

'That depends,' Patrick said. 'Surveillance is one thing, intimidation's another.'

'And that's what you think this is?' Robert followed Patrick onto one of those typical residential Berlin streets that felt desolate to him, its unbroken lines of apartment blocks, uniform as barracks, turned inwards to face their courtyards. Robert looked behind them: they were alone.

'Is he there?' Patrick said, refusing to slow his pace.

'No,' Robert said, but as he spoke he saw the man turn the corner, perhaps twenty metres behind them. 'He's coming,' Robert said. Surely it was only because of Patrick, he thought, that the man's implacable approach seemed threatening. He was just a man walking along the same street. They passed the entrance to a small park. 'Patrick, in here,' Robert said, walking through the gate.

'We should keep going.'

'He's not following us, Patrick. Trust me.'

Patrick's eyes shone with panic. Robert thought for a moment that he was going to bolt, but he stepped through the gate. There was a picnic table and Patrick sat down on its fixed bench, facing the street. He took a pack of cigarettes from his pocket. He lit one and passed the pack to Robert.

The man came into sight. He stopped by the entrance to the park, no more than five or six metres away. Without looking at either Patrick or Robert, he pulled a pack of cigarettes from his jeans. Unhurriedly he took one from the pack, lit it and exhaled with a loud sigh of pleasure. Smoke climbed through the sunny air. The man spat on the pavement. Robert and Patrick both watched him, but the man didn't look at them. Robert felt like laughing. He wanted to ask the man a question, anything to puncture this weird silence, but he didn't laugh and he didn't speak. The silence ran on for a minute, then two minutes. A lorry passed, its engine reverberating noisily in the narrow street. Robert tensed, fearing it might stop, that men would clamber from it and throw them inside. The man finished his cigarette, threw it on the ground and walked away in the direction he had come. Robert heard him humming something as he went. He hadn't noticed until then how rapid his breathing had become, as if he had been sprinting. 'That was . . . strange,' he said.

'You didn't believe me before, did you?' Patrick said. He lit another cigarette, his hand shaking.

'I didn't,' Robert said.

'They want me to know they know.'

'What do they know?'

'Where I am, what I'm doing, who I'm talking to. I'm sorry, it was a mistake telling you any of this. I should keep away.'

'No, I don't want you to do that.'

Patrick stood. 'Don't you understand? It's dangerous for you. For your family.'

Robert took another cigarette from the pack on the table. 'If you're worried, why don't you go to the police?'

'The police, the police,' Patrick mimicked. 'Why would I go to the police?'

'It's what I'd do.'

'Is it?' Patrick said. He fell back down onto the bench. He put his head in his hands. 'Would it really help? Like it helped Sergei? Like it helped Berezovsky and Perepilichnyy? Do you know who Stephen Curtis was? Or Paul Castle?'

'No, I don't know them,' Robert said. What he wanted to ask was if Patrick really thought he was the same as those people. He wanted to tell him that state security services didn't care about hacks who wrote footballers' memoirs, and that he was either a liar or delusional. Instead he said, 'Patrick, who do you know in Berlin?'

Patrick looked up. He was rolling his extinguished cigarette butt between his fingers.

'No one, right?'

Patrick nodded.

Robert sat down beside him on the bench. 'So, think of me as a friend, OK?'

Patrick was silent for a few moments. 'It might be dangerous for you,' he said.

Robert felt again the unease he had experienced when he saw the man advancing down the street towards them. But this wasn't real. It couldn't be real. 'How dangerous can it be for me? All I've heard about is some party you went to. Big deal.'

Patrick looked hurt. 'You asked,' he said.

Robert barged him with his shoulder. 'I'm taking the piss. I'm just saying, I don't think I'm going on anyone's hit list.'

Patrick looked at Robert in silence for what felt like a long time, but must only have been a matter of seconds. 'Let's go to my apartment,' he said.

He lived a ten-minute walk away, in a drab block on a bleak, treeless street. The building's brown concrete render looked like it had been raked by gunfire, but as they drew closer Robert realised that these ugly repeated scorings were attempts at decoration. At ground level the render was speckled with uninspired graffiti tags: initials, crude stars, random scribbles, as if the building were a piece of scrap paper used for practice. Patrick needed to jerk the front door to get it open, and the cracked grey tiles in the lobby and the dirty lino on the stairs added to the block's atmosphere of decay. Inside Patrick's apartment the walls were bare and the surfaces empty of the clutter of a lived-in space. To Robert it felt as sterile as a hotel room, especially compared to the chaos where he lived: the girls' overlapping drawings that covered the fridge, toys and discarded pieces of clothing littering the floor, books and papers stacked in high, unstable piles on the desk in the living room.

'Coffee?' Patrick asked, motioning for Robert to sit at the small breakfast bar that divided the kitchen from the living room.

'Please,' Robert said, putting his bag on the bar and sitting on a stool. He watched Patrick spoon instant coffee into mugs as the electric kettle began to emit a rushing sound. He didn't know what to make of him, or of what had happened that morning. 'You don't live in Neukölln, then?' he said.

Patrick shook his head. 'Sorry I lied. I thought it was better to take precautions.'

Robert didn't mention that he had headed in the wrong direction after their dinner. Yet this was the same man who claimed to have given Russian agents the slip.

Patrick opened a cupboard, then another. 'I'd offer you something to eat,' he said, 'but I don't seem to have anything.'

'I'm not hungry.'

The kettle clicked off and the rushing quickly receded, seeming to leave an echo in the small, dingy kitchen. Patrick put the coffees on the breakfast bar and sat down. 'I meant what I said. You might be putting yourself in danger by talking to me.'

Whatever the truth was, Patrick did seem genuinely scared. Robert could believe he was in some kind of trouble – maybe someone really was keeping an eye on him – but that didn't mean he was telling the truth; and whoever that man had been, Robert didn't think either of them would ever see him again. For a moment he wanted to tell Patrick it was OK, that he needed to just forget about all this stuff and stop thinking crazy thoughts. But he wanted to pressure him, too, and see where the cracks in his story might begin to show. 'You were telling me about your weekend in the country,' he said. 'Was it at the house where he died?'

Patrick nodded. 'In the Chilterns,' he said. 'An enormous place. Beautiful. He flew me there.'

'Flew you?'

For the first time since they had been in the cafe, a smile came to Patrick's face. 'Yeah, it was ridiculous. A chauffeur came to my poxy basement flat and drove me to the heliport at Battersea. In a Maybach.'

'I don't know anything about cars but I assume that's a nice one.'

'It costs more than most people's houses,' Patrick said. 'It was a weird trip. I remember being in the air, looking at London thinning out into fields, and not knowing what the hell to expect when I landed.'

As the helicopter descended, gravity tugging his stomach, Patrick saw a large house below him, nestled in a small valley at the foot of two hills. He saw a swimming pool and a cabana, a long greenhouse and a terrace on which a group of people sat at a long table, their faces turned towards the helicopter. Patrick saw them putting their hands on the papers spread across the table to stop them blowing away. The helicopter came down towards the far end of the garden. The plants in the borders thrashed wildly and the surface of the lawn pulsed like interference running across a TV picture, radiating out from the downdraught of the blades. The descent had been gradual, but suddenly the ground came up fast and they were down, the landing as smooth as a train pulling into a station – a moment's give was all Patrick felt before they settled. The pilot's voice came through his headset: 'Please remain inside the cabin for now, Mr Unsworth. I need to keep the rotors running for another thirty seconds, then I'll power down.'

Two men were crossing the lawn, their clothes whipped

by the slowing blades. The engine's bass hum thinned to a whine. Patrick heard the pilot's voice again. 'I'm just going to keep you hostage for one minute more, sir.'

'OK,' Patrick said, but at that moment he saw the handle flip upright as Vanyashin wrenched open the door.

'Patrick Unsworth!' he shouted above the noise of the slowing rotors. He pressed the button to release Patrick's seatbelt, grasped his hand and pulled him out of the helicopter, pressing his shoulder to make him stay low. 'How is this writing arm?' he said, pumping Patrick's arm up and down. Tom, standing beyond the rotors, smiled and waved. 'Toby!' Vanyashin shouted as the blades stilled and the pilot opened his door. 'Some people will go back to London in one hour. Come have coffee. Eat if you want.' He put his arm around Patrick's shoulders and they began walking towards the house. 'You and I will start writing today!' he said.

'I'm glad to hear it.'

Tom, walking ahead, turned to both of them. 'You're going to change the world,' he said.

Climbing the broad, moss-dotted stone stairs from the lawn, Patrick noticed two suited men, one at either end of the terrace. Their build and stance marked them out as bodyguards. Of the three men at the table, the remains of breakfast around them, two were dressed similarly to Vanyashin in loose linen shirts and chinos. The third man was more severe: thin and shaven-headed, his large, observant eyes gazed out from behind wireframe glasses.

He wore a white dress shirt buttoned to the neck beneath a thin grey cardigan and continued to stare impassively at Patrick as Vanyashin introduced him as 'the excellent British author Patrick Unsworth'. The introduction was one-way: Vanyashin didn't tell Patrick who the men were. 'Go inside and Tom will show you your room,' he said. 'We start in one hour.' As Vanyashin returned to his seat, the man in the white shirt began speaking urgently to him in Russian. Patrick caught the man's eye and had the uncomfortable sense that he was the subject of what was being said. Suddenly all of the men at the table began shouting in either enthusiasm or rage, he couldn't tell which.

'Business meeting?' Patrick said.

'No other kind with Sergei.'

Tom led Patrick along the terrace and into the house by way of a narrow, tiled corridor. This led to a large kitchen, made bright by the columns of sunlight that fell through a row of tall, churchlike windows. The air was filled with the sharp tang of frying garlic. A woman sitting at the kitchen table – long enough to seat ten or twelve – looked up as the men entered, gave a quick nod and returned to cutting the bacon slices that lay on the chopping board on the table. Behind her Patrick saw a copper-bottomed pan set on a range, and on the tile countertop beside it a large and ornate silver object that looked like a cross between a tea urn and a trophy. Through the kitchen they passed along another corridor that led to a large entrance hall, with a flagstone floor and stucco walls. A staircase of dark varnished wood curled around one side of it, leading to a wide landing. The stripe of carpet that ran up the middle of the stairs was intricately patterned with what Patrick thought looked like a Persian design. 'Is this Axminster?' he asked as they climbed.

'It's a carpet,' Tom said over his shoulder. 'How the fuck should I know what kind it is?'

'It's called scene-setting, Tom. People enjoy that type of detail.'

'It's whatever the most expensive one is.'

Tom sounded tired and pissed off, but Patrick got the sense now wasn't the time to ask why.

'The main bedrooms are on this floor,' he continued as they walked along the landing. 'You and I, and sundry other lickspittles, are on the floor above.'

At the end of the landing Patrick stopped beside a leaded window that looked over a lawn at the side of the house. It ran to a high stone wall, beyond which stood a dense wood of oak and ash.

'If you fancy a walk in the woods,' Tom said, 'be aware: he has men patrolling them night and day.'

'Does he really need to?'

'Don't underestimate the value of a good night's sleep,' Tom said, then lowered his voice to a whisper. 'And yes, I can think of all sorts of people who want him dead.'

'Who?'

'Listing who doesn't might be quicker.' Tom splayed his fingers and started folding them down: 'People he's done business with, people he's refused to do business with, the Russian state, the Russian mafia, and probably the Chechens. They want to kill everyone. We're up here,' he said, his voice returning to its usual volume as he began climbing another set of stairs, this one steep and narrow.

Patrick remained at the window a moment longer, searching the wood for a glimpse of Vanyashin's guards, but only saw leaves stir.

His room was small but comfortable. There was a desk in the corner and a TV on the wall opposite the bed. Patrick looked out of the window at the helicopter glinting on the lawn. 'How much would one of those cost?' he said.

'Four or five million, I think.'

'I'll probably get one, then.'

Tom grunted.

'You OK?' Patrick said. 'You seem a bit . . . depleted.'

Tom smiled wanly. 'Just dealing with the joys of Sergei being Sergei. It's nothing a bucket of vodka won't fix. I'll let you settle in.' He stopped at the doorway. 'The bathroom's next door on the right, if you need it. Part of the manor's old-school charm. Those guys Sergei's with are going back to London soon, so be downstairs in about thirty minutes, OK?'

'Who are they?'

'Two of them I don't know much about. They're something to do with mining in Africa. The guy in the glasses is Nikolai Donskoy. He was editor-in-chief of Moscow Voice.'

'The radio station?'

'He got fired after Sergei had to give it up. They're looking at starting something digital over here. They want to get back into Russia somehow.'

'He's got a lot going on, then?'

'My advice is don't let him go off on any tangents. You probably won't get a lot of time with him, so make it count. See you downstairs.'

Tom shut the door behind him and Patrick sat down on the bed. He listened to his breathing. A minute passed, then he stood and unpacked his bag.

He was leaning against the windowsill in his room, watching the helicopter's blades move from a crawl to a blur, when he heard a knock on the door. He opened it to see a very tall, very thin girl standing in the hallway. She had a large forehead and depthless green eyes that widened as Patrick looked at her, as if she had just asked a question and was waiting for him to answer. 'Hello?' he said, unable to keep a note of surprise out of his voice.

'Tom asked me to come and get you,' the girl said. 'I'm Alyona.' He could tell she was Russian, but her accent had a strong Californian lilt. From outside came the sound of the helicopter climbing into the sky: an aggressive buzz that smoothed into a purr.

Patrick returned her smile. 'Patrick,' he said. 'Pleased to meet you.'

'Are you ready to come down?'

'Sure, absolutely,' he said. He stepped into the hallway then remembered his voice recorder. 'Hold on,' he said. He went back into his room, took the recorder off the desk and put his notepad and pen in his jacket pocket. Back in the hallway he found Alyona standing in a one-legged yoga pose, her hands clasped behind her. She was barefoot, wearing loose black trousers that ended at mid-calf and a green hooded top with a glittering phoenix stitched into the back.

Remaining on one leg, she hopped around to face him. 'My last runway show I fell over,' she said. 'I'm working on my balance.'

'Seems pretty good to me.'

'It's easy barefoot,' she said, striding off down the hall.

She was the same height as him, he thought, and she looked about fifteen. 'I hope you enjoy walking,' she said over her shoulder. 'This place is about a thousand times bigger than my apartment.'

'Where do you live?'

'Out of a suitcase mostly,' she said as they descended the narrow staircase to the first floor. 'I'm always working. Which, y'know, I'm not complaining, but I get tired. New York is home for now, kind of. That's where the micro apartment is.'

'What about school?'

She laughed, turning to face him at the top of the grand staircase that curved down to the hall. 'How old do you think I am?'

Patrick suddenly felt that he was making a fool of himself. 'Seventeen?' he said.

'Two years off. But wait, am I fifteen or nineteen?' She took two steps backward down the stairs, looking up at him with a teasing look on her face.

'Please, I'm nervous you'll fall,' Patrick said.

'You're not sure?' Her eyes widened in fake shock. She took a step back, then another.

'Nineteen!' Patrick said. 'Definitely nineteen. Just turn around, OK?'

She laughed, hopped onto the banister and slid the rest of the way down the staircase.

'Your dad must love it when you're home for a bit,' Patrick said, the hall's floorboards creaking loudly beneath his shoes. Alyona's smile faded. She looked confused. 'I haven't seen him in years,' she said.

'Patrick of the pen!' Vanyashin shouted as he entered the hallway, followed by one of his bodyguards. 'You have met Alyona.' He stopped beside her, clasped the back of her head and pulled her towards him, his face angled up to hers.

Not his daughter, Patrick thought, as they kissed for what seemed a demonstratively long time, Vanyashin's belly pressed against her long, slight body, his hand gripping her neck like a clamp.

When the kiss finally ended, Vanyashin smiled and spoke quietly to Alyona in Russian, his hand kneading her hip and buttock. She looked at Patrick. 'Good to meet you. I'll see you around.'

'Likewise,' Patrick said. 'Good luck with the balancing.'

She pretended to stumble as she walked away, flashing a quick smile back at him before she disappeared through a doorway. He turned to see Vanyashin staring at him with eyes blank as a shark's. Then he put his hand on Patrick's shoulder and directed him into a long living room that ran the length of the house, from driveway to garden. Two large oxblood Chesterfield armchairs and a stone fireplace dominated the centre of the room. A small fire – needless on such a warm day – crackled within the deep, blackened hearth. The room's decor was traditional, with engravings of buildings and landscapes hanging in gilt frames, small hooded lights above them. The mint-green carpet was comfortably worn. There were no signs of ancient Rome here. Vanyashin settled into one of the chairs beside the fire. All he needed, Patrick thought, was some tweed and a pack of hounds flurrying around him to pass for an English country gentleman.

He indicated that Patrick should sit. 'My friend Kolya read your book. The one about the footballer.'

'Did he like it?'

'He says you are the wrong man for this job.'

'I'm sorry to hear that. Does he know who the right man is?'

'Sasha Yermilov. One of my reporters.'

'I've never heard of him.'

'A good writer. Good investigator.'

'Mr Vanyashin—'

'Sergei.'

'Sergei. It's your choice, you can hire this Sasha guy and write your book with him and sell it in Russia – if you can get copies into the bookshops there. But aren't we dreaming bigger than that?'

'Go on.'

'This is a story the world needs to hear,' Patrick said, leaning forward in his chair. 'You, a wronged figure, taking on the might of the corrupt Russian state. It's like . . . do you know *Star Wars*?'

'Of course. Skywalker.'

'That's right, Skywalker. And Putin's the Emperor. I'm sure Sasha would do a perfectly adequate job, but this is global, not local. And his name won't mean anything to publishers in London, or New York. Mine does.'

Vanyashin studied Patrick, a small smile on his lips. He didn't speak.

'What did Tom say? You're going to change the world. That's what I'm here to help you do.' Vanyashin watched Patrick again, but this time Patrick met his silence with his own.

After many long moments had passed Vanyashin said, 'My Alyona is something, isn't she? I met her when she came to my party at Cannes last year.' His tone was playful now, the conversation they had just been having seemingly forgotten. 'The best thing about having a party on a yacht,' he said, lifting his head slightly as though the thought had just come to him, but in a way that told

Patrick the line was rehearsed, 'is that you can make the people you like stay and throw the rest into the fucking sea!' He roared with laughter and Patrick chuckled dutifully. 'What do you think of Alyona?' Vanyashin said. His voice was still light, but Patrick detected hardness in the question.

'She seems like a great girl. Woman,' Patrick said. 'She's a model, I think she told me?'

Vanyashin laughed. 'There is a Russian story,' he said, 'about some foreigners visiting an art gallery. The guide shows them a painting, called *Lenin in London*. It shows a bedroom, a bed. A man and a woman are fucking on the bed, but only their legs can be seen. The guide points at the woman's legs: "These," he says, "are the legs of Nadezhda Konstantinova." Lenin's wife, you see? "And these," he says, pointing at the man's legs, "are the legs of Dzerzhinsky." "But where is Lenin?" someone asks. "Lenin," the guide says, "is in London."' Vanyashin leaned into the space between them and rested his hand heavily on Patrick's knee. 'Today,' he said, his smile gone, 'my wife is in London.' He sat back in his chair and stared silently at Patrick. Five seconds passed, then ten. Fifteen. Patrick resisted the urge to speak. Eventually Vanyashin raised his hand, his index finger extended towards Patrick. He smiled thinly. 'You really are like a ghost,' he said.

'I think the best way for this to work is if you feel like you're talking to yourself, Mr Vanyashin.'

'Sergei.'

'Sergei, sorry. I'm only going to interject when I need clarification. There might be things we need to unpack for people, certainly people in this country who aren't so familiar with Russia.'

Vanyashin nodded, but Patrick wasn't sure he was listening. 'They are on the streets, Patrick,' he said.

'They?'

'The people,' he said, sweeping his arm as if a crowd might be seen at the other end of the room instead of just one of his security detail, quickly straightening from a lean against the black body of a grand piano. 'The Russian people are finally coming out and saying "no" in numbers that mean something. Thirty thousand people on the streets of Moscow last week! Leonid Parfyonov, you know this name?'

Patrick shook his head.

'An absolute establishment figure,' Vanyashin said, his finger raised for emphasis. 'Now he speaks to huge rallies, protest rallies. "Russia without Putin," these crowds chant.' He wiped his eyes, although they appeared to be dry. 'How I wish to be there,' he said.

Patrick had read about the protests at Putin's inauguration. 'You think this could go somewhere?' he said.

'I absolutely believe this. This isn't like old protests. These aren't just communists, and it isn't only the young. This is the middle class rising up, Putin's base. So,' he said, standing, 'we must put our fuel on the fire too.' To Patrick's surprise he set his feet widely apart and began weaving his arms before him, like a wizard casting a spell. 'Stoop, Romans, stoop,' he said loudly, 'and let us bathe our hands in Caesar's blood to the elbows, and besmear our swords. Then walk we forth, even to the marketplace, and waving our red weapons above our heads we cry, "Peace, freedom, and liberty!"' He stood ramrod straight, his head angled up towards the ceiling, one arm raised as if he were holding a sword. He kept this pose for a moment then looked down. 'No applause?'

'I'm too stunned to clap, Sergei,' Patrick said.

Vanyashin smiled. 'I was director, not actor. But "let us besmear our swords." My friend Borya was talking about this for many years.'

'Borya?'

'Da. Borya. Boris Abramovich Berezovsky. He spoke with me about armed insurrection. Mercenaries. He has all his French Foreign Legion and ex-Mossad men. I have some French too. Good men. But now Borya only has time for high court and his fucking lawsuit. He can't talk about anything else.' Vanyashin looked into the fire. 'But there are other ways to start a revolution. Books start revolutions, too.'

'Sure, just ask Marx,' Patrick said. He stood to join Vanyashin. 'I was thinking,' he said, 'we want to make it as intriguing as possible, and we can do that by telling a very personal story: your story.'

Vanyashin moved his head from side to side. 'Perhaps yes, perhaps. But the important thing is the criminals in the Kremlin. We must bring justice to them. We will describe their crimes.'

'What do those files you sent me have to do with this?'

'Evidence. Gunpowder to blow them away.'

'Who are "they", precisely?'

'The siloviki. You would say "strongmen". The people in the state security services and the government – which since Putin is all same people – who own castles, islands, resorts, forests. Men with much, much bigger incomes than their official positions give.'

'Where does their money come from?'

'They steal it. Factories, refineries, banks, phone companies, laboratories. Moscow Voice. *New Times*.'

'Your radio station. Your newspaper.'

Vanyashin nodded.

'The siloviki own them?'

'The official owners are shell companies. But they are beneficiaries. A man called Adamov, ex-KGB, he's the real owner now. This I can prove. But my point isn't about that man or that man or that man, it's about a system.'

'And the documents you sent me show how this system works?'

'In some way. We need to publish this information.'

'You're going to have to get someone to walk me through it all. It doesn't mean anything to me.'

'Of course, in time you will be expert.' He glanced at

his watch. 'But financial lesson is for later,' he said, standing. 'Now is for lunch.'

They ate spaghetti carbonara on the terrace: Patrick, Vanyashin, Alyona, Tom and a German couple, Gregor and Jenny, who Patrick assumed were fellow houseguests. Vanyashin, who insisted Patrick sit beside him, kept refilling his glass with a potent red wine. He asked Patrick's opinion of Alexei Navalny, who had been arrested in Moscow the week before. When Patrick said he didn't know much about him except that he was an opposition leader, Vanyashin began speaking urgently. He called him heroic, fearless, ingenious. 'He publishes scanned evidence of money transfers online: black-and-white evidence of corruption. Simple. Brilliant. This example we should follow, show it for everyone to see. All our gunpowder.' Patrick listened, swallowing wine. By the time Vanyashin turned his attention to the Germans Patrick felt drunk, which was why he forgot the smoking ban. He had already pulled his cigarettes from his pocket, screwed one between his lips and sparked his lighter before Tom's hand signals alerted him to his mistake. Stuffing the lighter and cigarette in his pocket – like a furtive schoolboy, he thought – he stood and walked to the far end of the terrace. As he lit up the guard stationed nearby stepped down onto the lawn and moved a discreet distance away. The grass seemed to throb as Patrick stared at it. He looked at the wood and wondered how far it stretched and how many armed men it contained. He saw Alyona crossing the terrace towards him.

'Can I have one of those?' she said. Patrick took out the pack and folded back the lid. He held his lighter up.

She nodded thanks and blew out a stream of smoke. With her little finger she pulled a strand of breeze-blown hair away from her mouth. 'They're talking business,' she said. 'So boring.'

'Yeah, I don't really get it either.'

'I get it,' she said. 'That's how I know it's boring.'

They stood silently beside one another. Patrick felt Vanyashin's eyes on him. He was sure he was imagining it, but he couldn't bring himself to look and find out for certain. The silence grew until he had to break it. 'Doesn't he mind?' he said.

'Mind what?'

'You smoking.'

'I'm old enough, you know,' she snapped. 'It's not illegal.'

He turned to face her, thinking her anger was genuine, but she was smiling at him. 'I meant, y'know, his smoking ban,' he said.

She looked at him appraisingly. 'You don't know him at all yet, do you?' she said.

'That's kind of why I'm here.'

Alyona looked out over the lawn. She took short, shallow drags on her cigarette.

'Sergei told me you met on his yacht,' Patrick said.

She smiled, still looking straight ahead. 'Yes, that floating castle. Have you seen it?'

'I haven't.'

'You have to get him to take you, it's so cool. Much better than this ruin,' she said, looking over her shoulder at the house.

'It is a bit old-fashioned, I suppose,' Patrick said. 'But then I'm English. I'm programmed to like it.'

'It's pretty,' Alyona said, quoting the word rather than offering it as her own opinion. 'But it's so old and creaky. At night it sounds like the whole place is full of rats.'

'Thanks for putting that thought in my head.'

'Don't worry, they only go to the little bedrooms. On the top floor?'

'Oh great! At least they'll go for Tom first. He's a supersize meal of a man.'

Alyona laughed.

'What's so funny?' Tom said, coming towards them with a wine glass in one hand and a cigarette in the other.

'Patrick's scared he's going to get eaten by rats,' Alyona said. She gave him a complicit smile.

'I think concerned more than scared,' Patrick said.

'He's a writer,' Tom said. 'He's used to all sorts of vermin.' He swallowed the last of his wine then held the empty glass up in front of him. 'This Masseto is fucking delicious.'

A shout came from Vanyashin, followed by a laugh.

Robert saw him with his arms around the Germans, squeezing them against him.

'What are they talking about?' Patrick asked.

'I'm not sure, but it's above my pay grade,' Tom said. 'Which was why I came over here. Not that you both' – he inclined his head to Alyona and Patrick – 'aren't reason enough.'

'You speak so fast, Tom,' Alyona said. 'I only ever get half of what you're saying.'

'Half of it's bollocks, darling,' Tom said. 'And the other half is bullshit.' He was playing up his Welsh accent, Patrick thought. 'But this man,' Tom said, waving his glass at Patrick. 'This man might not say much, but what he says is always worth listening to.'

'The silent type,' Alyona said.

Patrick nodded. 'The strong silent type, I suppose that's true.'

Alyona looked him up and down. She cocked an eyebrow. 'Maybe,' she said. Tom laughed.

'I'll take maybe,' Patrick said, lighting another cigarette and offering the pack to Alyona. She shook her head.

'Alyona!' Vanyashin called. He snapped his fingers. She went to him and Patrick watched him pull her down into his lap. He rested one broad, hairy hand on her thigh.

'I don't think he likes you enjoying each other's company so much,' Tom said quietly.

Patrick watched as Vanyashin pushed his face towards Alyona's for a kiss, then grimaced and recoiled. 'Dick,'

Patrick muttered. 'When I met her, I thought she was his fucking daughter.'

Tom laughed behind his hand as he took a drag on his cigarette. 'His daughters are actually older than her.'

'Where are they?'

'One's at the Sorbonne, the other's at Oxford.'

'Smart?'

'Possibly smart. Definitely rich. I don't really know them.'

'And his wife?'

'Tatijana I know, but she's not up for spending much time with her husband these days. When he's here she's in the South of France, or Courchevel, and when he's in London she's here, or shopping in New York, and so on.'

'She knows about Alyona. He told me she does.'

Tom nodded. 'She's putting up with it for now.'

'I think it's disgusting.'

'Luckily for us you're not here to act as moral arbiter. And neither am I. You have to admit, though, she's a beautiful woman.'

'She's sharp. I like her.'

'Careful.'

'Not like that,' Patrick said, but he felt himself blushing. 'Anyway, she called me a weakling, so even if I did like her . . .'

'I wouldn't take it too hard. Where she's from they breed them stronger than most.'

'Where's that?'

'Norilsk. In the Arctic Circle.'

'What's in Norilsk?'

'Nickel mining, mostly. An ugly city filled with beautiful girls desperate to leave. I did a show about it. Scouts go to these places – Norilsk, Dzerzhinsk, Magnitogorsk – and scoop all these kids up and dump them in Moscow or Petersburg. A lot of them get sent to China. The lucky ones make it to the big leagues: Milan, Paris, New York. The scouts call the girls "cattle".'

'She's one of the lucky ones, then.'

'Clambering to the top of that heap is achievement enough. Bagging herself an oligarch into the bargain, that's like winning the lottery.'

Patrick felt uncomfortable hearing Alyona being talked about like that. 'Isn't that what you've done, too?' he said.

'Fuck off,' Tom said angrily. Then he laughed. 'Bastard. You're right, I suppose.'

For a moment the sun disappeared behind a cloud and the grass darkened, then swelled into brightness again. A breeze scurried across the terrace, plucking a napkin from the table. One of the women clearing the lunch things bent low to catch it.

'How was your chat with the big man?' Tom said.

'Spiky.'

'That's just him kicking your tyres.'

'I want to ask him how much money he has. Is that stupid?'

'Why do you want to know?'

'I want to understand where he fits in. If you're an oligarch you're defined by your wealth and power. So how much wealth and power does he have?'

'He isn't Berezovsky, or Abramovich,' Tom said, keeping his voice low. 'Not in their league. But maybe he's close enough that plenty of people wouldn't see the difference. In some ways he was smarter, getting his fingers in lots of different pies rather than, say, owning a Yukos outright. Getting that big attracts a certain kind of scrutiny, and maybe you have to be crazy to be able to get that big. You know, before he got arrested Khodorkovsky was negotiating his own pipeline deal with the Chinese and trying to build another from Murmansk to the US. Cutting the Kremlin out of the loop. Then he lectured Putin about corruption on live TV. What the fuck was he thinking? He left him no choice but to take him out.' Tom bent down to put his empty wine glass on the flagstones, then stood and lit another cigarette. 'Sergei was smarter than that, up to a point. But he couldn't stop himself mouthing off.'

'The *Kursk* stuff.'

Tom shook his head. 'That didn't help, but it wasn't the only thing. Sergei was complaining to people – people in business, people in government – about how Putin and his siloviki stole whatever they wanted and arrested anyone who tried standing up to them. When the person doing that owns a paper and a radio station, it makes people nervous.'

'He doesn't strike me as much of a reformer.'

'He's not. Or, he wasn't. What Putin was doing didn't offend him; he envied it. The moral crusader bit is a recent development. It's why he's got such a hard-on for Navalny now. I've told him he'd be better off working with Nemtsov, but he doesn't want to know. "United Russia is the party of crooks and thieves," that's Navalny's slogan, and that fits perfectly with Sergei's . . . well, not his morality, exactly, but his very selective idea of justice.'

Patrick laughed. 'What the fuck have you got me into, Tom?'

Tom dropped his cigarette into his wine glass, where it landed with a hiss. 'Your gratitude is noted.'

As tea was brought onto the terrace, Vanyashin said he had to make some calls and went inside the house. Alyona went upstairs for a nap and Tom said he needed to check his emails. 'I'll be in the kitchen if you need me,' he said.

'The kitchen?'

'I like to work in places where distraction is guaranteed. And where I don't have to move when I get hungry.'

Patrick spent the rest of the day wandering around, feeling self-conscious about not working but knowing that what he really needed to do was talk to Vanyashin. He heard him yelling at one point, but his voice faded as he moved into some distant part of the house. No interview took place. Patrick hoped he would encounter

Alyona again, but he didn't catch sight of her. He found the library, a shadowy, wood-panelled room, picked a book off the shelf at random – *Phineas Redux* – and listlessly scanned a few chapters. He took a walk in the garden and thought about going into the woods, but the possibility of encountering armed men put him off. Eventually he fetched his laptop and notebook from his room and worked in the kitchen alongside Tom. A little after eight o'clock the cook pulled a lasagne out of the oven and placed a bowl of salad at one end of the long, broad table and the two men sat down together to eat. 'Am I meant to just wait?' Patrick said.

'If you want the pay cheque,' Tom said around a mouthful of pasta. 'And the perks. Do you know how much Masseto actually costs?' He refilled Patrick's glass nearly to the brim.

'What are you doing here, anyway?' Patrick said. 'I mean, this weekend in particular.'

Tom took a long sip of wine. 'Sergei's developed some . . . trust issues,' he said. 'He likes me being around. And I've become very fond of his money, so everyone's happy. If we agree to reclassify his increasing paranoia as a kind of happiness.'

'Maybe it's not paranoia. You did say lots of people wanted him dead.'

'Lots, yes, but not everyone.'

'Imagine having all this and being so unhappy.'

Tom rolled his eyes.

'What?'

'Come on, what do you think a person with "all this" is like?' Tom waved his hands to indicate the array of Vanyashin's possessions. 'He could probably never be happy even if he hadn't lost all the things that made him his fortune, and which he's never going to get back bar several miracles taking place in his homeland. And,' Tom said, taking Patrick's arm and pulling him closer, his voice low, 'he might look like a billionaire to us, but I don't know that the figures add up. That helicopter you flew in on, it's rented. So's the yacht.'

'Maybe he's just prudent,' Patrick said.

'Does he seem prudent to you? You've seen his fucking campaign tent. You can bet Abramovich doesn't rent his yacht, and I don't see Sergei snapping up Bacons. But' – he held up his hands, palms out – 'my not inconsiderable wages keep getting paid, and this wine is real, so who knows, maybe I'm wrong.'

'Why didn't you tell me this before?'

'I wasn't this drunk, probably,' Tom said, lifting another slice of lasagne from the dish.

Patrick looked out through the long, narrow windows. A tangle of orange and purple clouds rose above the ragged black line of the woods. When they finished the bottle, Tom opened another.

The next day Patrick slept through his alarm and woke up at nine, groggy and confused, with someone knocking on his door. 'Come in,' he croaked, and a maid entered with a tray on which he found half a grapefruit, a bacon sandwich and a silver pot of coffee. He was downstairs twenty minutes later, but no one was around. Standing in the main hall, the only sounds he could hear were a vacuum cleaner somewhere upstairs and the deep ticking of the grandfather clock, an imposing, ancient-looking device that might have kept time in this same hallway for generations, or been snatched from elsewhere on one of Sergei's sprees – the last topic of conversation Patrick could remember from last night, and the point at which Tom had opened a third bottle of wine. He texted him now, his head throbbing as he looked down at his screen. A reply arrived in seconds: We're back in London. The typing notification showed. Something came up. Sergei says sorry. I'll be in touch. 'Fuck!' Patrick shouted. He went upstairs to pack and booked a taxi to take him to the train station in High Wycombe. He sat on the terrace steps with his bag beside him and lit a cigarette. The day was overcast and warm.

When he heard someone approaching he assumed one of the household staff was coming to tell him his cab was here, but was surprised to see it was Alyona. She sat down beside him. 'I thought you'd gone back to London with Van— with Sergei,' he said.

She frowned. 'His wife's in London. I'm staying here. Some friends are coming.'

'You're going to have a party?'

'No,' she said, sounding disgusted. 'No one has parties any more. We'll just do ket and have sex.'

He looked around and saw her smiling at him. 'You didn't get me,' he said stonily, then laughed. 'You did get me.' In the distance a gardener walked across the lawn, a spade in one hand and in the other a black plastic bag that floated out behind him, bulging with gathered air. 'Can I ask you something?' Patrick said.

'You can ask.'

'Is he good to you?'

Alyona stretched her legs out in front of her and looked at her feet as she flexed them alternately up and down. 'What do you mean,' she said. She wasn't smiling any more.

'I mean does he treat you like a person and not like a thing.'

'Yes, he treats me like a person. I—' she began and stopped. She lifted her thumb to her mouth and bit at the nail. 'I had this dream about us,' she said, and gave an awkward laugh. 'We were on the street, just being together. Then I heard this crazy loud sound and I knew there was something horrible coming for us. It wasn't anything I could see, it was just the sound, but I knew it was coming for us.'

'Us?' Patrick said.

'Sergei and me. And I knew he'd keep me safe. I believe my dreams. I've dreamed all kinds of things that turned out to be real.'

'That's good,' Patrick said. For a moment, when she said 'us', he had thought she was talking about him. He wanted to say something else but before he could decide what, the housekeeper came to tell him his taxi had arrived.

Days passed during which Robert worked steadily, his notes becoming scenes and then chapters, the pages beginning to accumulate. He thought about little else than the story he was creating, but just over a week after he had last seen Patrick something happened that made him recall the man who had, perhaps, followed them out of the cafe that day. It was a Sunday afternoon and he and Nora were on a tram, coming home from a birthday party in Pankow. Robert stood beside Nora as she knelt on the back-row seats, looking out of the window as the vehicles on the road fell behind and drew closer. She was pretending the cars were wolves and had been relaying details of their pursuit for the length of the journey.

'They're catching us, Pappa!' she shouted, her voice loud in the packed but quiet carriage.

'Oh no!' Robert said quietly, trying to coax her to match his volume.

She twisted her head to smile up at him. 'They're chasing us!'

The tram jolted across a junction with a deep clang. 'Bong!' Nora said, and chuckled.

The movement made Robert stumble. As he regained his balance he looked behind him and saw a man, standing a few metres away in the crowded central aisle, staring at him. He was about thirty, tall and wide-shouldered, with a black beard and a flat, twisted nose that gave him the look of a boxer. His gaze was intent and persisted even as the tram went around a curve, its articulated carriages swaying woozily away from each other, then drawing back into alignment. At the next stop, as people jostled off and on, he moved closer. He was only a couple of metres away, but now the curved bill of his black baseball cap hid his eyes. He typed something into his phone. Robert watched him as the tram accelerated. He lifted his head once, looked directly into Robert's eyes, then returned his attention to his phone screen. Robert remembered the glance of the man in the cafe; heard a snatch of the tune he had hummed as he walked away. He looked around at the other passengers but all he saw were the vacant stares of Sunday afternoon travellers, a mother telling her son to stop treading on a man's feet, a pair of teenagers, the girl's head resting on the shoulder of the boy's camouflage parka. He felt Nora's hand tug at his trouser leg. 'Look at I, Pappa, look at I,' she said.

'What is it, älskling?'

Nora turned away from him, wrapped her hands around a railing and made a minuscule jump into the air. She smiled proudly.

'Well done!' Robert said, reaching out to steady her as the tram slowed to a halt.

'Do we get off now?' Nora said.

'One more to go.' Looking around to see if the man might have come even closer, Robert saw him step off the tram and walk quickly away.

It took a long time to travel the short distance between Schönhauser Allee and their apartment because Nora threw herself to the ground and protested that it was impossible for her to walk any further. Robert cajoled her, telling her if she got up there would be time to watch TV before bed. When she collapsed again, this time because she suddenly wanted the rest of a croissant she had been eating that morning, which Robert had thrown away hours before, he didn't have the patience to talk her round. He picked her up and carried her the last fifty metres home, as she bucked and thrashed in his arms.

He was so flustered when he got into the apartment, doing everything he could to resist yelling at Nora as she continued to flail, that he didn't notice the window. It was only when she was in the bath, chattering happily to her plastic animals, that he realised the window in the girls' room, which always stayed locked because they were four floors up, was wide open. He didn't think Karijn, who had taken Sonja to a birthday party in Neukölln, would have left it open, and Nora couldn't have done it – even if she had been able to climb up and reach the handles, which were aggravatingly stiff, the key was kept in a jar on top of the fridge. But there the key was, in the upper handle's lock. Robert put his head out and looked down at the cobbles far below, his pulse quickening as he briefly but irresistibly imagined falling. He pulled the window closed, locked both handles and returned the key to the kitchen. Thinking of the hallway thefts he checked their laptops and Karijn's jewellery. Everything was there. He opened the front door, stepped out and examined the lock. The brass plate around the doorknob was dented, but he was fairly sure it had always been like that. He couldn't see any sign the door had been tampered with, although he didn't really know what he was looking for. He thought about calling Karijn, but Nora shouted for him and he went to towel her dry.

He was getting her into her pyjamas when he heard a key in the lock and the door banged open. 'Tomorrow,' Karijn said as she came in. 'Tomorrow.'

'No, now!' Sonja screamed. 'It's not fair. You will not be my best friend and you will not come to my party!'

Robert smiled. It was extraordinary, he thought, how easy it was to be amused by one of these arguments when you stood outside it, yet if it had been him in Karijn's place he probably would have been shouting in fury. 'Hej,' he called. 'Nora, say hej to Mamma and Sonja.'

'Hello!' Nora shouted, close enough to Robert's ear to make him flinch.

'Pappa!' Sonja shouted as she ran into the bedroom, her voice rising with a plea, 'Mamma won't let me finish my treat!'

Behind Sonja, Robert saw Karijn cross the hall and go into the kitchen carrying something wrapped in a napkin. 'You can have the rest tomorrow, sweetheart,' she said. Sonja started to cry.

'They gave her a lollipop the size of her head,' Karijn called from the kitchen. 'She's eaten half of it already.' She leaned out of the kitchen doorway and smiled at Sonja. 'Now come and have your tea,' she said.

That evening Robert and Karijn watched a film, but soon after it began Robert fell asleep. He walked the darkened hallways of Vanyashin's country house. There were men in the house; they walked alongside him but were apparently unaware of his presence. They were looking for Vanyashin. He woke to Karijn nudging his foot with her knee. 'Thanks for another electric night,' she said. 'I'm going to bed.'

'Night, my love,' he said, rousing himself. 'I'm coming too.' He sat for a moment longer and when he next opened his eyes and looked at his phone, frowning at its painful brightness, he saw it was just after three in the morning. He sat up, took his glasses off and rubbed his eyes. He switched off the living-room light and staggered into the bathroom to brush his teeth.

He stripped down to his underwear, got into bed beside Karijn and fell instantly asleep. When the bedside alarm clock blared it felt like he had only been out for a few minutes. Looking at the clock he realised that was true: 3:34, the green digits read. He stared at them in confusion.

'Turn it off,' Karijn said into her pillow. 'What time is it?'

'You don't want to know,' Robert said, pushing buttons at random on top of the clock, its harsh beep unrelenting. Karijn moaned. He couldn't remember how to turn it off – they both used their phone alarms; he had no idea when either of them had last touched the clock. The beeping stopped, but Robert didn't know if he had turned it off or only snoozed it. He reached down between the bedside table and the wall, fumbling for the plug, and pulled it out of the socket. The green digits vanished. He sighed and lay back in bed. It must have been one of the kids, he thought, and as if summoned Nora then Sonja shambled into the room, climbed onto the bed and squirmed between Robert and Karijn. They usually jostled to be beside Karijn, so Robert often ceded his space and slept in the living room. Tonight, though, they simply lay down and returned to sleep as if they had never been awake at all.

The next morning, eager to get back to work, Robert got the girls out of the apartment unusually early and had them at the Kita just after eight. By eight thirty he was at a table in Balzac, his laptop open and a cup of black coffee steaming beside it. It had been a couple of days since he last worked and he wasn't sure about the scene he was in the middle of, so he spent some time scanning the notes he had written up after his last meeting with Patrick. There were pages of them. When Patrick had gone to the toilet, leaving Robert alone in his kitchen, he had taken the opportunity to switch on his voice recorder and hide it in the pocket of his jacket. As soon as he did so it seemed to become incredibly heavy and for the rest of the conversation he had sat in an unnaturally rigid position, paranoid that any movement might trigger an incriminating noise from the device. It had been a foolish risk to take, perhaps, but even though some of what Patrick said was drowned under the rasp of fabric rubbing against the microphone, the recording gave Robert so much more than his memory alone would have provided. Patrick had spoken about how dejected he felt travelling back to London from High Wycombe that Sunday afternoon, despairing of ever getting anywhere with Vanyashin, only to receive an invitation to join him the next day at Sotheby's for a sale of Russian paintings. That was the scene Robert was trying to write when a beggar approached his table and rattled a cup in his face.

'Entschuldigung, ich habe nichts,' Robert said.

The man took a step towards Robert's table. He was wearing ragged Adidas tracksuit trousers and a quilted jacket with a long gash down one side. The grimy, once-white synthetic padding showed through it like sinew. He rattled the cup again. His lined face was tanned the ruddy brown of someone who spent most of their life outdoors. His patchy grey beard was stained yellow.

'Ich habe nichts,' Robert said again.

The man gave his cup a last shake, very close to Robert's face, and drew it away. Doing so he caught Robert's cup, which toppled and sent a wave of coffee across the table's surface, sheeting over its edge and down onto his bag. 'Jesus,' Robert shouted and stood, stepping around the table to snatch the bag away. The beggar bent down and fumbled at the bag as Robert lifted it.

'Leave it,' Robert said, pulling the bag away, but the man tightened his grip and pulled it back towards him, trying to wipe the coffee from it with his sleeve.

'Entschuldigung,' he said. 'Entschuldigung.'

'Stop it!' Robert shouted, ripping the bag from the man's hands. He became aware of other people around them. A barista put a hand on the beggar's shoulder, but the beggar pushed him away. 'Ich gehe,' he said angrily. He picked up his cup, the loose change clinking inside it, and limped rapidly to the door. The small crowd dispersed. The barista handed Robert some napkins and wiped the table with a cloth. Robert picked up his laptop so the man could clean the entire surface. 'Danke,' he said. The barista nodded.

Sitting back down, Robert saw faces here and there turned towards him. Embarrassed at the thought of what his struggle with the beggar must have looked like, he tried to get back into the scene he had been writing but kept hearing those coins rattling in the man's cup. He decided to leave. Saving his work, he noticed that his thumb drive wasn't plugged into his laptop. He looked underneath the table, on his seat, and checked inside his bag, even though he was certain he had plugged it in when he first sat down. 'Fucking bastard,' he said, looking at the door the beggar had walked out of five minutes ago.

A couple of hours later, still brooding about the theft, Robert was sitting at the kitchen table trying to read a magazine when a Facebook Messenger notification lit his phone. It was from Bea, a colleague from the ad agency where he used to work. He hadn't spoken to her for at least three years, since she moved to the New York office and he left the company. Bad news, he read in the message preview. He thumbed it open. There's no good way to say this. Liam is dead. Liam and Bea had been a couple, but they had broken up after she moved to the States – something Liam revealed with typical indirectness in an email sent months after it happened. The composition dots appeared. He always admired you, Bea wrote. I think he thought of you as one of the few people that understood him.

Bea, I'm so sorry, Robert typed. How did it happen? The dots reappeared. It was four thirty in the morning in New York. Perhaps she was back in London. The dots disappeared; a few seconds later they returned.

He killed himself

Oh god, Bea, I'm so sorry.

Yeah me too. What can you say?

He emailed me. He said he was coming to Berlin.

When was that?

Robert switched to his mail app and searched. 6 weeks ago. End of September. Bea didn't reply. Where are you? Robert typed.

New York

What time is it?

Very early. Very late. Can't sleep.

Dots.

Anyway the funeral's in Ireland on Saturday, but his family are coming over to collect him. There's a thing in London on Wednesday. A viewing they call it. I know it's short notice but I wanted to tell you.

His first impulse was to lie. To invent some obligation that prevented him from going. But this urge dissolved, replaced by the certainty that he would go. Thanks Bea, he typed. I want to be there. You'll be in London?

Flying tomorrow

If you need anything, if there's anything I can do, just let me know OK?

Sure

Robert sat back in the chair. He felt disembodied, as if he might put his hand on the table only to see it pass through. He had forgotten how it felt to hear that someone he knew had died: weightlessness edged with something like excitement. A fizzing emptiness. He saw Liam sitting on grass beside water in early-morning light. He started as his phone buzzed against the table. He picked it up and turned it around, intending to dump the call, but saw it was Patrick. He tapped to accept and lifted the phone to his ear. 'Hello?'

'Robert, it's Patrick. Can you talk?'

'Sure,' he said and looked out of the window at the block across the Hof, a white strip of sky visible above it.

'I was wondering when we could meet next,' Patrick said. He was walking. He sounded short of breath.

'I'm not sure,' Robert said. 'I have to go to London for a couple of days.'

'What's in London?' Somewhere near Patrick a car horn sounded.

'A friend of mine has died. I have to go to his funeral.'

For a moment there was only the sound of the connection and the surf of traffic. 'I'm so sorry, Robert. What happened?'

'Suicide.' It didn't sound real when he said it.

A long exhalation came over the line. 'I'm sorry. You were close?'

'Yeah. Kind of. I hadn't seen him for a long time. Actually—' he said, laughing.

'What?'

'Just something I was thinking about when you called. He was the last person I ever got really fucking high with.'

Patrick made a sound that might have been laughter.

'A few years ago now,' Robert said. 'He was a good person.'

'I'm sorry.'

'Thanks. It's . . . yeah, I don't know what it is.'

'You're not meant to know,' Patrick said. 'You shouldn't feel like you were supposed to know something you didn't.'

'With all due respect, you didn't know Liam and you don't know anything about my relationship with him.'

'But I know you. I've got no doubt you were a good friend to him. You're a good listener.'

Robert didn't know what to say. He hadn't ever considered what Patrick thought of him. 'Let's meet up when I'm back,' he said.

'Please, we need to,' Patrick said. 'Take care of yourself.'

'And you.' Robert ended the call and sat with the phone in his hand. The screen went black. He tapped it into life and opened the email Liam had sent him a couple of months before. The last message he would ever have from him. I'll be in Berlin soon. A beer? Karijn had never met him. Robert had been looking forward to that happening. He read the email over and over again, until the letters grew strange and stopped making any sense at all.

The train crawled into the station and stopped with a strangled gasp. Robert looked out of the window at the flaking red brick of a derelict warehouse, weeds like grasping fingers coming through the walls. On a crumbling ledge a small, twisted tree pointed towards a grey sky so featureless it looked like a ceiling suspended just a few metres overhead: London in November.

He had flown from Berlin early that morning and dropped his suitcase at a cheap hotel in King's Cross. He took a tube across the city to Victoria station, where he met Sam and Gilbert, two old colleagues. Bea had begun a group email chain not long after Robert spoke to her and some of those on it had shared their travel plans. The three said hello just as the train was about to leave; a harsh alarm blared from the closing doors as they hurried aboard.

'Thanks for this, Liam,' Gilbert said, looking out at the scrappy, sooty backs of buildings as the train rolled slowly out of Victoria. 'I'm pitching on Friday. This is unbeatable timing.'

'What's the account?' Sam said.

'J and J. It's a combined dose thing for HIV. Pretty interesting, actually.'

'When did you see Liam last?' Robert cut in, not wanting to hear anything more about Gilbert's pitch strategy.

'I ran into him at an awards thing a few months ago,' Sam said. 'We had a laugh. He was bossing it at BPP. He was their secret weapon.'

The train stopped and the doors hissed open. The morning rush hour was over and only a couple of people got on. A newspaper lay on the platform just outside Robert's window, the pages moving in the breeze as if turned by an invisible hand. 'I tried to nick him off them when I got made account director at Pine,' Gilbert said. 'Offered him a ton of money. He was very loyal.' The train left the station, some part of it screaming in protest. 'The last time I saw him,' Gilbert said thoughtfully. 'It must have been in the summer. Lovebox. We got absolutely cunted.'

Robert thought of the night he and Liam had shared. He didn't want to talk about it now. 'Did you go out together a lot?' he said.

'A fair bit. He'd drop off the radar now and then, but he always popped back up. Until now.'

The words hung between them as the train limped through the low-rise sprawl of south London. Sam received a text and tapped out a reply, sinking deeper into his seat. Gilbert pulled out his phone and said he needed to send an email. Robert looked out of the window at concrete yards stacked with pallets; loops of barbed wire strung along corrugated fences; a small, barren park inhabited by a lone drunk. He had always found London bleak, but hadn't allowed the thought any oxygen when he lived here. Now he felt relief that he had left. Karijn had suggested he ask one of his friends to put him up for the night, but he had been bad at staying in touch with people since the move to Berlin and anyway, he didn't want to reconnect with anyone on this visit. A hotel reinforced the sense that this wasn't his city any more. It was a casing he had shed.

Looking at Sam and Gilbert, who were immaculate and whose mingled colognes filled the carriage, Robert felt self-conscious. His suit was ten years old. The white backing material showed through the tears in its lining. A moth had eaten a hole in one of the sleeves and a cigarette burn marked the lapel. None of this would have bothered Liam, though. For as long as Robert knew him, whether he was meeting clients or dancing to techno, he had always worn the same uniform of untucked shirt, baggy chinos and battered brogues.

'What is this thing, anyway?' Gilbert asked. 'Is it a service or what?'

'It's a viewing,' Robert said.

'Meaning what?'

'I think we just look at him.'

'At his coffin?'

'At his body, assuming it's an open coffin.'

'And if it's not?'

'Then we look at the coffin.'

Gilbert began to say something, then stopped and looked out of the window. The train's brakes whined, then squealed. Robert saw the ruined warehouse and the twisted tree.

'This is us,' Sam said, standing.

The doors shuddered open and the three men stepped down onto the platform. They descended a steep, dirty staircase to the windblown ticket hall, where dead leaves and empty crisp packets trembled in the corners. The station's exits opened onto two different streets. Gilbert looked at his phone. 'This way,' he said. They walked along a narrow strip of pavement beneath the vaulted brick arch of the bridge their train had just crossed. A van rattled past followed by a stream of cars, their engines echoing loudly beneath the bridge. Gilbert led them away from the noise of the main road, down an empty residential street that felt less peaceful than abandoned. The pavement was uneven, its grey slabs rising at foot-catching angles. The semi-detached houses were identical in design, but in varying stages of rot. Many of them had wooden fences that sagged, or were missing slats. The small front yards held sun-paled plastic trikes, rusty barbecues and maimed dolls tangled in stands of dead grass. In some of the windows strings of Christmas lights flashed hectically. In one of the gardens a dog was barking with the insistence of an alarm.

'Did Liam live round here?' Robert asked.

'I think he was in Islington,' Sam said. When he heard

that, Robert remembered visiting Liam there, a tiny place off Rosebery Avenue.

'So what the fuck are we doing here?' said Gilbert as he stepped over a torn bin bag, a bulging nappy and a sauce-smeared foil tray spilling out from it. 'Do any of his family live here?'

'No,' Robert said. 'Bea told me they've all come over from Ireland.'

'Do either of you know how he did it?' Sam said.

Robert and Gilbert shook their heads.

'Is it wrong to want to know?'

'I want to know,' Robert said.

At the end of the road ran a much busier one. On the other side of it they saw the funeral home. *Harmon Brothers*. At a glance its sign made it look like a solicitor's, or an estate agent, but slat curtains screened the interior and beneath the name, in a much smaller font, were the words *Family Funeral Directors & Monumental Masons*. Liam would have enjoyed the ambiguity of 'monumental', Robert thought. He had liked the malleability of words, how the same ones could be sublime or ridiculous, or both things at once. He had enjoyed finding the absurd in things and would have undoubtedly found the absurd in this: people coming to pay their final respects at a miserable stand of shops somewhere near Croydon, for no reason anyone could provide. For the first time Robert felt anger at what Liam had done. He hadn't known he was depressed, but he wasn't surprised. Even so, he still found it hard to believe he had killed himself. He had wanted to ask Bea how Liam did it but he didn't know how to and he worried about what sort of state she was in. The time stamps on her replies to messages sent over the last couple of days told him she wasn't sleeping.

The door of the funeral home was heavy and opened grudgingly. It made Robert think of pushing at the door of a crypt. He held it open for Sam and Gilbert. The lobby's walls and carpet were a neutral colour that made it difficult to gauge the room's precise size, as if its walls were obscured by mist. A group of people, all in black, stood beside a reception desk made from cheap yellow wood. A few looked over as Sam, Gilbert and Robert came through the door. One of them, a heavy woman in a long, grey woollen coat, was crying, a hand gripping a corner of the desk, the other held to her face. They looked young, reminding Robert that he was ten years older than Liam. The door closed and as the traffic noise reduced to a hum, Robert heard what seemed to be several people weeping. It was coming from a corridor to the left of the lobby. Turning away from it, Robert was confused to see, through an archway, another lobby apparently identical to the one he was standing in, as if he were looking into a mirror from which his reflection was impossibly absent. The difference, he realised with a momentary relief, was that the floor of this duplicate version was covered with a dustsheet. He watched as a workman in white, paint-spattered dungarees walked past the archway and said something indistinct. From somewhere out of view came the loud laughter of several men: a wild-seeming sound in this muted space. The receptionist stood and walked around the corner. The laughter cut off like she had closed a tap. She spoke, but too softly for Robert to tell what she was saying. She returned to her seat, her face impassive, and resumed her swift, quiet typing. Her phone rang once before she picked it up. 'Harmon Brothers?' she said calmly.

Robert turned to see Bea coming out of the corridor from which the crying still came. He heard it grow louder and more ragged. Bea looked exhausted but somehow serene. She came to Robert and he opened his arms. 'Hey,' he said, as she folded herself into his embrace.

She hugged Sam and then Gilbert.

'Oh, you!' Gilbert said, his mouth downturned in a pantomime of grief.

'These are friends of Liam's from university,' Bea said, indicating the other group. 'Robert, Sam and Gilbert all worked with Liam,' she told the university friends in turn. 'He's—' she began, then stopped and swallowed. 'He's through here.'

They followed Bea around the corner. Ahead of them, beside an open doorway, stood another small group of people, all dressed in black. Through the doorway Robert saw the pine and gold of a coffin, lying unsealed on top of a table. He glimpsed a brown shoe. That's Liam's shoe, he thought, somehow surprised that Liam should be wearing his own shoes, shoes he had worn when he walked beside Robert, and that he should see one of them and recognise it despite Liam being dead. He saw the shoe being polished and brought to a room and slipped onto Liam's foot. The sight of it almost sent him back down the corridor and out into the street, but Sam and Gilbert were moving ahead of him towards the group of people standing outside the room, the crying people who must of course be Liam's family, and he found himself following them, grateful to simply follow someone else and do what they did. The mother's face looked peeled by grief. Had she polished the shoes? Had she worn them on her hands as she worked in the polish, feeling on her hands the rub of the creases made by her son's feet? The father, his piercing blue eyes moist and rimmed red, smiled at Robert and took his hand in both his own. Liam's brothers and sister stood beside them. It was the sister who looked like him. Her dark eyes were swollen. She dabbed at them with a twisted shred of tissue paper.

Then Robert was in the room, looking down at Liam's remains. The word seemed entirely wrong. This was Liam, not some leftover piece of him: the green-checked shirt, the blue chinos, those shined brown brogues. This was him, only sleeping, despite the white veil covering his face. Beneath it Robert saw some beard growth, ginger on the cheeks and moustache, black, the colour of Liam's hair, at the chin. He had a book resting on his chest, the cover showing two boats on a blue sea viewed through arches. *Balcony of Europe*, Robert read. Pinned beneath a hand was a Blackwing pencil. Robert remembered giving Liam one when they worked together and telling him it was the best pencil in the world. 'Get over yourself,' Liam had said. Robert had completely forgotten about it until now. The walls of the room buckled as his eyes filled with tears. He crossed his arm over his chest, held the other up towards his face and pressed his fingers into his eyes. He moaned. The body in the box looked so lonely. He wiped his eyes and leaned back against the wall. Sam and Gilbert had come in and gone out. Two of Liam's university friends were beside the coffin. Robert looked around the room, at its varieties of beige. The lid of the coffin leaned against the wall. On the floor beside it stood an unlit tea light and a bottle of bright blue hand sanitiser. He looked into the coffin again. He had the ridiculous sense that Liam might wake up. Seen through the veil's gauze the lines of his checked shirt seemed to move as if his chest were rising and falling. The veil made him look like a bride. If he were to sit up, the veil would slip from his face and pool in his lap. As he clambered from the box, well again, the pencil and the book would fall to the floor.

Liam's mother was crying. 'My boy,' she said. She didn't shout, but somehow the words sounded as harsh as a scream. They came from some part of her that existed only to produce that hoarse, hollow sound. She cried out and it sounded as if she were coming apart. Robert wanted to say something but there was nothing he could say. They were all crying, the mother and the family. He walked past them in silence.

The foyer was crowded with people now. Robert saw Danielle and Rosie, whom he used to work with. They had both moved to the same agency as Liam. Maybe they could tell him what happened. Some people were having muted conversations, but most stood and listened to the awful sound of Liam's family. It sounded as if they had just that moment been told. Robert didn't know where to look. He stared down at the carpet, his vision narrowing, the carpet seeming to pulse as Liam's shirt had pulsed, as everything had pulsed on that weekend with Liam long ago, the last lost weekend Robert ever had. Someone said, 'Shall we find a pub?' and a murmur of agreement passed through the room. 'I'll tell them,' Bea said, going back down the corridor towards that sound.

Outside, the rumble of traffic and the cold, gritty wind came as a relief after the tense hush of the funeral home. People consulted their phones as they made their way along the street. 'Anyone know this area?' Sam asked. No one did.

One of Liam's university friends was staring at her screen. 'There's a place up by Thornton Heath station,' she said. 'Ten minutes. It's a Wetherspoons.'

A tall woman with attractive, angular features laughed and said, 'We owe it to Liam to get as drunk as fucking possible.' Her voice shook a little as she spoke.

A text came through from Karijn. Hej, I hope it's OK today. Not too awful. I saw Heidi and we spoke about dinner tomorrow night at ours. I could ask Ernesto too. I know you'll be tired, but I thought it could be fun. What do you think?

Hej, Robert typed, very sad but lots of love too. Dinner sounds good. As he sent the message he fell into step with Danielle and Rosie. 'I still can't believe it,' Rosie said, and told a long, garbled story about the first client meeting she attended with Liam, when she realised he was, she said, 'some kind of genius'. By the time she finished speaking, several members of the group were listening to her and in the pub, a rectangular cave at the foot of a grimy seventies office block, dominated by a bank of glimmering fruit machines, people continued to share their memories. Robert found himself standing beside the woman he had noticed earlier. Her name was Molly. She had known Liam since university. She pushed a strand of lank brown hair away from her face. Her bright green eyes were large. Her nose was large, too. Her hands were constantly moving from her hair to her face to her arms. 'How do you know him?' she asked. 'Did,' she said, and laughed in a disappointed way.

'I used to work with him,' Robert said. 'I hadn't seen him since I moved to Berlin, but we emailed a lot. Actually, he'd just written to say he was coming over.' Even as he spoke the words he wanted to take them back. What did it prove, how recently he'd received an email? What even needed to be proven? He heard Patrick's question, *Were you close?* 'What about you?' he said.

'We were at Cambridge together,' said Molly. 'We went out with each other for five seconds in the first year.'

'You always know when someone's gone to Cambridge,' Robert said.

'How?'

'Because they tell you.'

She had a loud laugh. 'Fuck you,' she said.

'I can see why Liam liked you,' he said.

'Because I drink and have a foul mouth?'

'Because you seem smart and kind,' he said.

His words seemed to surprise her. She took a moment to answer. 'That's true, I am,' she said with mock conceit, an eyebrow arched. Her expression changed. 'That's actually a very nice thing to say.'

'I'm going for a cigarette. Do you want one?'

'Don't smoke,' she said, a lilt in her voice as if he had tried to trick her and she had spotted it.

He had one Guinness, then another and another. Someone bought a round of Jameson. He saw he had missed a text from Karijn: OK great. Call me later x. He put his phone away. People were switching places; more and more tables were pulled together to make room for everyone as they arrived. In the fruit machines' flicker Robert saw that apart from Liam's mourners the pub was mostly empty: a few solitary men hunched over papers and two women sharing a plate of nachos, a drift of shopping bags at their feet.

Robert skirted the edges of conversations as he drank. At times he felt a strange certainty that he couldn't be seen. He spoke briefly to one of Liam's brothers and then with someone called Marcus who had lived with Liam first at university, then for their first few years in London. He had been with him the night he killed himself. 'He wanted one more drink, but my wife,' he said, indicating a pregnant woman sitting a couple of seats away. 'We're having a baby,' he said. 'She wanted to go home.'

'There's nothing you could have done,' Robert said. 'Don't think that there was.' But he wasn't sure he believed that was true. Maybe another drink might have made all the difference. Perhaps actually killing yourself, the momentary action that pushed you from life into death, was only ever a split-second decision. If that was true, then not doing it, deferring it, was always a possibility. Maybe another drink would have stopped him that night, and something else the next time, and something else the time after that. He would still have been suicidal, but alive for another year, two years, ten years. 'It was Liam's decision,' Robert said.

Marcus shook his head, but Robert didn't know if he was disagreeing with what Liam had done or with what Robert had just told him. He went to the toilet and on his way back to the table he ran into Bea, took her elbow and directed her to the bar. He ordered two whiskeys. 'Down in one,' he said. She nodded. He upended his glass and a moment later she did the same. They winced, gasped, laughed. They leaned back on the bar. Robert watched a man feed pound coins into a fruit machine. 'How did he do it?' he said.

Bea was silent.

'I'm sorry,' Robert said. 'I wasn't going to ask you that.'

'He hung himself,' she said. The tears on her face shone red in the light from the fruit machines.

'Where?' Robert said.

'In his wardrobe. With a belt.' She wiped her face. Robert reached behind him for a napkin and handed it to her. She blew her nose.

'Who found him?'

'Marcus.' Bea pointed at the man Robert had spoken to earlier. 'They'd been for a drink. He called him the next morning. No answer. Called his work, found out he hadn't come in. He went over and broke down the door. He said he'd never thought Liam would do something like this, but as soon as they said he wasn't at work he knew. He knew he'd done it.'

'Did you ever think he could?'

A group of men in cheap suits came in from the street. Robert looked at them as they crossed loudly to the bar, obviously excited to be free of work. Bea was looking at the men too, but her gaze was unfocused. She crossed her arms over her chest and lifted her shoulders as if she were cold. 'It's unbelievable and completely unsurprising,' she said.

'Is it something he talked about?'

'He said things,' she said, sounding impatient. 'But there's saying and doing, right? He'd say something stupid and I'd just roll my eyes, like, "come on, you're the smartest person I know." But that turned out to be beside the point, I guess. Or it is the point. Oh god.' She began to cry again but shook off Robert's arm. She looked up and touched her little finger to the bottom of her widened eyes, trying to dry them. 'Maybe,' she began, and stopped. 'Maybe it's always this way, and it always feels like something that'll never happen until it does.' She tutted. 'You want to know what the worst thing is?'

'What?'

'It turns everything I say into a fucking banality.'

Robert laughed, then Bea did. It was relieving to laugh.

'Did you ever tell your parents about Liam?' When Bea and Liam started going out she had told Robert that her parents, who had come to Britain from Nigeria, only wanted her to date someone who attended their church.

'Never,' she said. 'Isn't that pathetic? They don't even know I'm home right now.'

'What was he so upset about?' Robert said.

Bea arched an eyebrow. 'How long do you have?'

'Long enough,' he said. He raised a finger to attract the barman and ordered two more whiskeys.

'No, I've had enough,' Bea said.

'You haven't,' Robert said. 'None of us have.' He recognised the feeling inside him. He would either leave now or stay and drink himself to a standstill. He didn't want to go back to his hotel.

The barman slid the whiskeys across the bar and Robert handed him a note. He lifted his glass and waited until Bea, reluctantly, lifted hers. He didn't know why he was making her drink. 'To Liam,' he said. 'Despite him being a thoughtless fucking arsehole.'

'To Liam,' Bea said. They drank.

'You were saying,' Robert said.

Bea swallowed and shook her head. 'Was I?'

'Liam's woes.'

'Oh Robert, I don't want to do this. Sometimes he detested himself. He thought he was the worst person, the absolute worst person. Logic didn't apply, you couldn't persuade him otherwise. It was like he was in a hole, and the hole was so deep he couldn't hear what you were saying. He could only shout out of it at you, it was all one-way. But after some random length of time had passed something would happen, what I don't know, and apparently he didn't know either, but then he'd climb out and be brilliant again and we'd forget that the hole had ever been there.'

The fruit machine nearest them blurted out an ascending sequence of chords. The man playing it pushed more coins into its ember-red slot. At the other end of the bar a group of mourners laughed loudly.

Danielle approached. 'Robert,' she said urgently, 'will you help me? Gilbert's got Liam's folks cornered and he won't shut up about him and Liam getting wasted together. They need to hear something else.'

Robert put a hand on Bea's shoulder and left her, following Danielle away from the bar, stumbling up the steps to where Liam's parents sat. Gilbert was seated beside the mother, one hand on her knee and in the other the dregs of a pint. His voice was loud. He said something and threw his head back and laughed and the harrowed-looking woman with cropped blonde hair smiled vaguely. Beside her was her husband: chubby, pink-skinned, white-haired, his blue eyes shining even in the pub's twilight. He was looking straight ahead, not reacting to what Gilbert was saying at all. Danielle leaned in towards him. 'This is Robert,' she said. Her Australian twang, combined with the deliberate slowness of her speech – she enunciated as if Liam's parents were senile – cut through the chatter around them. 'He and Liam shared a love of writing.'

Liam's mother turned to him. 'Robert,' she said, her eyes focusing on him. 'Is it you that wrote a book?'

'Yes,' Robert said. 'I'm so sorry for your loss.'

'Sit down, please,' she said, indicating the chair where Gilbert was sitting. Beaming insincerely, Gilbert stood and waved Robert towards the chair.

Robert sat. Liam's mother smiled at him. She touched her husband's leg. He started and looked at her. His arms were crossed tightly at his chest, his back completely straight. 'This is Robert,' she said to him. 'The writer friend Liam told us about. Do you remember?'

'Robert, thanks for coming, pal.' Liam's father smiled warmly, but there was still a vagueness to his gaze. Robert wasn't sure he had any idea what his wife was talking about.

Robert told them how sorry he was. He told them how, although he hadn't seen Liam for a long time, they had remained in touch and that he had always been happy to hear from him. 'He had a remarkable mind,' he said.

The mother nodded and smiled, then pursed her lips as tears spilled from her eyes. She swallowed, looked up to the pub ceiling and nodded, her tears stopped from falling only by the tilt of her head. She smiled again, still looking up. 'Always with his head in a book,' she said, her voice shaking.

'You couldn't get his head out of them when he was a lad,' the father said. He pointed at his wife. 'Orla could talk to him about that stuff. Not me. I'm an engineer,' he said, holding Robert's gaze. 'So are Ryan and Brendan.' He motioned behind him, where his sons were standing chatting in a circle of mourners. 'I could never fill my head with all that stuff. Fiction. I couldn't,' he said and shrugged, as if Robert had challenged his claim. 'What's the point of it? He could never explain it to me.'

Orla had turned to Liam's sister, Siobhán, who was weeping silently, her shoulders quaking. Orla ran her hands up and down her back.

Liam's father leaned in. 'I don't think,' he said, as if sharing a secret.

Robert waited for him to finish the sentence, then realised he had. 'You don't think?'

'I don't think,' he said. 'When I'm not working, my mind just stops.' He held his fingertips together, then moved them apart, suggesting an explosion – or, Robert supposed, the expansion of nothingness. 'And when I sleep, I don't dream. These last eight days, though, I've dreams every night. Awful dreams. But Liam, he thought all the time. I love him, but it's like he isn't my son. With me it's about rationality. Absolute rationality. He was irrational. He had a brilliant mind, but it was haunted.'

'What's haunted, Declan?' Orla said. Siobhán's head was in her mother's lap now, and Orla's fingers gently searched her daughter's hair until they found a particular strand then smoothed it to her scalp. Then they searched for another. It was such an incongruously intimate act that Robert had to look away. Someone put another Guinness down in front of him and he lifted it and drank. His vision was swarming. Chords rang out from the fruit machines and coins rattled into their troughs. He heard the beggar's coins in his shaken cup. The voices around him clustered and became indecipherable.

'I was telling Robert here about the way my mind works,' Declan said.

Orla's smile was bleak. 'That old mystery machine,' she said.

'No mystery,' Declan said, and tapped his forehead with a short, straight forefinger. 'It's a mechanism is all, and you want to treat it so it doesn't break.' He smiled at Robert. 'When I switch off, I switch off. I don't even remember my family's faces. My wife, Brendan, Siobhán,' he said, gesturing towards each of them as he spoke. 'If I walked out of this pub, the next minute I wouldn't remember any of their faces. I don't know the colour of Orla's eyes. I don't remember the colour of my daughter's eyes. The only one of them I remember right now is Liam, and the coroner's photograph Orla showed me last week.'

A noise escaped Orla, a sharp intake of breath as if she were sipping something hot. Siobhán lay still in her lap, hair covering her face.

'Is it—' Robert began. 'Does it help, being that way?'

Declan put his hand on Robert's shoulder. 'You're a terrific fella,' he said. 'Liam thought the world of you and it makes me happy to know he had you for a friend.'

Orla reached out her hand and placed it on top of her husband's, increasing the pressure on Robert's arm. She smiled. Two tears fell down her cheeks, one fast, the other slow.

Declan squeezed Robert's arm tighter still, nodded and released him. He felt dismissed. He knocked the table as he stood, setting glasses of wine and beer rocking, spilling slops onto the table. 'Thank you,' he said, not knowing what else to say. Declan's words had upset him. Robert never knew the depth of Liam's sorrow, had never thought that the irony he found so amusing might have been a marker of despair. Robert saw him dangling in a wardrobe beside his suits and shirts. Did he empty it first? Lay his clothes on the bed? He didn't know if he arranged them neatly or threw them down in a pile. Add it to everything he didn't know. Staggering a little, he walked to the bar. 'Hey, Cambridge,' he said.

Molly, standing with a knot of mourners Robert didn't recognise, turned to look at him and paused, her eyes widening in panic. 'Person!' she said.

'I'm touched you remembered.' He raised his glass and she met it with her own, and they laughed as some of their Guinness and red wine splashed onto the floor. 'Robert,' he said.

'I knew that! I was going to say that!' she said, reaching for his arm and squeezing it in apology. She took her hand away and pushed back her hair, then scratched her neck. Her clavicles stood out like handles, holding the straps of her thin black dress suspended. 'Well,' she said. Her hand ran up and down her arm then plucked at her dress, as if her body were an instrument from which it might pull music.

'Let's go somewhere,' Robert said.

'Where?'

'Somewhere less . . .' he looked around him, 'here.'

'You and me?' she said.

'Yeah. Unless . . . I just want to get drunk somewhere else.'

'Are you not drunk already? I'm drunk already.'

He laughed. 'Not get drunk, then. Continue to be drunk.'

She hesitated, then she walked away. Robert stood dumbly beside the bank of fruit machines, watching their lights pulse. Then Molly was beside him again, wearing her coat. She held out her hand. He took it and they walked towards the door. Someone called his name but he didn't turn around. Outside he was stunned there was still some drab light left in the sky. He pulled out his phone. It was only four o'clock. The traffic ground past. In front of them stood a confusion of roadwork barriers; he couldn't see where to cross for the station. He saw a black cab with its light on and he waved his arm, pulling Molly along behind him. She laughed and cried out, 'Taxi!'

The driver lowered his window and leaned over. 'The West End,' Robert said. The man nodded and Robert opened the door and they threw themselves down beside each other on the back seat. The cab moved slowly through the traffic at first, but they picked up speed as they headed towards Streatham, the pavements growing busier with people. 'I haven't been here for years,' Robert said.

'I don't think I've ever been here,' Molly said.

'Where do you live?'

'Finsbury Park.'

'With someone?'

'No. Do you live with someone in Berlin?'

Robert thought he had already told her about Karijn and the kids, but perhaps that had been someone else. 'Pub, bar or hotel?' he said.

'Pub,' Molly said, decisively. 'No, bar. Wait, what's the difference?'

'Bars are darker,' he said.

'Bar, then,' she said. 'Pub. Oh, I don't care. Where's your hotel?'

'King's Cross.'

'Let's go to King's Cross.'

He thought of a pub he used to go to near the British Library, but he had forgotten its name. It was across the street from a good Chinese restaurant, where the menus were tacky with fried grease. 'Are you hungry?' he said.

'I don't eat when I drink.'

'What are you, fifteen?'

'Thirty-three. Sorry to disappoint.'

Robert twisted his wedding ring between his thumb and middle finger. He thought she must have seen it, then wondered, if he knew she hadn't, whether he would remove it. She was staring out of the window. He looked at her legs, sheathed in thin black tights that showed white where they stretched across her kneecaps. On her feet, which were turned slightly towards one another, she wore scuffed black ballet flats. Her thin black dress was short and she wore a long black coat over it. This too had begun to wear, the wool pilling in places. She gathered her hair and twisted a band around it. Her hands dropped, her left hand lying slightly curled in her lap and her right upturned on the seat between them. He thought about putting his own on top of it.

'Poor Liam,' she said.

He put his head back on the hard plastic headrest. 'Yeah,' he said.

'He hanged himself, you know. In a wardrobe. In a fucking wardrobe.'

'Would somewhere else have been better?'

'I don't know,' she said, lifting her hand off the seat and letting it fall back again. 'Maybe.'

'Where? Where would have been better?'

She looked at him. She smiled then her face clouded. 'Fuck you,' she said. 'You know what I mean.'

'I don't.'

'Well I do.'

'Would a tree have been better? A majestic oak?'

'Fuck. You.'

Robert didn't know if they were flirting or fighting. They were in Brixton now, where he had lived more than a decade ago. The red neon light of the Ritzy shone in the darkening afternoon.

'So what do you do in Berlin?' Molly's head was turned away, towards the passing streets.

'I'm a writer,' Robert said.

'What do you write?'

'Books. Stories. I'm writing something about an oligarch.'

'Fiction or real?'

'Fiction. I met someone who worked for one. He's been telling me what it was like, and I'm turning it into a novel.'

Molly smiled. 'And what's the oligarch going to say about that?'

'Nothing. He's dead.' They were coming through Oval, past the dim expanse of Kennington Park.

'How did he die?'

Robert hesitated. 'He was found hanged from a tree on his estate.'

Molly sighed. 'Right,' she said.

Robert remembered the photographs he had seen of the oak where Vanyashin was found. He thought of Liam's foot and how pathetic his body must have looked dangling from a clothes rail. He had found the circumstances of Vanyashin's death grimly exciting and had been looking forward to writing about it. Now the prospect sickened him. 'Sorry,' he said. 'We can talk about something else.'

'No, it's OK. Why did he kill himself?'

'Well that's it. My guy says he didn't.' In the distance Robert saw the peak of the Shard. 'He says he was killed.'

'Killed? Who by?'

'Take your pick. Russian mafia, his enemies in the Kremlin, the Chechens.'

'Who kills him in your book?'

'I don't know. It's not really about that.'

'Oh. What is it about, then?'

'It's more about this guy, Patrick, who's working for the oligarch. After his boss dies, he thinks he's next. He goes on the run and ends up in Berlin.'

'And he's getting chased by the killers?'

'Yeah, only he's not. No one actually cares about him enough to kill him.'

'And what does he think of that?'

'Who?'

'The real-life version of Patrick. Does he think he's going to be assassinated?'

'He says he's being followed.'

'Really?' Molly said, turning to face him. 'But you – what, you don't believe him?'

'I didn't. Or I don't. I mean, at first I thought he was just making shit up, but now I think maybe he believes what he's saying. Like, he's playing out some fantasy.' Robert could see the appeal of it, the freedom in telling Molly anything he wanted about himself, editing out whatever he didn't want to think about or admit to. All those times when he had hidden away from people rather than have to see himself through their eyes: maybe he should have just lied instead, said things not because they were true, but because that's how he wanted them to be. 'Can I tell you something I haven't told anyone else?' he said.

Molly smiled, her teeth flashing in the glow of a passing streetlight. 'Definitely,' she said.

'The guy who's telling me all this, he doesn't know I'm using it for a book.'

'What does he think it's for?'

'Nothing. He doesn't know anyone else in Berlin, so we meet up and talk. I'm his friend.'

Molly laughed. 'You're not his friend.'

'I'm the closest he's got to one.'

'Why haven't you told him what you're doing?'

'He'd tell me to stop.'

'Even if it's made up? You don't want to call his bluff?'

'Like I said, I think maybe it's real to him. And even if he is just spinning bullshit, why piss him off by calling him a liar? I don't care if he is or isn't. I just want the story.'

Molly considered him. 'You've trapped him in your web.'

Robert looked out of the window. He didn't like the phrase she had chosen. He didn't know why he had told her about Patrick.

'And you aren't worried there really might be people after him?' she said. 'That doesn't freak you out? That would freak me out.'

Robert shook his head. The cab bounced in and out of a pothole, the movement drawing them together on the back seat. Their arms pressed against one another and neither moved away. Lambeth. The streets drew tighter around them.

'I could really use a drink,' Molly said.

Robert leaned forward and rapped on the divider. 'Driver, my friend desperately needs alcohol.'

Molly laughed. The driver turned on the intercom. 'Is that right, love? I know how you feel.' He made the cab surge in speed for a moment and Robert and Molly cheered. After that they really did move faster: lights changed in their favour and the traffic opened before them as they passed over the river, running low, flat and dull as iron in the twilight. Across the water and back into the city: Aldwych, Holborn, Bloomsbury.

Robert found the pub on his phone. As they got out of the cab the last light was draining from the sky. A soft violet band hung above them. The tables on the street were full, each one bathed in red light from the space heaters suspended above them. Inside it was even busier. Once they had their drinks they went back out and squeezed onto the end of a table filled with a loud group of men and women, all smoking and talking over one another. The table was cluttered with bottles of wine and half-eaten plates – olives, white beans, glistening fried peppers speckled with salt crystals. Molly asked one of the men for a cigarette and he lit it for her.

'So you do smoke,' Robert said.

'Only when I'm this drunk.' She lifted her chin and sent a thin stream of smoke into the air. Some people can really smoke, Robert thought. It was dark now and as Molly moved her head she alternately obscured and revealed a burning white streetlight a little way past the pub. These dazzling flashes of light seemed to contain some message, some confirmation or warning about what Robert was doing: if he saw the flash in five seconds, he would kiss her. If he didn't, he would get up and go back to his room alone. As the smoke of her cigarette passed through the light it became a thick white cloud rushing up into the darkness. The side of his face turned towards the heater prickled with warmth. Someone at the table was laughing with manic intensity. All around he heard chatter, but it sounded reversed. How long had he been listening to it? How long had it been since he spoke? Molly smiled at him and raised her eyebrows in a questioning way. 'Can't decide?' she said.

'What?'

'Do you want another drink, I said.'

He pressed his fingers to his temple. 'I don't know if I can,' he said.

She nodded and looked away, then glanced at her phone. 'Getting late,' she said.

'We could go to my hotel.'

She looked into the road, down at the pavement. 'We could,' she said deliberately.

Robert was surprised he had said the words. Say no, he thought.

'OK,' she said.

He lost his balance as he stood, almost falling back onto the table. 'Jesus,' he said and laughed. He felt foolish.

'Which way?' Molly said.

He looked left and then right, getting his bearings. 'This way,' he said. 'It's the other side of the station.' Walking down the street he felt insubstantial, as if he could do anything, go anywhere, and it wouldn't matter or mean anything. They turned onto a broad but quiet street, at the end of which he saw a ruby stream of brake lights oozing along Euston Road. At the junction they lifted their faces to the spires of St Pancras. Molly said something that Robert couldn't hear above the noise of the traffic. He reached out and put his hand on her shoulder. She looked at him. He moved his face towards hers and their noses met. They both angled their heads the same way at the same time. She laughed, cupped his jaw and held it while she turned her head again. Her mouth was warm. His hands moved to her waist and held her. One of her hands went around his neck, the other gripped his shoulder. As their mouths moved together, Robert heard the rumble and gasp of a truck and the wasp-like drone of a scooter; he heard a woman repeating the words, 'Got no credit,' as she passed by; he heard the rasp of a lighter's wheel. With his eyes closed the world seemed to swing as if he were in a hammock. He pulled away. Molly looked up. He felt the press of her long, bony body. They were still at the roadside, a crowd of people around them waiting to cross. They moved apart. She took his hand and squeezed it. The lights changed, the crowd moved and they were carried with it. Robert found the density of people around him suffocating. It was as if the entire city were on the move. He felt the mass of people thicken around him. A band tightened at his chest. Soon the crowd would come to a complete standstill and he would be trapped, no space ahead of him and none behind, like an animal caught in a snare. Molly's hand felt alien in his, oddly heavy. He wanted to shake it off. He wanted to be somewhere quiet. Somewhere empty. He wanted to sleep and put this long, strange day behind him. He pulled his hand from hers and began to run. He shoved a pair of men out of his way, whatever they shouted at him lost to the pounding of his blood. He heard Molly call his name but he didn't turn. To escape the crowded pavement he stepped off the kerb and onto the road, but had only gone a few steps before a horn sounded, loud and close behind him. He jumped back onto the pavement as a bus rushed past, sideswiping him with a hot slab of displaced air. 'Robert!' he heard. He ran on without looking back. He gained speed as he crossed the plaza outside King's Cross, darting between people smoking last cigarettes before boarding their trains, a man selling the *Big Issue* with a dog lying at his feet, some teenagers sitting cross-legged in a circle drinking cans of beer, as if it were summer. He ran past them all, moving faster and faster. His legs were beginning to burn, his breath was getting ragged, but he wanted only to run and to never stop. The pain was the only thing he wanted to feel. He ran up Pentonville Road beneath towering plane trees. He was almost there. He slowed to a walk, his lungs burning. He looked behind him: a few people stood at a bus stop; a man was walking a dog down the hill the way Robert had come. There was no sign of Molly. He put his hands on his hips and took deep breaths. He laughed. 'You fucking idiot,' he said. He looked up to clouds washed a grimy purple by the city's lights. A group of young men and women were coming down the road, laughing and talking loudly, swigging from bottles. Instead of altering their direction to avoid him, they moved past him as if he wasn't there. For an instant he was amid them all. In that moment, and as he stood on the street watching them move away, their voices fading, he felt for the second time that day as if he were a ghost.

His hotel was on a short, dead-end side street; a nondescript new build slotted between black-brick Victorian townhouses. The lobby was cramped and grubby, a staticky puce carpet on the floor and a brown-leafed cheese plant dying in a corner. A large man in a strained shirt and skewed tie sat behind the reception desk eating a wrap. 'You see me?' Robert said, sharply enough that the man flinched. He stared, his mouth slightly open.

'Do you see me?' Robert repeated.

The man nodded.

'Because I'm here,' Robert said.

'OK,' the man said uncertainly.

Robert crossed the lobby to a door that led to the stairwell.

'There's a lift,' the man called out.

Robert ignored him and went unsteadily up the stairs. His legs throbbed from running. His blood hissed in his ears. He staggered against the wall. He was hungry but he wasn't going out there again. He opened the door to his room, pushed the keycard into the light switch and collapsed onto the bed. Water and painkillers, he thought, but he only lay there. He needed to get undressed but couldn't stand up. He saw Liam in the wardrobe, the wood patterned with flashing blue light. Karijn was there, her back to him. She turned, a puzzled look on her face. 'You didn't know him,' she said. Liam's face was obscured by a veil, a single hair from his beard curling up through the fabric. 'See you,' he said, and entered the wardrobe that opened onto a street: Hanbury Street, off Brick Lane, the end of a two-day session that began with a drink after work one Friday, a pub just off Piccadilly Circus, then a place in Soho and another in Holborn. Liam mentioned a night he was going to, something round the back of Angel tube station, and it was on the way there, not far from where Robert lay at that moment, that they started in on the MDMA. Liam had it in a bag, divided into twists of Rizla. Robert texted Karijn, pregnant with Sonja then, to say he'd be home late, then sent another message saying he wouldn't be back until the morning. They stayed in the smaller room downstairs, a brick cellar, dancing to techno that was mostly space and echo: the kind that drew Robert deeper inside it the longer he listened. The only light was a strobe that would occasionally flicker to life before plunging everything back into darkness. Robert lost any sense of time. Liam pressed another twist of Rizla into his palm and after that there was only the music, the darkness and the beacon of the strobe signalling danger or salvation. He saw immense, detailed landscapes in the retina burns left by each burst.

It felt like no more than an hour had passed when a raw, racing beat faded into silence and the lights came up with brutal immediacy. The room Robert had thought was still dense with people turned out to be largely empty. He and Liam put their arms around each other as they climbed the steps and walked out into the pale morning light. It was just after six and already getting warm. They bought cigarettes and bottles of Lucozade and walked down to the canal and followed it east. Liam said he knew about an after-party somewhere in Hackney Wick, across the water from the vast construction zone of the Olympic site. When they could see the stadium, a half-built bowl with a cluster of green and yellow cranes rising from it, they stopped to rest. They sat on the grass verge beside the towpath as joggers and cyclists swept by, the sun burning white streaks onto the water.

'You do this a lot?' Robert asked.

'Every once in a while,' Liam said.

'Who with?'

'People. On my own.'

'On your own?'

Liam moved his head as if to say, 'So what?' His legs were stretched out towards the water, an arm thrown behind him for support, his hand pressed to the turf. In the other hand he held a cigarette. His white shirt was stained brown with brick dust from the walls of the cellar. Robert's eyes felt gritty. His guts were knotted. Thrills ran through his body, partly from the MDMA and partly, he supposed, from tiredness. He thought of texting Karijn, but when he looked at his phone it was dead.

'A question,' Liam said, reaching into his shirt pocket and pulling out the glassine bag, cloudy now with creases and escaped powder. 'What are we going to do with these?'

Robert looked at the bag. The twisted cigarette papers looked like white tadpoles. There were still a lot of them left. They squirmed against one another as he tried to focus on them. 'What do you think we should do?' he said.

'I think we owe it to ourselves to consume them,' Liam said.

They wandered around Hackney Wick for a couple of hours but couldn't find the after-party. Robert smoked compulsively. He felt enormously high: his skin crawled with a moment-by-moment anticipation, but he was restless too – dissatisfied, aware of some huge but obscure disappointment that was relentlessly approaching. They found a canalside pub opening its doors and sat drinking at the water's edge. Every so often they swallowed more MDMA. Liam went to the toilet to snort some and came back to the table looking like he'd been slapped. Robert went and did the same: it felt like inhaling powdered glass. He was certain that blood was about to begin pouring out of his nose, but when he wiped it all he saw on his hand were flakes of powder. He felt as if he were set at a different angle to the rest of the world. The flattest of surfaces wouldn't stay straight; everything he looked at for longer than a couple of seconds began breathing. He couldn't remember what they talked about, but they laughed a lot. Every time he felt the day's end drawing nearer – a void towards which they were, every second, sliding – he pushed the feeling back with another drink, another cigarette, another twist of paper from Liam's supply.

Evening came. There was another club somewhere, then someone's apartment off Brick Lane. He remembered a deep marmalade light coating everything in the living room, and music that sounded Arabic. He remembered talking intensely to a very thin woman wearing bondage trousers, buckles running up and down them and canvas straps running from one leg to the other. Robert woke up on a couch and found Liam asleep at the foot of a bed on which four people lay clothed and tangled smoking joints, the duvet speckled with burns. They walked out of there into the blaze of midday. A few white clouds passed the brick chimney of the Truman Brewery. A minicab driver slept in his car, his beaded seat reclined, one shoeless foot slung out of the rolled-down window. At the end of the street they watched two women in knee socks and furs throw themselves into poses in front of a wall of graffiti, while a third woman, crouched low to the ground, took photographs.

Liam rubbed the stubble at his jaw, said, 'See you,' and walked up the street towards Brick Lane, which was thick with people. Abrupt goodbyes were the only kind he knew.

The last time Robert saw him was a couple of summers later at a production of the *Oresteia*. In the interval they went out onto the hot street and smoked beneath the blazing lightbulbs of the theatre's porch. Liam took a book of Samuel Beckett's letters from his satchel and read Robert something that made them laugh. At the end of the evening Robert said how much he had enjoyed it, that they should do it again soon. Liam only said, 'Sure,' and crossed Whitehall towards Charing Cross. In Robert's memory he carried on watching Liam for a long time, until he completely lost sight of him in the crowds. But he knew the memory wasn't real. It had only existed since he heard that Liam was dead.

Robert woke up fully clothed. His eyelids were sticky. His throat felt scorched. When he sat upright the room sloshed towards him then drained away. He stood, wanting only to lie back down and fall asleep, but he had a plane to catch.

Hangover paranoia got him to Stansted and through security with nearly three hours to spare. He bought a sandwich and a coffee, found a seat in the departure lounge, opened his laptop and looked through his folder of research on Vanyashin. There were Word documents filled with notes, PDFs of newspaper articles, lists of links. He supposed much of what he had collected was the same material Patrick would have read through when Vanyashin commissioned him. It made him feel a kind of kinship with the other man and at the same time gave him the sense he was again tailing him, not along city streets this time, but through a series of documents and articles.

Tom's warning about the amount of time Patrick would get with Vanyashin had proved accurate: between his first trip to Buckinghamshire and the Russian's death Patrick was only granted another four or five meetings, most of which were hastily convened and brief. But there was one, he had told Robert, that was different. On that night Patrick was summoned to the Lanesborough, where Vanyashin liked to hold informal meetings in the hotel's Library Bar. Patrick didn't recognise any of Vanyashin's companions that night except for Uri and Aleksey, who had been at the Holland Park house the first time Patrick met him and who, he now knew, were two of his oldest business partners. Everyone was speaking Russian. Patrick drank a vodka tonic, then several glasses of mineral water, and wondered why he had been told to come. In fact there was one other man there that he knew, although this person was so quiet and still, sitting back in a deep armchair, that at first Patrick failed to notice him at all. But when he leaned in, his large, bald head thrust forward, Patrick recognised him at once: Boris Berezovsky.

He looked an older and lesser man than the one Patrick had come to know in the course of his research. He had enjoyed reading about him and became especially captivated by a long interview filmed at the Frontline Club that he found on YouTube. That man had been tanned and robust. A glass of white wine stood on the table beside him. He was intelligent, charming and quick to smile. But Patrick encountered him just a couple of months after he had lost his High Court case against Roman Abramovich, when he had been ordered to pay tens of millions for Abramovich's legal costs. He was gaunt and unshaven, his movements laboured. The only time he conveyed any sense of his old vigour was when he seemed to disagree vehemently with something Aleksey had said, making a repeated cutting motion with one hand against the open palm of the other. His fingers, Patrick noticed, were surprisingly long and thin. His point made, he sank back into his chair, apparently exhausted. But a little later, when Patrick thought Berezovsky had fallen asleep and was taking the opportunity to study the oligarch's face, his eyes flicked open and held Patrick's. He winked at him, smiled briefly and reclosed his eyes.

Around midnight, when the meeting broke up, Vanyashin told Patrick to stay. The bar was thinning out. Two of Vanyashin's bodyguards sat at a neighbouring table. It was five months since Patrick had visited him in the country, and since Sotheby's – where Patrick got to see Vanyashin at his most ferociously acquisitive, spurning the private room they began the auction in and moving to the main hall, where he wielded his paddle like a mace – they had seen each other just once. 'I think the book had sunk pretty low on his list of priorities,' Patrick had told Robert. 'But that night, for whatever reason, he wanted to talk. He told me to hit record and he just went on and on. I don't think I asked him a single question.'

He spoke about the early days of making money, during perestroika, when one scheme fed into another: copper bracelets, banking, a consultancy that helped Western investors understand – and exploit – the newly opened Russian economy, property deals, a radio station, a newspaper. 'I saw a different man that night,' Patrick said. 'Not humble exactly, he wasn't ever that, but more vulnerable maybe. He seemed to want to go back to a time when things made more sense.'

Robert read an interview Vanyashin had given the *Guardian* in 2006, in the aftermath of Litvinenko's assassination; it included that extraordinary image of the hairless ex-FSB man lying in his hospital bed, looking serene as he was eaten away by a massive dose of radiation. The article, which described Vanyashin as 'the oligarch you've never heard of', began with a summary of the various stands he had made against Putin's regime. 'My Russia,' he was quoted as saying, 'has been hijacked by gangsters in sombre suits; their hideout is the Kremlin.' It was a decent line, one Robert assumed had been prepared in advance, but the journalist – James Siddell, the paper's Moscow bureau chief – wasn't impressed by Vanyashin. He took time to describe the opulence of his lifestyle and challenged him on the double standards some of his actions seemed to reveal. Hadn't he started his own bank when working on property deals with the mayor of Moscow, using it to pocket money that should have gone back into the city? Hadn't he taken the proceeds of those dubious deals out of the country, just like those 'thieves' he was accusing? Vanyashin dodged the question about his bank and tried his best to make his exile sound principled. 'In Russia the state is all,' he said. 'If you don't play Putin's game you lose everything. They put you in a prison cell, like Mikhail Borisovich [Khodorkovsky], or a box in the ground like Sasha Litvinenko. In this situation I think you, me, many other people would leave.'

Vanyashin came out of the piece badly. There was a pomposity to his statements, and the parallels Siddell drew between him and Berezovsky were patronising. 'In both his criticisms of Putin and his wealth,' Siddell wrote, 'Sergei Vanyashin is like a pocket Berezovsky.'

Six years later, another parallel: Berezovsky and Vanyashin were both found hanged, half a year apart. Were they murdered by the same people? For the same reasons? Perhaps. But if it were possible, even likely, that they had been killed by their own government, Robert couldn't see someone like Patrick being included on the same list. There was something he remembered Vanyashin saying, though, that made him go back to the *Guardian* article. Siddell had asked how harmful words alone could really be to someone like President Putin. 'Maybe not so harmful,' Vanyashin replied, 'but I don't only have words. There will be more to say soon about the crimes Putin and his government commit against the Russian people.' Vanyashin wouldn't add anything to this. Siddell theorised he might be establishing a foundation, like Berezovsky's International Foundation for Civil Liberties, which highlighted human rights abuses in Russia and produced a stream of anti-Putin material. But the thing that occupied Robert's thoughts, as he walked from the terminal to his gate, was that what Vanyashin told Siddell was almost exactly what he told Patrick five years later. What was it he had and why had it taken him so long to do something with it? Did it even exist? He wanted to know, even as he told himself that for his purposes, the truth didn't matter. Only the story mattered.

After finding his cramped seat and tensely enduring take-off – with a hangover he was an even more nervous flyer than usual, certain that every shake and turn of the plane, every hydraulic whine and thud from somewhere beneath him, was the beginning of a nosedive – Robert read a report on Vanyashin's death he had found on a website called *Crosshairs*, the luridly designed homepage of which claimed that it provided 'the lowdown on political assassination'. On the day he died Vanyashin took the unprecedented step of giving all but one of his security detail the day off, sending the remaining guard into High Wycombe on an errand and then going running on his own along the lanes and through the woods around his country house. Why would he go alone? To Robert his actions, as well as various anecdotal reports of how unhappy he was at the time, supported the coroner's verdict of suicide. The *Telegraph*'s report of his death noted his feud with Putin's administration, but put more emphasis on the fact that he had suffered heavy financial losses in the last year of his life. The police also said there was no suspicion of foul play, but a few articles written in the following days and weeks questioned that judgement. One, from just a couple of days after Vanyashin's death, summarised the criticisms he had made of Putin and his officials, and wondered whether his name belonged on 'the growing list of out-of-favour Russian businessmen and ex-security service officers who appear to have been executed on foreign soil by or at the behest of the Russian state'. Several weeks later a *Guardian* editorial criticised the Thames Valley Police for their handling of the scene and the subsequent investigation, listing several puzzling facts that it said no one had been able to adequately explain: the area around the tree was never searched, no photographs were taken until Vanyashin's corpse had been cut down, and a forensic post-mortem wasn't carried out until fifteen days after his death. The editorial drew parallels with the deaths of Berezovsky and Alexander Perepilichnyy and was critical of Putin, whom it called 'the world's bully, playing an intimidation game with the western liberal democracies he loathes'. 'Whether or not Sergei Vanyashin is another victim of Mr Putin's regime,' it ended, 'this sequence of apparent executions, largely ignored by the British authorities, is an affront to our democratic way of life and its protection by the rule of law. If we wish to demonstrate our disapproval then stronger measures – not least the adoption of the Magnitsky Act, signed into law in the US by the Obama administration last year – are necessary at both a British and European level'.

The mishandling of the crime scene was suspicious, but things like that did sometimes happen. The question Robert kept returning to, though, the only question that really mattered, was whether, if Vanyashin had been murdered, the same people would want to kill Patrick. The only reason Robert could think that they would, based on what Patrick had told him and what his own reading had pieced together, was because of the files Vanyashin had sent him – files Patrick said he couldn't even read, which were probably evidence of nothing more than the impotence of Vanyashin's desire to revenge himself on the people who stole his businesses and sent him into exile: a pocket Berezovsky with a point to prove, but apparently no way to prove it. He was a fantasist. What other conclusion could be drawn from five years of hints that he had some career-ending dirt on Putin? He imagined Vanyashin, depressed and desperate, clambering into the oak tree, killing himself in the hope that suspicion would fall on the Kremlin and that he would find some relevance as another victim of a corrupt state. He saw Liam's shoes pointing at five to one. Men stole through a wood in blue early-morning light. In the heart of the wood they approached not Vanyashin's mansion, but Robert's own Berlin apartment block. Noiselessly the men climbed the stairs and flowed along the corridor towards him. He woke up beside Karijn knowing the men were there, drawing nearer, but he couldn't move; he was frozen in his bed. He jolted awake, the plane descending.

Walking past the smokers who always lined the terminal at Schönefeld, he texted Karijn: Landed! Home in an hour. Do you need me to pick anything up? He walked along the colonnade that ran between the terminal buildings and the railway station, past the currywurst van that had become a welcome signifier of coming home. It was cold. In the field that ran alongside the colonnade he saw several figures bundled in sleeping bags under a small, bare tree, a large blue Ikea bag hanging limply from one of its branches. He walked down into the underpass and climbed to the platform to wait for his train. The empty, dilapidated station made him feel desolate in the way of Sunday afternoons. It was a terminus, and trains stood at several platforms as if abandoned. Robert gazed across the tracks at the brick wall of a factory, remembering Croydon and the funeral home. He was glad he had put a sea and a few hundred miles between him and it, and everything else in London. His train rolled slowly into the station. A few people got off, tugging their suitcases behind them. He validated his ticket and boarded the train, sitting with his case wedged between his legs. He stared absently at his phone. He was still hungover, which he knew was why, alongside his physical dishevelment, he felt so melancholy. He didn't want people over for dinner tonight. He only wanted to sleep. The train's doors clattered shut and air hissed from its brakes. It rolled slowly past the scrubland around the airport. Robert put his head against the glass. The train began to pick up speed. He saw residential grids, sports pitches, a closed-down supermarket covered in graffiti. A few trees still clung to their leaves, yellow and red, but most were bare.

His phone shook. A reply from Karijn: OK here. Holding it together with puzzles and ice cream. Don't need anything, only you. It was just past four. He would be home in half an hour. As the train swung around on its approach to Ostkreuz the low sun found a rent in the clouds and the carriage filled with an intense red light. There was something mournful about it, and getting off the train, dazzled by the same red light cutting across the station platforms, Robert was struck by another great charge of sadness. He looked down through the station's dirty glass sides into a sumac-choked lot. Half the lot lay in shadow, half glowed red. The sunset was devastating. Karijn and the girls felt so distant that he might never reach them and the thought of all these people around him going home, or out, or to work beneath this molten light was intolerable. He couldn't say why. It was a wave of feeling that sometimes rose and engulfed him, that was all. He recognised it but was never able to shake it: it ended when it ended.

The light subsided while he rode the rattling S-Bahn train to Schönhauser Allee. It was night. Turning onto his street he smelled burning leaves and heard the sound of a piano from an open window. It was dark. The streetlights were so spaced out that he entered a patch of absolute darkness before reaching the glow cast by the next light. Robert passed the Japanese barista as he closed up his shop. He nodded but the man didn't notice. He unlocked the door to his building, walked down the entrance hall and crossed the Hof. The gate to the wooden shelter that housed the block's bins had been left open, as it often was – something that infuriated him, to Karijn's amusement. He shook his head as he slammed it closed, as if the culprit might see him from an apartment window and feel remorse for their carelessness. It was such a ridiculous thing to do that he started to laugh as he went up the stairs to the apartment and was still laughing as he knocked on the door, clutching in one hand the Beefeater bears he had bought the girls at the airport.

Standing at the sink peeling potatoes, Robert listened to Karijn sing the girls to sleep. He had come in as they were finishing their tea and given them a bath before she put them to bed. Their friends were due at eight thirty. He rinsed the potatoes, filled a saucepan with water, salted it and tipped them in. He took a bottle of wine from the small rack above the fridge and poured a glass. He closed the kitchen door and switched off the light so he could see into the apartments of his neighbours across the Hof. Karijn said it was creepy, but Berliners rarely drew their curtains and he couldn't resist looking into all these other lives the building contained, a score of stages on which new work was performed daily. The only sound in the kitchen was the soft rush of gas from the stove. In the window directly opposite an old man, whom Robert had cast as a university professor, was chopping something. The light in his kitchen was golden and warm. Robert imagined bright, intricate music filling the room; the Goldberg Variations, perhaps. A few windows to the left he saw a football match playing on a small TV. One floor below, three women sat talking around a kitchen table. One of them was smoking and after every drag her hand darted towards the open window and flicked her cigarette, sending brief red sparks into the evening air. There were opaque windows belonging to toilets and bathrooms, behind which vague phantoms sometimes appeared. A few had shut curtains or blinds. Many others were dark, the residents out or away, or, like Robert, standing in the darkness watching. He liked to elaborate narratives from the scenes he saw, but when he wasn't spectating he forgot these people even existed and that their mundane or perfect or disastrous days continued to unfold around him. Glancing down he saw a man in the Hof looking up towards his window. Robert's instinct was to step back out of sight, even though he didn't actually think he could be seen.

'What are you doing in the dark?' Karijn said. He started and she laughed.

'Jesus,' he said. 'Not paying enough attention to my flanks, I guess.'

'One day you're going to get arrested,' she said. 'Put it away, I'm turning the light on.'

The brightness made him blink.

Karijn lifted the lid off the casserole dish and steam bloomed from it.

'That smells great,' he said. The wine had sharpened his hunger and he found he was looking forward to seeing their friends. He scooped up the potato peelings and dropped them into the food recycling. He suddenly felt extraordinarily happy.

'Heidi and Frank are bringing dessert,' Karijn said, stepping towards him and hugging him tightly. 'Tell me. How was it?'

He sighed into her hair. 'It was sad. And weird.'

'Were there a lot of people there?'

'Quite a few. His family, some workmates, friends from uni.' He thought of Molly, of her face in the half-dark of the taxi. He remembered holding her beside the road.

'Were you at a church?'

'No, it was a viewing.'

'What's a viewing?'

'It's when the body's at a funeral home, an undertaker's, and you go in and see it. Them. And you say goodbye, or say a prayer, or whatever takes you.'

'What did you do?'

'I tried to say something, but I couldn't think. I just stood beside him. We don't have to talk about it. But thank you for asking.' When Karijn was eleven her father had contracted bacterial meningitis and died in a matter of hours. He knew how much she disliked talking about death.

'There's never anything to say, that's the most horrible part,' she said. 'No, it's all horrible.' She shook her head.

'Oh Rob, I'm sorry. Did you get a better idea of what happened?'

'Not really. Depression. Anxiety. A shit state of affairs.'

There was a knock at the door. Karijn hugged Robert tightly again and went to answer it. He heard her speaking German to Heidi and Frank while they took off their shoes. He took the pan off the stove and poured the hot water from it. Steam spread up the window, leaving a thin film of condensation behind.

Frank came in and shook Robert's hand. 'It smells good,' he said in English.

'The part that smells good is Karijn's work,' Robert said. 'Unless you love the smell of boiled potatoes.'

'I love everything about potatoes,' Frank said gravely.

'He loves them more than he loves me,' Heidi said, squeezing past Frank and hugging Robert. 'Where's Ernesto?'

Heidi and Frank lived a thirty-minute tram ride away, up in Pankow. Ernesto was in Mitte, which was closer, but he always seemed to be coming from something and leaving for something else, and rarely arrived on time. There was no one this irritated more than Heidi.

'Give him a chance,' Karijn said. 'Maybe he'll surprise us. Let's have a drink.'

But they spent so long waiting that eventually they started without him – 'I might actually die if you don't give me food,' Heidi said after her second glass of wine – and had almost finished the main course when he knocked at the door. 'Sorry, Robert,' he smiled. 'I got held up.'

The others stood to greet him – Frank with a handshake, Heidi with kisses on both cheeks and Karijn with a powerful hug. They had quickly become close after Robert introduced them, and when Ernesto was suffering through a bad breakup, something that happened several times a year, it was Karijn he turned to. They would sit in the kitchen and drink tea and talk, often for hours after Robert had gone to bed. Karijn had told Robert how much she enjoyed those conversations. 'Ernesto always, always thinks with his dick,' she said. 'But his dick is unusually smart.'

'I'm amazed you could make it, Ernesto,' Robert said. 'A single day's notice? Are you finally starting to slow down?' Even when Robert came to Berlin solely to visit clubs Ernesto, who never took drugs and barely drank alcohol, could always outlast him. He was born in Munich, days after his parents emigrated from Eritrea, but had come to Berlin when he was seventeen and seemed like more of a Berliner than anyone else Robert had met. He didn't just know every club and bar, but every bouncer, too. Robert had been with him when he jumped the line at Berghain, something so unlikely that whenever he told the story, Robert felt like he was lying.

Karijn brought Ernesto some stew and Robert poured him a glass of wine. Ernesto told them about the opening party for a gallery he had just come from. Robert went to the kitchen to check on the strudel Heidi and Frank had brought. He looked at his phone and saw he had received a text from a number he didn't recognise.

We need to talk

P

When's good? Robert replied and put the phone back in his pocket. He was surprised when he felt it buzz almost immediately: 9 tomorrow night. I'll tell you where nearer the time. What was he up to now? They had spoken briefly before Robert went to London, but their last meeting had been two weeks ago. During that time, Robert realised, he had often thought about Patrick, but Patrick the character in his novel, not the actual person in Berlin.

In the living room Robert found Ernesto and Frank having what sounded like a stilted conversation, while Karijn and Heidi were standing in the far corner, beside the bookshelves, looking at a large book about upholstery. Heidi had started taking weekly lessons from Karijn.

'Dessert!' Robert said.

'Amazing,' Ernesto said around a mouthful of food, wiping up the last of the stew with a piece of bread. Karijn and Heidi sat down as Robert cut slices from the strudel and handed them down the table.

'Karijn told me you were working on something new, Robert,' Heidi said. 'Can you talk about it?'

'There's not much to talk about,' Robert said. 'I'll see if it goes anywhere.'

'Come on, Rob,' Karijn said. 'Tell them about "the Russians".' She spoke the words in a mock-dramatic tone.

'Russians?' Ernesto said. 'Gangsters?'

'Not all Russians are gangsters,' Frank said.

'The ones buying up Mitte are.' Ernesto waved his fork in the vague direction of his neighbourhood. 'Putting my shop rent up. Bastards.'

'This one's a gangster,' said Karijn.

'Oh!' Heidi said. 'You have to tell us now.'

'Or maybe you can't?' Frank said. 'You'll be in, ah, danger?'

Robert laughed. 'You sound like someone I know. OK, has anyone heard of Sergei Vanyashin?' Three blank faces looked back at him. 'Well, he was a very rich Russian businessman,' Robert said.

'Rich like . . . an oligarch?' Frank said.

'Yeah, like that. Rich enough to have helicopters and houses in London and the Côte d'Azur, and an army of bodyguards.'

Heidi nodded. 'I feel strangely attracted to this man.'

'If he isn't a gangster,' Ernesto said, 'where did he get all his cash?'

'He did a lot of things. When perestroika happened he was a taxi driver, but he made some money through hustling, then property deals, then banking.'

'Property and banking? Gangster moves,' Ernesto said, wagging his finger.

'Fair enough,' Robert said, pouring more wine into his glass and passing the bottle down the table. 'But he set up a radio station, too, and a newspaper.'

'Oh shit, Russian media,' Heidi said. 'Propaganda all day long like fucking GDR mind control. I grew up with this.' She had been twelve when the Wall came down.

'Maybe now, yeah,' Robert said. 'But the station, the paper, they were independent. They criticised Putin before he took them over. Vanyashin's not a hero but, I don't know, Russia was a lawless place then. Or at least they didn't have laws that applied to a lot of the stuff that was happening. They went from a completely controlled economy to a free market in a few months, it was insane.' Robert saw Frank nodding. 'Vanyashin actually made some stuff – put up some buildings, created a radio station that broadcast things other than propaganda' – he looked at Heidi – 'to millions of people, whereas other people, people like Berezovsky, gamed the system and ripped people off, maybe even had people killed. Vanyashin didn't do that. And when he had all his businesses taken away, he went to the UK and claimed asylum – he would have been locked up otherwise, or worse.'

'If you're rich you get asylum,' Ernesto said. 'If you're brown and poor you drown in the Mediterranean.'

'What is your connection to this man?' Frank said. 'Why are you writing about him?'

'I – we,' he said, indicating Karijn, 'met someone who worked for him, a writer. He came to Berlin after Vanyashin died. He thinks he was murdered.'

'Oh!' Heidi said.

'Gangster,' said Ernesto.

'Thinks?' said Frank. 'What was the official cause of death?'

'Hanging. He was found hanging from a tree.'

'So he killed himself,' Heidi said.

'He might have,' said Robert.

'He was murdered,' Karijn said. 'Isn't that what Patrick says happened?'

'Why?' Heidi said.

'Because men,' said Karijn, the words a strangulated cry. 'Wanting to be richest, have the biggest boat, write the best book. All those men crawling over each other to grab the factories or the oil or the copper. It's disgusting. Why can't they collaborate without killing each other? Make things better for everyone, not just themselves every second. There's no' – she grabbed at the air, trying to find the word – 'no dignity.' She sat back. Everyone was silent. 'Fuck,' she said and laughed. She clutched the stem of her glass. 'Pour me some wine.'

'Apart from the shittiness of men,' Heidi said, 'which, yes, I absolutely agree with, why was this rich man found in a tree?'

'My guy, the writer, he thinks he knows why,' Robert said. 'I don't know if he's telling the truth or not. I don't think his story is totally reliable, but he wanted to tell it and I'm helping him do that.'

'No, you approached him,' Karijn said. 'It was your idea to tell the story.'

Robert shrugged and silently willed the conversation to move on. He didn't want to talk about Patrick or Vanyashin any more. 'It might not go anywhere,' he said. 'It'd probably be a better magazine article than a novel.'

'Why?' Ernesto said.

'Maybe it's better to lay out the facts. In a story you always need to twist them to fit.'

'Robert,' Frank said, 'if I am telling a child or their parents about an illness or a procedure I must perform, do I tell them what I understand medically? No. I take what they need to know and I put it into a story. This is important for everyone. It's a tool to help us understand.'

'But you're a doctor. The kinds of stories I tell don't help anyone.'

'I'm sure this Patrick would disagree,' Heidi said. 'He chose you to do this. That is a great responsibility, yes, but I think he is lucky.'

'Me too,' Frank said.

'And me,' Ernesto said.

Karijn raised her glass to Robert. 'Despite my recent comments about men working together, I agree too. He couldn't be luckier.'

Robert could barely return their smiles. He saw Molly's streetlight-yellow mouth pulled into a grin. Patrick lying on the pavement at his feet. He wanted to tell them he was a liar. That it wasn't luck but misfortune that brought Patrick to that bookshop. He could tell them and then tell Patrick. He could atone. But all he did was duck his head in a show of modesty. 'I don't know about lucky,' he said.

Karijn began to speak but something behind Robert caught her attention. 'Baby!' she said.

Nora stood in the doorway in her nightshirt rubbing her eye, the other opened to a slit against the living room's light. Her hair stood wildly from her head. Robert opened his arms and she padded over to him and climbed into his lap, while Heidi and Frank and Ernesto cooed hellos. She burrowed her face into Robert's chest as he rocked her back and forth. 'Shhh,' he whispered into her scalp. She was warm and smelled thickly of sleep. Eager to leave the conversation, Robert stood and hefted her so her cheek came to rest on his shoulder. He could tell from how inert she was that she would go back to bed without protest. As he came through the open door of the girls' room he angled his body to protect Nora's head from the doorframe. Sonja was splayed on the top bunk, one foot thrust through the ladder's gap, suspended in air. He knelt down and eased Nora off his shoulder and onto the bottom bunk. As he stood to go she moaned, 'No,' and held onto his hand.

'One song,' he whispered. He started singing 'Yesterday', her current favourite.

When he sang the line about the shadow she murmured, 'That's his ghost.' She did it every time. He had no idea where this notion had come from.

Her eyes rolled back, her breathing slowed and she was asleep. He stayed by her side. He wanted to stay in the simple calm of the moment. He was singing the song so quietly now that it was more a rumbling in his chest than a sound coming from his mouth.

When he came out of the girls' room, Heidi and Frank were in the hallway putting on their coats. 'Thank you, Robert!' Heidi whispered. 'So nice. You must come and eat at our house next time. Frank will make you potatoes.'

'I'd love that,' Robert said. He embraced Heidi and shook Frank's hand.

'Good luck with your story,' Frank said. 'Karijn is hopeful it will make you into millionaires.'

'We'd be better off trying to be gangsters,' Robert said.

He closed the front door and turned to go back to Karijn and Ernesto in the living room but changed his mind and went into the dark kitchen. The room smelled pleasantly of the stew, and he listened to the soothing churn of the dishwasher. He crossed to the window and looked out, but most of the apartments were dark now and the few that were lit showed only empty rooms.

In the living room Karijn was pouring Ernesto a brandy. 'Here he is,' she said. 'Ernesto was just telling me about all the places he's yet to visit tonight.'

'Tonight?' Robert said.

'I'm going to a friend's bar, that's all. It just opened.'

'My god,' Robert said. 'Did we really use to go out to bars at this time of night?'

'It's not even twelve!' Ernesto said.

Karijn patted Ernesto's hand. 'You keep us young.' She tilted her brandy glass towards Robert. 'You want one?'

'No, I'm good.'

'Come on,' Ernesto said, pouring a glass and pushing it towards Robert. 'I want to drink to your new book!'

They held their glasses together. 'What's the toast?' Karijn said.

'Murdered Russians,' Ernesto said.

Karijn laughed. 'Murdered Russians!'

Robert touched his glass to Ernesto's and to Karijn's, looking each of them in the eye in turn. 'Murdered Russians,' he said.

Hunched into his coat against the cold, Robert saw the rain fall in wild stripes through the streetlights' glare. Through his hood it felt like fingers drumming across his scalp. The short walk from the U-Bahn station at Samariterstrasse was a battle fought against barrelling wind that seemed intent on keeping him from his appointment.

He had received his instructions an hour earlier, when he had started to think he might not hear from Patrick at all. Antilope turned out to be a dark Friedrichshain cellar bar. It was Friday night and when Robert came down from the blustery street into the crowded, low-ceilinged space, lit almost entirely by candles, it took him a few seconds to regain his equilibrium. One of his contact lenses wasn't sitting right on his eye, which made the candlelight flare and gave the bar a smeared, dreamlike haze.

He found Patrick in a side room sitting in a deep, low leather chair, a baseball cap pulled down over his eyes. On the table in front of him a tea light flickered in a jar, a glass of red wine beside it. When he saw Robert, Patrick motioned to the chair on the other side of the table.

'I'll get a drink,' Robert said.

'Sit down,' Patrick said. 'This won't take long.'

'Won't it?' Robert said, unzipping his jacket. Patrick sounded angry. Coming from the wind and rain into the warmth of the bar had made Robert's nose run. He searched his pockets, flustered by the way Patrick was silently staring at him. He found a balled-up tissue in his jeans and blew his nose. 'So?' he said.

Patrick looked up towards the ceiling, eyes searching, one hand kneading his throat. 'When the Albie Cooper book came out I got called a few things.' He laughed a tired laugh. 'See, the thing people loved about that book was Albie's sensitivity. His vulnerability. And that's what some people hated about it, too. Especially his friends, his family. They thought it made him look weak. His brother said if he ever saw me again he'd break my legs, did you know that?'

Robert shook his head. Patrick was speaking calmly, but on certain words his voice seemed to tremble. His hands were now gripping the arms of his chair.

'I can understand,' Patrick said. 'No one likes the version of themselves they find on the page. It's like hearing your voice on tape, you know what I mean?'

'I think so.'

'If I'm being honest, I did stitch Albie up. He's eloquent, and very reflective – not normal for a footballer. I took advantage of that. I made him come to see me as a friend' – Robert heard the pressure Patrick put on the word – 'and that made him tell me all sorts of things I don't think he'd have said otherwise. It made him feel safe, when really he wasn't safe at all. But,' Patrick said, raising a finger, 'differences: Albie knew I was writing a book. There was a contract with both our names on it. He even got to sign off on the finished text – although apparently neither he nor anyone around him bothered reading it, but he had the opportunity. So while I understand his brother wanting to break my legs, and his fiancée calling me a wanker in the papers, and Albie feeling let down by what I did, I still don't feel, on balance, that I acted like an utter cunt.' He took something from his pocket. Robert recognised it: his thumb drive. 'But this,' Patrick said, 'this is theft.'

Panic swarmed in Robert's chest, his throat. 'How do you figure that?' he said.

'It's my story,' Patrick said, sounding incredulous. 'Or do you think this shit you've written belongs to you?'

'Yes, I do. It's mine, Patrick.' Robert leaned forward in his chair. 'And that drive is mine, so how the fuck did you get it?'

'What happens in your story? Do I meet you?'

'What?'

'Patrick, in the story. Does he meet someone like you?'

'You want to find out what happens next,' Robert said, smiling. 'That's a good sign.'

'Fuck you, tell me.'

Robert stared at Patrick, who held his gaze. Conversations went on all around them. A cork popped, followed by cheers.

'Tell me,' Patrick said, the words inflected like a plea.

'I haven't figured that part out yet.'

'I think you know.'

He did know. It had come to him after his conversation with Molly. 'What I thought was, maybe, the ghostwriter—'

'Patrick,' said Patrick.

'Patrick flees to Berlin and meets another writer there.' He felt foolish telling Patrick the story, his own story. He was angry with him for staging this ambush.

'And what does this other writer make of what Patrick tells him?'

Robert stared at Patrick. He wasn't going to talk about it any more.

'Come on,' Patrick said. 'Tell me.' Silence. 'Tell me.'

'The other writer,' Robert began, then stopped. 'Look,' he said, 'I can understand why you think what you think.'

Patrick tilted his head and narrowed his eyes. 'You don't believe anything I've told you, do you?'

Robert hesitated before answering. 'I believe some of it.'

'About why I needed to leave? About my being in danger?'

'No,' Robert said. 'I don't believe you.' He was surprised by how terrible it felt to say it. Like it was a betrayal.

Patrick placed the thumb drive on the table and looked at it. He picked up his wine and took a long sip, then put the glass back on the table with deliberate care. 'She's dead, you know,' he said.

'Who's dead?'

'Alyona. Another name you fucking deigned to leave unchanged.'

'When? How?'

Patrick waved his hand dismissively. 'You're a real fucking prick, you know that? All that Mills and Boon shit at Vanyashin's place, your version of me hoping she's dreaming about him. A nineteen-year-old girl, for fuck's sake.'

'I've heard the way you speak about her. You liked her.'

'Is that what liking a woman means to you? I don't want to be in your wank fantasy, OK? I don't want to be in your shitty book at all, and I definitely don't want my fucking name all over it!'

Heads turned at the sound of Patrick's raised voice. His eyes flicked around the room.

'All I was doing there,' Robert said, speaking slowly, 'was introducing another source of tension. It's important to the story.'

Patrick looked at Robert and moved his fingers back and forth across his chin. He remained silent.

'I don't see what you're getting so angry about,' Robert said. 'You told your story to a novelist. This is what novelists do. They take things that happen to people and they . . . tweak them.'

'Steal them. Cheapen them.'

Robert dropped his head back and sighed as he looked up at the ceiling. 'Yes, fine, cheapen them.'

'I thought I was talking to a friend, not a novelist.'

'Tell me where you got that USB,' Robert said.

Patrick tapped his fingers against the table. 'I got a feeling when you were at my place,' he said. 'Something felt off. So I followed you. I followed you back to Prenzlauer Berg and into a coffee shop, and I watched you tap away on your little fucking laptop and save whatever it was you were writing onto your little fucking stick. I stood on the street, in the dark, watching you through the window, and I knew. I fucking knew.'

'You followed me,' Robert said.

'Yeah, I followed you. More than once. And a couple of weeks later I took that' – he pointed at the thumb drive on the table – 'and it was easy. So think about this: what you've done is going to have repercussions. You might have me down as a nutter who's dreamed all this up, but there are real people out there that want something, and it doesn't make any difference to them whether or not you believe they exist.'

'Are you threatening me now?'

'Not me,' Patrick said, pointing his finger at Robert. 'You, mate, this is on you.'

'How much did you give that homeless guy to nick it?'

A smile flitted across Patrick's lips. 'He didn't take it, I told him to distract you. I took it when you were flapping about with your bag. I was right beside you and you never even saw me. Trust me, if you're being followed you'll be the last to know about it.'

Patrick was sitting forward, his chest puffed out. Robert

wanted to get out of his chair and shove him backward. 'If you think I'm some kind of parasite, so are you,' he said. 'Albie Cooper sold all those books, not you.'

'It's my job to tell other people's stories, Robert. And they know I'm doing it.'

'But you didn't tell the story Cooper wanted told.'

'Everything in that book is true.'

'But some of that "truth" is the truth according to you,' Robert said, stabbing the tabletop. 'You drew out the connections, you applied the cod psychology, you threaded all those apparent obsessions of his into one complex. Not him.'

'It's not the same.'

'It is the same!' Robert said, his finger almost touching Patrick's face. 'He told you things, then you decided if they were important, or what he really meant by them, and you wrote what you wanted to write.' He sat back, drew a long breath in and held it. Released it slowly. 'You knew when you called me, then?' he said. 'When you said we needed to talk?'

'I had the stick but I hadn't looked at it. I didn't need to look. I knew.'

'Then why didn't you say anything?'

Patrick frowned. 'Because your friend had just died. It could wait.'

Patrick's words were unexpected. Robert looked away, first to one side of Patrick then down at the floor. 'Thank you,' he said.

'How was the funeral?'

'Awful. It was awful in every way.'

'I'm sorry.'

Robert nodded. A few moments passed. He listened to the clamour of talk around them. The meaningless noise. 'He hanged himself in a wardrobe,' he said. 'Can you believe that?'

'I guess once the decision's been made the location doesn't really matter.'

'That's what I thought too, but now I don't know. Something about it bothers me.'

'About it being a wardrobe?'

'It's the smallness of the space. Putting himself away like that. It feels wrong. More wrong.'

'It's horrible, but he was your friend. Anywhere else would be just as bad.'

'Maybe. How did Alyona die?'

Patrick took off his cap and dropped it onto the table. He bowed his head, lifted his hand and began massaging his temples with his thumb and middle finger. 'She went off her balcony in New York. Full of drugs and booze.'

'But you think . . .'

Patrick looked up. 'I think what?' he said, his voice sharp.

'I don't know. You have a theory about everything else: Vanyashin was murdered, you're being followed.' He was overtaken by a sudden fury at Patrick's delusions. 'Are they here right now? Are we about to get snatched?'

'Robert, you saw someone following me. He followed both of us.'

'I saw a guy acting weird. I don't know what I saw.'

'Believe me, this is real.'

'Why are you still here then? If you're being followed or threatened or whatever the fuck's happening to you, why are you still here?'

'I've got a plan. If I need to leave, I've got somewhere to go.'

'Where?'

Patrick scoffed. 'Like I'd tell you,' he said. He drained his glass and fell back in his chair. He seemed exhausted. Robert thought he should get up and leave but something held him there. Patrick pointed at his glass. 'You want one?'

Robert hadn't expected the question. For a moment he didn't know what to say. He stood. 'Let me get them.'

The place was even busier now, and Robert joined a crowd at the bar. While he waited he searched alyona model nyc death. A *New York Daily News* article came up: Russian Model Plunges to Death. He tapped it and stared into the bright white of the screen, waiting for the story to load; the signal was weak down here. He refreshed but the screen remained a dazzling blank. He glanced up and saw the bartender pointing at him.

Robert carried the drinks carefully through the crowd. He handed Patrick his and sat down. 'Cheers,' he said.

Patrick touched his glass to Robert's, swallowed half

the wine in one go and breathed out heavily. 'I was thinking about this story Sergei told me,' he said. 'Back in the early seventies his dad kept a little boat moored on a lake just outside Moscow, and whenever he got the chance he'd take Sergei and his brother out there. The problem was the boat's motor was knackered, always breaking down. Whenever that happened they had to wait weeks for a new part. One time the dad got hold of some water skis and told Sergei and his brother to invite some friends to the lake that weekend. It was all they talked about for days. But come Sunday, the boat wouldn't start. Sergei kept telling his dad to try it again, try it again, but his dad knew that boat and he said it was pointless. But Sergei wouldn't let it go. He wanted to strip the engine. "Have you become an engineer overnight?" his dad said. Sergei didn't care about not knowing what he was doing, he just knew that he had to try. So, Sergei's brother and their friends go off and swim while Sergei and his dad strip the engine. It takes them three hours to pull it apart, inspect it and put it all back together. The others have made a fire. Sergei's brother brings them sausages. He tells them they're missing the party, but Sergei doesn't care – and I guess by this stage his dad doesn't care, either.' Patrick paused and took another large draught of wine. 'Once the engine was back in one piece, they tried to start it again and . . . nothing.'

'Shit,' Robert said.

'Right?' Patrick lit a cigarette. 'And then he asks me: did I think that was a happy story or a sad one?'

'What did you say?'

'I didn't know how to answer, but I couldn't say nothing. I said I thought it was a happy story.'

'And?'

'He didn't say anything. He just gave me that blank look he had sometimes.' A woman standing close beside them stepped backward and trod on Patrick's foot. She turned and raised her hand in apology. 'No problem,' he said, but without looking at her; he was still looking at Robert. 'He told me that story the last time I ever saw him.'

'When was that?'

'A month before he died. He called me out to Buckinghamshire.'

'Another helicopter ride?'

'One of his security guys got me from the station. He'd had to get rid of the helicopter by then. And the yacht, and the London house. The weather was terrible. You couldn't even see out of the windows. It was like the house was sinking.'

'How did he seem?'

'Completely drained. He showed me a letter from Tatijana's solicitors. He said she wanted everything he had left. He kept calling her the love of his life, "how could the love of my life do this to me?" That kind of thing. It was weird, given how he treated her.'

'Was . . . sorry to bring her up again, but was Alyona still around?'

'No, they'd split up.'

'What about his friends?'

'He said everyone was gone. I know Tom was. He'd taken a job with RT, Putin's propaganda channel. That killed Sergei.'

'Why would Tom want to work there?'

'Money. Which is the answer to most questions about Tom.' Patrick smiled mirthlessly. 'I could understand why he got frustrated with Sergei, though. He had all these schemes going on, but they never went anywhere. He couldn't focus for long enough. I was two years in and the book was nowhere. We'd had a handful of meetings about it, that was all. He kept paying me and yeah, that was great, but I was sick of spinning my wheels. I wanted to work but I couldn't commit to anything in case he suddenly wanted . . .' Patrick waved his hand. 'Tom's a producer. That's what he loves to do. RT offered him the chance to do it.'

'Have you spoken to him?'

'He hasn't spoken to me since Sergei's death. Won't answer my calls, won't reply to my emails.'

'Not much of a friend to either of you, then.'

'A man after your own heart,' Patrick said, but with little venom. He stubbed out his cigarette. 'I think Sergei really did think of him as someone he could trust, and there weren't many of those. By the time I went to see him it was all falling apart. The marriage was finished, obviously, but so were his businesses. He'd just lost some deal he'd been counting on, something to do with diamond mines in Sierra Leone, I think. He told me the word was out. That everyone was turning their back on him.'

'What word?'

Patrick shrugged. 'That he was finished, I suppose. He used to think British decency and the rule of law would protect him, but he didn't think that any more. "Money is everything here," he said. That was good when he arrived because he could buy his safety. But when the money runs out, so does the safety. He was scared. He didn't want to be in the city, he preferred staying in the countryside. But that house was like a husk. Most of the rooms were closed up. He was alone. It was just him and his security guards eating frozen pizza.'

'Did he tell you his life was in danger?'

'Not in so many words. But he talked about the report Litvinenko wrote for some security firm before he was killed, and Perepilichnyy's dossier on money-laundering schemes, and all the people Berezovsky had pissed off. He said it was all linked, and it all involved that Adamov guy.'

'The one he said took the radio station and the paper?'

Patrick nodded. 'He was fixated on him. And he didn't think it was a coincidence all these people were dying.'

'What did you think?'

'Back then I thought he was going crazy. He didn't have any evidence that I'd seen.'

'What about the files? All that gunpowder stuff?'

'I couldn't make any sense of it. He'd said someone would explain it to me, but no one ever did. We didn't talk about it that day, but it wasn't really that kind of conversation. He was rambling. It was like he'd taken a tranquilliser or something. And he was drinking a lot.'

'So why did he ask you to come?'

'I don't know,' Patrick said. 'He wanted company. Maybe I was the only option he had left. He talked about business deals he wanted to make happen, bad investments, death. He said a year earlier he'd thought Putin was finished, but now it looked like he might go on forever. Then he told me the story about the boat.'

'It must have been important to him.'

Patrick smiled. 'That's what I thought, for a while.'

'What do you mean?'

'A few months after he died, I was reading a book about Berezovsky and I found the story there. A few details were different but it was the same story. Vanyashin stole it.'

'Why?'

'That's what I was going to ask you. Why would someone ever do that?'

Robert didn't take the bait. 'Did you like him?' he said.

Patrick looked up at the dim ceiling. His throat glowed with candlelight. 'Did I like him,' he repeated. He lowered his eyes to Robert's. 'No, I didn't like him.'

'Why?'

'If you were his friend then great: helicopter rides,

Breguets for your birthday, whatever. And he was interesting to talk to because he was interested – he wanted to share stuff, hear what you thought about things. But he'd do anything if he thought it would make him money, and if you got in his way he'd get you out of it.'

'Don't you have to be like that to get where he did?'

'Maybe, but how is that an excuse?' Patrick rested his elbows on his knees, his hands dangling. 'That stuff doesn't really matter, though,' he said. 'I hated the way he treated Alyona.'

'You cared about her,' Robert said.

Patrick scowled. 'Not the way you mean,' he said. 'She was a kid. A smart, beautiful kid who deserved a better life.'

The music jumped in volume: the night was entering a new phase. Shouts and laughter filled the smoky air. 'What were you doing in that bookshop?' Robert said.

Patrick picked at a gash in the arm of his chair. 'I was walking past and I looked in and saw you. You looked like you really belonged. I was lonely, I guess. And I was drunk. I thought, I could talk to that bloke. So, when you reached for a book I reached for it too.' He looked up at Robert. 'Do you know that you're the only person I know in this city?'

'Yeah.'

'The only person I know and you lied to me. You used me. Fuck you.'

'Patrick,' Robert began, 'I'm genuinely—'

'Genuinely what? You wouldn't know genuine if it fucking . . .' Patrick writhed in his seat, searching for the word.

It was then that Robert noticed a man seated a few tables away, directly behind Patrick. He was staring. Robert's pulse surged. The man stood. Robert waited for him to step towards them. He wanted to act, but could only look. Then the watcher smiled and embraced another man, who took off his jacket and sat down beside him.

'What?' Patrick said, turning to follow Robert's gaze.

'Spooks and phantoms,' Robert said, his fear transforming into anger. 'Haunted houses. All this FSB, SVR, UFO bollocks. Vanyashin might have been murdered, but even if he was, who are you for anyone to bother about? You write fucking footballers' memoirs.'

'And you're a thief,' Patrick said. He picked up the thumb drive and tossed it at Robert. It bounced off the arm of his chair and fell to the floor.

Robert bent down to pick it up. 'I didn't want to piss you off by writing this, Patrick. The more you told me, the more important I thought it was to tell it. I just didn't know how to ask you. I'm asking you to trust me now.' He was surprised by how much, suddenly, he wanted Patrick's permission.

'Alyona Kapelushnik,' Patrick said.

'What?'

'The people you're writing about are real. Alyona Kapelushnik,' he said, over-enunciating the name, 'was real. She was twenty years old and she fell nine floors from the balcony of her apartment.' Patrick stood and pulled on his jacket. 'Her body landed so far into the street the police said she must have taken a running jump. I don't care if you need another source of fucking tension. You can't write whatever you like about people. You just can't.' He turned and walked away, and although Robert called his name he didn't stop. He kept walking, through the press of people filling the bar and up the stairs, out into the night.

Stories are like coins, Robert thought, passed from one hand to another. When you tell someone a story, you give it to them. Patrick and Vanyashin; Caesar and the Aedui; Bolaño's heroin addiction; Robert's own pilgrimage to Blanes: some stories spread, others wither. He told himself what he was writing didn't diminish Patrick's experience; it was a tribute to it. If Patrick couldn't see that, it was unfortunate, but it wasn't his problem to solve.

Robert was walking his daughters to the Kita. Frost glittered on the pavement. The girls, pretending to be dragons, puffed white clouds into the sunlight. He thought about where to go after he had dropped them off. He was eager to continue working on the book. He wouldn't let Patrick stop him.

He decided to get breakfast at a cafe he liked on the other side of Mauerpark. The park was empty except for a few dog walkers and Robert enjoyed the solitude as he walked along the broad cobblestone path that ran its length, its stones glittering with frost. He was passing the amphitheatre where, many years before, he had gone to the raucous Sunday karaoke parties, when his phone started ringing. Taking it out of his pocket he saw the ID was withheld. 'Hello?' he said.

'Mr Robert Prowe?' a man said in thickly accented English. The line was choppy with static and the voice was distorted: it sounded unnaturally deep.

'Yes?' Robert said, pressing the phone more tightly to his ear.

'This is Dr Schreiber from the St Hedwig hospital. Can you confirm that you are Robert Prowe, husband of Karijn Jonsson?'

Fear grasped at Robert. He stopped at the threshold of the park, where the cobbled pathway met the pavement.

'Can you confirm?' The voice warped like something heard on a shortwave frequency.

'Yes, I confirm. What is it? What's happened?'

'I'm afraid your wife was involved in a car accident this morning, Mr Prowe.'

'Oh my god.' The voice was his and yet he didn't feel as if he had spoken. 'Oh my god,' the voice said again.

'I'm afraid her injuries are extremely serious.'

'What does that mean?' he said. 'Where is she?'

'Your wife is at the St Hedwig hospital,' the doctor said slowly. 'I am very sorry, Mr Prowe. You must come now. Her injuries are extremely serious.'

'Where are you? Where's the hospital?' Robert said.

There was a pause. 'This is the St Hedwig hospital,' the voice said. 'You must come now.'

The line went dead. With shaking hands, his thumbs hitting the wrong keys, Robert entered st hedwig hospital into his map. It was in Mitte, ten minutes in a car.

He launched Uber but it wouldn't load: the blue dot that was him hung in an empty grey field. He struck the screen repeatedly but nothing changed. The street he was on was large and usually busy, but he saw no cabs. He thought he should probably wait, but he couldn't stay still. He ran across the road and down the street that opened ahead of him. The pavement was narrow, the paving stones pushed crooked by tree roots, so he ran on the road between the bare lindens. He pumped his free arm, the bag containing his laptop clutched under the other. The low sun flashed at his left, appearing and disappearing behind buildings. He crossed blinding channels of light and plunged into cool blue corridors. He turned a corner and nearly collided with a pushchair. The woman behind it spoke angrily at him. He stared at her, stunned, then ran on, continuing to sprint as he crossed the road beside a church—the Zionskirche, he realised, his surroundings snapping into focus. He ran up a path onto the church grounds then down a sloping cobbled driveway, slipping and almost falling on the frost-slick stones. His breath was ragged, his chest burning. The road sloped downhill and he let it carry him on. Sunlight flared from the tramlines embedded in the road. Eyes narrowed against it, he saw a park up ahead. Realising he could cut through he tried to take the entrance without slowing. He caught a metal bollard near the top of his thigh and his leg went out from under him. His cheek cracked against the jagged cobbles and they tore his palms. He tried to stand, but as he pressed his arms to the ground they shook and collapsed. His cheek was against cold stone. He sucked in air and coughed, feeling fragments of grit in his throat. Scribbles of colour filled his eyes. He looked around him and remembered where he was and what had happened. Karijn was hurt. She needed him. But someone had taken the street and rotated it to a strange new angle. He tried to work out what he needed to move to get himself upright. His stomach lurched; as he pushed himself onto his knees he felt something throb in his leg. Blood was pumping from his thigh. He looked but saw nothing: it was his phone vibrating. He fumbled for it, unable to work his stiff fingers into the pocket of his trousers. By the time he had pulled it from his pocket the caller had rung off. Missed call: Karijn Jonsson, the screen read. He was aware of people moving past him on foot and on bikes, leaving a broad span of ground between themselves and the man sprawled across the entrance to the park. He looked at the screen in confusion. Had someone found her phone? He swiped the notification and went to missed calls. He pressed his thumb to her name. He staggered to a low metal railing around a flowerbed and lowered himself onto it, crouching more than sitting. He pressed the phone to his ear as it rang. There were tears in his eyes now. His breathing was shallow.

'Hello?'

Karijn's voice.

'Hello? Rob?'

Her voice.

'Karijn?' he said.

'Hej, I just tried to call you. It's about tonight.'

'Karijn, are you OK?'

'I'm fine. What's up? You sound strange.'

'Someone called me,' he began, breaking off to stifle a sob. He took a long breath and held it in lungs still raw from running.

'Rob?'

'Someone called me from the hospital,' he said. 'They told me – they said you'd been in an accident.' For a moment he heard only the gentle static of the open line.

'What? I'm fine. Are you sure that's what they said?'

'They said it was serious. I thought you'd been knocked off your bike. Fuck.'

Her tone changed from bewilderment to worry. 'Could they have meant one of the girls?'

'No. I mean, I don't . . .' Could he have misunderstood? He was sure the doctor had said that Karijn was hurt, but that wasn't true.

'You're sure?'

He wasn't. 'I am sure,' he said. 'But let me call and check, OK?' He hung up and found the Kita's number. He dialled and waited. He spoke to a woman who told him the girls were fine, she had just seen them in the playground. He asked her to go and check again. 'Please,' he said. 'Please, I know it's, ah, nervig, aber bitte machen Sie es für mich.'

She was gone for thirty seconds. When she came back on the line she sounded irritated. 'They're playing,' she said. 'Just where I saw them.'

Robert called Karijn.

'Oh thank god,' she said, her voice descending in relief. 'Thank god for that.'

Robert stood and gasped.

'Are you OK?' Karijn asked.

He laughed. 'I'm a little beaten up.' He examined his free hand. Poppy seeds of gravel were embedded in his palm. A cut ran across the meat of his thumb.

'What happened?'

He looked around him. 'I got the call, I was running to get to you. I ran into a . . .' He couldn't find the right word, his thoughts were still warping and scattering. 'Into a . . . thing, a post, and I wiped out.' He looked down and saw that one leg of his trousers was torn, the black cotton hanging in a flap. He bent over to examine his knee through the tear. Only when he looked did it begin to burn: there were dark fragments of gravel held in the wet redness of the graze. 'Took some skin off my knee,' he said, 'and – shit, where's . . .' He cast around him for his laptop bag and saw it several feet away in a flowerbed beside the path, its contents spilled. 'Jesus,' he said.

'Rob, what did this doctor say?'

He bent down and, with his free hand, weakly gathered his things, his palm stinging. He moved hesitantly towards a bench, each movement revealing new pain.

In his relief the pain seemed wonderful. 'He said he was from the St Hedwig hospital and that you'd been hurt. Seriously hurt.'

'My god,' Karijn said.

'Fuck, Karijn, it's good to hear your voice.'

'Oh Rob,' Karijn murmured. 'How fucked up.'

He brought his arm up to his face and wiped it across his eyes. 'Ah!' he said, as if exasperated, and laughed and shook his head. 'What were you calling about, anyway?'

Karijn was silent for a moment. 'Oh god,' she said, 'it was about picking the kids up tonight, but forget about it.'

'Why? I can do that.'

'It seems beside the point after this.'

'Älskling, trust me, I am so happy to be talking domestic banalities with you right now.'

She laughed. 'Better than having to decide whether to switch off my life support?'

'That's not funny.'

'It is, but fair enough. I just need a couple of extra hours to finish this ottoman. But I can do it tomorrow.'

'No, let me do this,' Robert said, wincing as he rose and put weight on his bruised leg to test it. 'I love you asking. I love the ottoman. I love whoever it's for. I would love to pick them up.'

'Well, that's excellent. If you're sure. Let me know if you're in too much pain, or completely crippled. Or if that person calls you again.'

'I love you. I'll see you tonight.' Ending the call, Robert

eased himself back down onto the bench. He felt the cold air against his burning knee. His thigh ached. His hands throbbed. His cheek was numb. The sky was a harsh, fluorescent white. The thought arrived: Patrick did this. This was his revenge. Robert picked up his phone and called the new number Patrick had texted him from the week before. It rang through to a generic voicemail message. He killed the call and tried Patrick's old number. Disconnected. 'Fucker,' he said. He sent a text to the other number, repeating the message Patrick had sent him the night he got back from London: We need to talk.

He found a toilet and did what he could to wash his wounds. He crossed the park to Rosenthaler Platz, where he took a train up to Gesundbrunnen and changed for Schönhauser Allee. His bruised thigh burned as he climbed the stairs from the station. He crossed the road, walking through the darkened space beneath the U-Bahn and stepping back into the light. The smell of grilled meat from the kebab shop beside Balzac made him realise how hungry he was.

Robert stood beside the counter waiting for a shish kebab and watched people walking past on the street and getting off and on the tram. It calmed him. He took his kebab to a standing table on the pavement. He ate it fast, washed it down with coffee and dumped his cup and wrapper in a bin. Back at the apartment he took off his torn, stained clothes, his body protesting each time he stretched or bent. In the shower the hot water stung his cheek, his knee, his palms. He leaned back against the tile and lifted his face to the jets. The surging fall of the water stopped his thoughts.

After drying off he put antiseptic on his cuts and grazes and a large plaster on his skinned knee. There was an angry red patch on his thigh where he had struck the post. He got dressed, took a couple of painkillers and drank a pint of water. He looked for cigarettes in his coat pockets but couldn't find any. He went to the bureau in the living room, where he found an old pouch of tobacco. The powdery tobacco sifted from either end of the paper as he turned it. To stop the cigarette from emptying completely he needed to twist the end closed, as if it were a joint. He lit it as he unlocked the balcony door and stepped outside. He dragged deeply, lost for a moment in the satisfaction that unfurled from his lungs. The temperature was dropping. The Hinterhof was barren, the vegetable patches scraped back to bare earth. Clumps of long grass lay flat and bedraggled. Despite the glaring white sky, a gloom pervaded. He looked towards the empty gym, where every light burned brightly.

On the way home from the Kita, Robert bought the girls gingerbread men. In spite of the deep cold they wanted to eat them at the playground on the corner of their street. They lay down in a concrete tube, their favourite place to rest in between sliding and swinging, and Sonja dictated to Nora the order in which they would eat the limbs.

Bending down, Robert put a hand to the concrete and yelped in shock that was only partly faked. 'You're crazy, it's freezing in there!'

'You're silly, Pappa,' said Sonja, seemingly more out of politeness than amusement.

'All right, little icicles,' Robert said, straightening up stiffly. 'I'll leave you to it.' An old song came back to him as he watched them eat, one he had sung when they used to read a picture-book version of the old fairy tale: 'Run, run, as fast as you can, you can't catch me, I'm the Gingerbread Man.' 'If I need to leave, I've got somewhere to go,' that's what Patrick had said. Had he, perhaps, already left the city? Robert would go to his apartment in the morning and find out. He wouldn't let him get away with what he had done.

The playground was mostly dark now, lit only by the streetlight on the corner. Robert's breath showed as white rags as it passed through the light. 'Come on, girls,' he said. 'Spaghetti for tea.'

'With ketchup?' Nora said.

'With lots of ketchup.'

'Yay!' The girls rolled out of the tube, gingerbread falling from their coats, and Robert limped after them as they ran down the street.

Heidi had taught Robert the recipe for kindergarten spaghetti: frankfurters, cream and ketchup. It was punishingly sweet, but he liked eating it with the kids. Karijn could barely look at it.

As the sauce bubbled, Robert poured water and spooned coffee into the espresso pot and set it on the stove. Karijn texted to say she might not be back until nine, was it OK? Fine, Robert replied. Stay as late as you need. Everything's under control here. Kindergarten spaghetti! Her reply came through a moment later: You disgust me.

Robert and the girls ate together, then Robert brushed their hair while they watched cartoons, read them stories in their bedroom, their warm bodies pressing on either side of him, and sang to them in the soft rose glow of the nightlight. For a long time after they were asleep he lay dozing against the side of Nora's bunk, listening to their snores.

He was reading a book, a second large glass of wine on the coffee table, when Karijn came home. He heard her keys clatter in the Bakelite dish on the hall table. She leaned through the doorway. 'Hej!' she said, smiling. Her hair was up, the bun skewered with a pencil.

'Hej,' he said. 'You look beautiful.'

'How much have you drunk?'

'Less than half of what I'm going to drink.' He stood, dropped the book on the chair and crossed the room to her, Karijn wincing in sympathy when she saw his limp. 'I'm so glad you're alive,' he said. He put his arms around her.

She hugged him back. 'What was that? So weird.'

'I have no idea, but it scared the shit out of me.' He pulled away, his hands gripping her shoulders.

'Did you talk to someone at the hospital?'

'I didn't. I was going to, but . . . Once I knew you were OK, I really didn't want to think about it any more.'

'They need to know about it, though, don't you think? What if it happened to other people? Or, I don't know, if there was someone else there that they thought was me?'

'How would that even be possible?'

She shook her head.

'I'll call them,' he said. 'Are you hungry?'

'I had hard bread at the workshop.'

'How about wine?'

'Yes. Yes yes yes. I'll take a shower and get these chemicals off me.'

They drank the rest of the bottle. Karijn told Robert about the ottoman, Robert told her about the girls' picnic in a frozen concrete tube. They discussed what they needed to do before they left for Sweden, Karijn taking the pencil from Robert's book and making a list as they talked. They were at opposite ends of the couch, one of his feet on the floor and hers in the space between his thighs. They were both too tall for the couch; when they lay on it together it often felt like they would tumble to the floor. He gripped her calf and kneaded it through the cotton of her pyjama trousers. Her hair, water-dark and hanging straight as a curtain, left lines of moisture on her T-shirt. 'Anything else?' she said.

'No, come here, my organised love.'

Karijn rose to her knees and straddled him. 'You consider being organised trivial,' she said, inspecting his grazed hand. 'But without the organisers among us, no agriculture. Without agriculture, no civilisation. Thus, no leisure time. Thus, no time for writing or reading. Without people like me, you wouldn't exist.'

She brushed his closed lips with hers. He opened his mouth and they kissed. He held her head between his hands. 'I was so scared, Karijn.'

She lifted a finger and brushed a tear from his face. 'You need to stop crying and take me to bed,' she said. 'Resurrection has made me horny.'

From the train window, Robert looked at the neat plots and brightly painted huts of a large allotment garden. It rolled out of view, replaced by the metal canyons of the container terminal at Westhafen. He tried to formulate what he would say to Patrick, but the words wouldn't remain orderly – phrases kept pushing ahead of one another in their eagerness to be chosen. When he noticed an old woman staring pointedly at him he realised he had been nervously slapping a rhythm on his thighs.

Walking out of Jungfernheide station, Robert passed a group of teenage boys playing football on a concrete pitch at the foot of a tower block. Their breath steamed in the cold air. A powerful shot went wide and a sound like sleigh bells rang from the chain-link fence surrounding the pitch. He couldn't remember the way to Patrick's apartment. He took off a glove, brought up the map on his phone and typed in Patrick's street. In the distance he saw a tall church spire he remembered from his previous visit. He crossed a busy road and turned onto a quiet residential street. Walking between tall, marzipan-yellow apartment buildings, birdsong falling from the birches that lined the pavement, he could almost forget the unpleasant task that had brought him here. He heard a window opening, the ring of a bicycle bell. At the bottom of the street he passed a grand, fortress-like building. Beside its entrance stood a man in a very baggy pinstripe suit and duffel coat. He was smoking a joint, its sweet, groiny stench strong in the cold air. The man smiled at him and Robert felt strangely certain he was about to offer him a drag. He put his head down and hurried on, turning left and then right onto a treeless stretch of road: Kamminer Strasse. It had only been three weeks since he was last here, but it felt much longer than that. Everything before London seemed long ago. A cold gust struck him; he dug his hands deeper into the pockets of his coat and worked his chin into his scarf. His breath moistened the wool. The scored render of Patrick's block looked even more dismal in the bitter cold. Some residents, he saw, had tried to brighten the building's exterior with window boxes, although these, containing dead or dying plants or nothing at all, only added to its desolation. As far as he remembered Patrick's balcony was unornamented, a narrow space occupied only by a dirty plastic chair and a beer bottle filled with cigarette butts.

Robert walked up the crumbling steps to a wooden double door, the paint at its foot cracked and flaking. Robert scanned the names on the buzzer. There were twenty buttons and nametags. He remembered Patrick saying he hadn't wanted his real name on the bell, but for a moment couldn't remember what he had used instead.

Then he saw it: *Bracknell*. He pressed the buzzer and waited. He pressed it again, but there was no sound or light that suggested it was working. 'Come on,' he muttered into his scarf and stamped his feet, pressing the button a third time, but the intercom remained silent.

An old man pulling a wheeled grocery bag, the kind Robert remembered his grandmother having, approached the steps. He began to laboriously climb them: one step, then a turn to lift the trolley up behind him, then another step. 'Entschuldigung,' Robert said, climbing down the steps. 'Kann ich . . .' and he mimed lifting the trolley.

'Ja, bitte,' the man said, smiling.

The trolley was heavier than Robert expected, so heavy that for a moment he thought it was going to drag him down the steps after it. As he carried it to the top of the short flight the old man followed behind, puffing and repeating 'Bitte.' Gaining the top step the man smiled at Robert. He was very short, and his round, red face and watch cap gave him a gnomish look. Robert motioned towards the door. The man's smile faltered as he pulled a set of keys from his pocket. He slotted one into the keyhole. Before turning it he looked at Robert. 'Wohnst du hier?' he said.

'Ja, ja,' Robert said, patting his pockets to mime forgetting his key. The look on the old man's face suggested his lie wasn't persuasive, but he pushed open the door. Robert carried the trolley over the lip of the doorway and set it down in the hall. As he began to ascend the stairs the front door slammed shut. The old man called out, but Robert didn't hear what he said.

Three flights up he opened the door off the stairwell. Patrick's was the second apartment along the corridor. There was a buzzer beside the door, the nameplate beneath it blank. Robert heard the thin, aggressive buzz bleed back through the door. He released the button. He waited, listening. He still didn't know what he was going to say. Part of him wanted to do no more than hit Patrick, turn around and leave. He buzzed again, two quick squawks. Silence. Hopelessly, he knocked at the door. As his knuckles struck the wood the door gave and swung part way open. He pushed it open further. 'Hello?' he called. He stepped into the small hallway, where a sports bag, some clothes and a few coins lay scattered across the carpet. He went into the kitchen, where the drawers and cupboards had been emptied onto the floor: it was littered with food, broken glass and smashed crockery. Something had been burned in the sink – a lump of wet ash, slick as seaweed, lay beside the plughole. The room still smelled of smoke. Perhaps whoever did this was still here. He looked around for something to defend himself with. The knife block was empty. He bent down and took a dinner knife from the floor. He felt ridiculous and scared. Cautiously he entered the living room. Sheets of paper lay scattered across the floor, covered in printed text. He crouched down to pick a handful up then heard something and looked towards the bedroom. The bed had been stripped, the mattress tossed from the bed's base and slashed open: dirty yellow fibre, the colour of a used cigarette filter, spilled from two jagged tears. He heard water trickling. He moved slowly towards the bathroom door and put his ear to it. The water was the only sound he could hear. He placed his hand gently against the door and pushed. It would not move. His breaths were fast and shallow. He made himself breathe slowly, deeply. He gripped the door handle and slowly pushed it down. The door began to move. With a small cry he threw it open as powerfully as he could. It hit the wall and bounced back. He had to hold out his hand to stop it slamming shut in his face. He pushed it open again and saw the tap running hot. A bloom of steam lay on the mirror. He shut off the tap. He saw a towel lying in a mound beneath the rail, a pair of boxer shorts balled up in a corner. 'Was machst du hier?' a voice said. Stepping out of the bathroom he looked down the hallway and saw the old man standing at the front door. 'Ich ruf die Polizei,' the man said.

'Nein, bitte, nein,' Robert said, dropping the knife to the floor. 'Freund.'

'Doch, ich rufe die Polizei.'

For a few seconds panic held Robert where he stood, then he ran down the hallway and out of the apartment, shouldering the old man aside. He felt him crumple and heard him fall and cry out. He wrenched open the door to the stairwell and took each flight in a couple of jumps, colliding into the wall at each turn of the stairs.

He crashed into the building's front door and rammed it twice with his shoulder before he saw the release button on the wall. He smacked his palm against it and heard the lock click. He thrust the door open and stumbled down the stairs to the street, losing his footing and slamming his knees into the pavement. The bruises from the day before flared painfully. He got to his feet and began to run again, jerkily now, his joints protesting every time his feet struck the pavement. He turned onto a side street, then onto another. After a couple of minutes he stopped, out of breath, beside a poster pillar. He looked at his phone and tried to get his bearings. A siren wailed into life as a bright orange van sped past: an ambulance. The old man will call the police, he thought. He had knocked him down, assaulted him. He began to run again, heading for the river. A busy main road ran between him and the water. When he saw a gap he sprinted across, a horn blaring as he reached the other side. A strip of vegetation lay between the roadside pavement and the dirt towpath. He moved towards it and was shunted violently to the ground. He saw the sky. He sat up, confused. His right arm felt heavy. A few metres away a man was picking up a bike. He was wearing a large, dirty ski jacket and jeans and he was shouting something at Robert but everything was scrambled, Robert couldn't tell what he was saying. He didn't even know what language he was speaking. The man leaned down towards Robert and very deliberately gave him the finger, then got on his bike and rode away.

Robert stood. His right leg shook and his right arm was dead. He limped through a cluster of bare bushes, their sharp, rigid branches pulling at his clothes as he forced his way past. The riverside path was matted with rotting leaves. A warmthless sun shone on the water. A woman with a dog walked past. The woman looked uncertainly at Robert as the dog sniffed frantically around his feet. He walked as fast as he could without breaking into a run. He thought he would be broadcasting his guilt if he ran. As he passed a moored glass-roofed river cruiser the two men mopping its deck stopped their work to look at him. Green railings ran along the river's edge. Red buoys floated in the water. He wanted to be on the other side, where he felt he would be safe. He began to run. There must be a bridge, he thought, but he didn't want to waste more time looking at his phone. He wanted to keep moving.

The river curved and he saw the green metal arch of a bridge ahead. The path rose towards it. His vision throbbed in time with his heartbeat. He was over the water, running across the striped shadows cast by the bridge's arch and supports. He heard another siren, a police car driving towards and then past him, speeding across the bridge. On the other side of the water he stopped, hands on knees, beside a family posing for pictures with a fibreglass Berlin bear. Gradually his breathing slowed and the pressure in his lungs ebbed. He felt sweat running down his body. He felt it begin to chill on his face in the cold air. He looked at his torn trousers and scraped hands, the black crescents of his nails. He was on the corner of a narrow, tree-lined street. He walked down it and found a small, sheltered square between two apartment blocks. There was a bench there and he sank down onto its cold slats and tried to make sense of what he had just seen. Who had done that? What had they been looking for? Where was Patrick? He took his phone from his pocket and opened the call list but hesitated before tapping Patrick's number. What if someone else had Patrick's phone? He ran his hand back and forth through his hair. He didn't know what to do. Karijn would know, but he couldn't tell her about all this now. It was too late. 'Fuck,' he said to the empty square.

Sitting back, he felt something in the back pocket of his trousers. He pulled out the sheets of paper he had found on Patrick's living-room floor, creased from his pocket. He put one of the sheets on the bench and smoothed it with his hand. Reading the words, he recognised them immediately. He had written them himself.

An hour later Robert was turning onto his street, having expected at each stage of his journey, first on foot, then U-Bahn, then S-Bahn, to be stopped and arrested. But apart from the occasional glance prompted by his torn and muddied trousers, or his strained movements – his right leg felt incredibly heavy and throbbed where the bike wheel had collided with it – the journey passed without incident.

Crossing the Hof to his block, Robert saw the door to the bin shelter was again standing ajar. As he reached out to push it closed he heard movement from behind one of the large steel bins. A man emerged and came towards him. 'Jesus!' Robert said as he recoiled, realising as he did so that the man was Patrick.

Patrick held his hands out in front of him. 'I'm sorry,' he said. 'I wasn't trying to scare you.'

'Well you fucking failed,' Robert said, his face hot with shock.

'Are you OK?' Patrick said.

'You shouldn't be here.'

'Forget about the other night,' Patrick said. 'Something's happened.'

'I know. I've just been at your apartment.'

'Shit.' Patrick shrank from Robert, as if he was going to return to his hiding place behind the bin. 'Were they there?'

'There was no one there,' Robert said. 'But it's been trashed.'

'You're sure no one was there? Someone could have followed you. Someone might have seen you leave.'

'No one was there. Just an old man.'

'What old man?'

'One of your neighbours. He said he was calling the police, so I ran.'

'Fuck, this isn't good,' Patrick said. He paced the shelter, his hands clutching the back of his head.

'Were you burgled?' Robert said. 'Is that what this is?'

Patrick stopped pacing. 'Burgled?' He laughed. 'Fucking burgled? It was them, Robert. Don't you get it?' He hissed the words as if a hand were gripping his throat.

A vision came to Robert of Patrick wrecking his own apartment, of this being part of some trap Robert had blundered into, but he didn't believe it was possible. What if he really was telling the truth? He felt lost. He heard a click and thud as the street door unlocked: someone was coming. Looking at Patrick and holding a finger to his lips, he pushed the door of the shelter almost closed. The door leading from the entrance hall to the Hof creaked as it opened. Footsteps approached the shelter. Robert looked through the fissure between door and jamb. A woman he recognised, wearing a long leather coat and carrying a bulging Kaiser's shopping bag, passed the shelter and let herself into his block. His head pulsed as he rested it against the chill, rough wood of the door. He wanted to send Patrick away, never see him again. He knew it was the smart thing to do. 'You'd better come up,' he said.

'I saw them,' Patrick said. 'I was on the balcony having a smoke. I saw them crossing the street and I knew who they were from the way they moved. I was ready. I keep a bag packed. I grabbed it and waited down the hall.'

'Why didn't you leave?'

'I didn't have time to get out. I waited. I heard them knock on my door. Heard them whisper to each other. They opened the door somehow – they didn't force it – and when they went in, I ran.'

'They didn't see you?'

'No.'

'And you're sure they were your Russians? They couldn't have been . . .'

'Been what?'

Robert hesitated. 'Burglars,' he said.

Patrick shook his head. The suggestion didn't anger him the way it had before. 'I heard them talking. It was them.' He sounded exhausted. He slowly lifted his coffee cup and sipped. They were sitting at the kitchen table in the thin light of mid-afternoon.

'And there wasn't anyone outside?' Robert said. 'Could someone have followed you here?' He would go along with it for now. He didn't know what else to do.

'No,' Patrick said. 'I would have seen them. I've been all over. I wouldn't have come here but I wanted to tell you. I didn't want to call. I don't even want to turn my phone on.'

'Why?'

'Maybe they've hacked it.'

'You really think they've done that?'

Patrick shrugged.

'Someone called me pretending to be a doctor,' Robert said.

'When?'

'Yesterday. They told me Karijn had been hurt. It wasn't real. I thought it was you.'

'Me?'

Robert studied Patrick's reaction. It wasn't him. 'Because of how angry you were,' Robert said, embarrassed by the words. 'About what I'd written.'

'So, you thought—' Patrick said and stopped. He lifted his cup, brought it halfway to his mouth then carefully set it back down on the table. 'You think I could lie about your wife being hurt? You think I would do that?'

'I don't know you, Patrick. You don't seem like the kind of person that would do that, but I don't know you.' Robert looked at the small black rucksack propped beside Patrick's chair. It seemed ridiculous to think that it was apparently everything he owned now. If all this really was true, Patrick didn't stand a chance. 'We need to talk to the police,' Robert said.

'No.'

'Why? If this isn't all made up, why won't you talk to them?'

'Look what they did for Alyona,' Patrick said. 'Look what they did for Sergei. They knew about the threats that had been made against him. He told them himself. But when he dies, there's no murder investigation. There's barely even a crime scene – yep, hanging, must be suicide,' he said, clapping his palms together. 'That doesn't seem suspicious to you?'

'And the Berlin police are in on this conspiracy too? Come on.'

'I don't know what you expect them to do, Robert. Are they going to assign you a security team because you got a fucking phone call? And you think I'm the fantasist.'

'Are you really not going to report that someone broke into your apartment and tore it apart?'

Patrick shook his head.

'Christ!'

'You disapprove,' Patrick said, with scorn.

'Do what you want,' Robert said. He looked into his coffee. He could feel Patrick's stare without needing to look up. 'What?'

'You still don't believe me, do you?'

'Does it matter?'

'How can you not believe me?'

'I don't disbelieve that you believe,' Robert said. 'But I think this stuff . . .'

'This "stuff"? Tell me about this stuff, please, I'm listening.'

'You let it get under your skin, and that can make you see things that maybe aren't there.'

'You saw my apartment. That was "there", right?'

'I did. I saw your apartment, and maybe it was a couple of Russians who broke into it, but even if they were Russian, it doesn't mean they're who you think they are. This stuff messes with your head. You kept talking about being followed, and then I started thinking I was being followed. I saw someone on the tram and I was convinced he was keeping tabs on me, but then I realised I was being paranoid.'

'Robert, please listen to me,' Patrick said, speaking slowly, his eyes locked on Robert's. 'If you think you were being followed then you were. I was the same as you, I thought Sergei was exaggerating, or playing things up for the drama. But then he died and that scared me. Really scared me. But a couple of months went by and I read the papers and even though they got certain things about him wrong, I believed some of what they wrote. I started thinking maybe it was suicide, like the reports all seemed to say. Then I got a text: "Patrick, we follow you. We are behind you." And I knew. So trust me,' he said, leaning closer to Robert. 'The phone call, the tram, it's them. You need to get out of here.'

'We're going to Sweden. We'll be safe there.' He wasn't going to argue any more.

'That's good,' Patrick said. 'I'm leaving too.'

'Where will you go?'

Patrick looked away. 'I've got a place,' he said.

'That's right, you wouldn't tell me where it was.'

'You'd laugh if you knew,' Patrick said as he stood. 'My train's leaving soon. Thanks for the coffee.'

Robert walked Patrick to the front door. 'Listen,' he said. 'I know you probably don't care, but I'm sorry about what happened with the book.'

'You're wrong, I do care,' Patrick said, turning to face him. 'I enjoyed our talks. Finding out it was a set-up was . . . well, it doesn't matter any more.'

'Do you need anything?' Robert said. 'Some clothes?'

'No.'

'Money?' Robert tried to think of what else he could offer. He wanted Patrick to accept something from him.

'I don't need anything,' Patrick said. He held out his hand. 'It would have been good to meet you in different circumstances, Robert.'

'Some other time, maybe.'

'Some other time.'

At the first landing Patrick looked back and waved. Robert held up his hand in reply and shut the door. He went into the kitchen and put the dirty coffee cups in the dishwasher. It was getting dark. The apartment windows opposite were lit in a patchwork. Patrick, his rucksack slung over one shoulder, walked across the Hof, emerging into and disappearing from panels of thrown light. Where was he going? Robert wondered if he had friends or family who could help him. As the door to the entrance hall slammed he felt, with a plummeting certainty, that he was the only person who knew Patrick, not just in Berlin but anywhere. That he was someone the world had forgotten.

It was five below and as they left the airport it started snowing. Karijn drove. The way the flakes danced in the headlights made it seem as if the car were speeding through a tunnel of infinite length. It was just after nine o'clock when they turned off the highway. They climbed a ridge, the frozen lake a smooth indigo plain below them. They passed a shaggy-maned horse standing in a floodlit field, then their headlights ran the length of a yellow barn. Beyond the farm they entered a darkness broken only by the glimmer of distant houses. These dis appeared too, as the road made its twisting descent to the lake. Then all that the headlights illuminated were the unmoving boughs of the pines.

Robert inhaled sharply as he got out of the car and was clenched by the frozen air. His breath caught in his throat with a mentholated burn. The girls were asleep.

'Let's open the door before we get them out,' Karijn said.

Robert nodded and went to the boot to get their bags. It had stopped snowing and as he walked towards the house he looked up and saw, through a gap in the cloud, stars high above. They glinted as if they were turning in a breeze. The shock of the cold felt cleansing, and the great open space of the lake, out of sight but tangible, charged the air. Berlin felt very far away.

The house was warm. Lars had stopped by a few days before to heat it for them. 'The pump seems to be working OK,' Robert said as he put the bags down inside the door. His eyes were drawn immediately to the lake, a pattern of darknesses beyond the picture window, but then Karijn flicked on the lights and it was replaced by the indistinct reflection of the living room, including a faint version of himself. The girls ran past him, shouting excitedly. 'Shoes!' he called after them. Karijn pulled the door closed behind her. 'Did you lock the car?' he said.

'You know I never do.'

'You're too trusting.'

Karijn was crouched over one of the smaller bags, taking out their toiletries. 'If someone comes all the way out here to steal a car,' she said, 'they can have it. And my admiration. Girls, kom nu då! It's time to brush your teeth. Are you OK with putting them to bed? I can unpack.'

Sonja punctuated the bedtime story with questions about what they were going to do the next day, and the days after that: 'Will we go to the swimming pool? Is Mormor coming to see us? Will the lake stay frozen? Are we staying here for a long time?'

'Do you want to hear the story or not?' Robert said, after the fifth failed attempt to read a page. 'Shall we just go to sleep now?'

'No!'

'Then no more questions, OK?' Robert knew Sonja's hyperactivity was a sign of how tired she was. Nora had her head in his lap and was almost asleep, sucking noisily on her dummy.

He finished the story and Sonja climbed up to her bunk while he slid Nora off his lap and covered her with a duvet. She sucked her dummy once and briefly tightened her closed eyes. Robert switched off the lamp, leaving only the nightlight's amber glow. 'Shall I sing?' he whispered to Sonja.

She shook her head, which was buried beneath her arm.

'Shall I go?'

'No,' she said, her voice muffled, 'stay.'

'OK,' he said, stroking her hair and listening as her breathing deepened.

A few minutes later he found Karijn in the kitchen, surveying the cupboards. 'I'm going to get some groceries,' she said. They had decided not to stop on the way from the airport in favour of getting the girls to bed.

'You don't want to wait until morning?'

'We need breakfast things. I won't be long.'

After Karijn had left, Robert made his own inspection of the house. He thought about building a fire, but Karijn was much better at that than he was. He went down into the basement and turned on the light, the fluorescent tubes stuttering to life. It was cold in the utility room.

An icy draught seeped in through the small window that stood just above ground level, against which a small drift of leaves had accumulated. The pump hummed quietly. He picked up his cold-weather boots, switched off the light and went back upstairs. In a kitchen cupboard he found a half-full bottle of whisky and poured himself a glass. He put on his boots and coat, took the key from the row of hooks beside the front door and opened the sliding door onto the terrace. He shut it behind him, crossed the apron of light cast from the living room and stepped gingerly down the steps towards the lake. Below the terrace the ground was treacherous with fallen leaves, slick from recent rainfall and that evening's snow shower. The cloud had continued to break up and the moon shone blue on the frozen lake. Further out he saw patches that hadn't frozen yet, the silvered water being pushed along in these channels by the wind. Standing on the stone pier he heard a sound like the chirrup of crickets: the newly formed ice moving as water shifted beneath it. While the surface looked solid enough, he knew if he put his weight on it when it was this fresh he would almost certainly plunge through. If the forecast was right and the temperature didn't rise it would be thick enough to walk on in a couple of days. Daredevils would be out on it tomorrow, but for now it was pristine and unpopulated. He loved the way the logic of the lake disappeared when it was frozen and it became instead a vast, featureless territory around which, for some unknown reason, a ring of roadways and dwellings had been built.

He looked at the distant lights of cars on the highway. One of them was Karijn. He wanted to tell her about everything that had happened since he met Patrick. Over the last two months he felt as if another person had grown up inside him, a shadow-self whose existence she knew nothing about. It made him feel ashamed, but part of him remained curious and wondered if he had the ability to sustain it; to live a hidden life. He could do anything, provided he had the nerve to twist and distort as necessary and could live with the dishonesty. The idea made him see life not as a vast sprawl, but a series of stacked realities. People could ascend or descend through these levels of life as they chose, although most never did. Someone like Vanyashin knew this was how life worked and exploited it, but Robert's experiment with living this way, his relationship with Patrick, was something he didn't think he could have maintained if it hadn't already come to an end. He wasn't strong enough. Or was his unwillingness to live that way a form of strength in itself? If it was, it gave him no satisfaction. He shivered at a dagger of wind thrusting off the lake. He sipped the whisky and felt it surge within him. He looked back at the house and saw the warm light from the girls' bedroom. He felt like a guard at his post, defending the house against whatever was out there in the darkness. He tensed his thigh to feel his bruise twinge, the ache almost pleasurable now. Off to his right, to the east, he saw the lights of Sandared, where Karijn had lived when she was a child. The lights seemed to wink off and on as they carried over the surface of the lake. The stiffening water chirruped. He gulped the last of his whisky. With its burn in his throat, its heat threading his cheeks, he climbed the slope to the house.

The morning was dull, with dark grey clouds jumbled at the horizon like a rockfall. The frozen lake might have been a vast concrete rink. At the breakfast table they made plans for the day. Robert said he would clear the leaves from the lawn and terrace and empty the gutters. The girls wanted to see if the camp they had built in the woods last summer had survived. 'Maybe there's a bear living in it now,' Karijn said. 'Or a family of wolves.' Sonja mouthed the word to Nora, her eyes wide.

'Or a bunch of teenagers,' Robert said.

'The most terrifying creatures of all,' Karijn said.

The frozen leaves on the lawn snapped under Robert's boots. The temperature had dropped another couple of degrees and he thought the bay, a small, sheltered inlet at the western edge of the garden that was always the first patch to freeze, would probably be solid enough to walk on. Stepping onto it, his boots sliding a little, he heard deep thrums from the ice below, like muffled laser bolts flying back and forth. He had learned to find these eerie sounds reassuring. It was the high, tinkling cracks that Karijn had told him to be wary of: they were the ones that signalled the ice might give way. After a few tentative steps his confidence grew, and he began to stride. When he turned back he was surprised at how far from the shore he had gone. The house looked small from here, the stilled lake vast.

He fetched garden sacks and a rake from the carport. He started at the far end of the lawn, beyond the rotting friggebod that had been in bad repair when they bought the place and was now on the verge of falling down altogether. The spinney of trees that stood between the lawn and the road, a mixture of oak, birch and pine, looked skeletal now, the bare oak and birch branches forming a lattice that cut the sky into a chaotic grey mosaic. Fused together, the leaves came up in flaps as Robert raked. He gathered a series of piles as he made his way from the lake edge up towards the house. The lawn was large; it took him half an hour to clear it and the terrace was still to be done. He was putting the leaves into the sacks when Karijn came outside with two mugs of coffee. He took his gratefully and blew across it, the steam billowing in the frigid air.

'You should take the girls out before lunch,' Karijn said. 'It'll be dark by three.'

'We'll go to the camp.'

'I'll make a thermos of hot chocolate. Don't keep them out for more than an hour.'

'You think they'll get bored?'

'I think they'll get hypothermia. The British half, anyway.'

Soon afterwards they were climbing into the forest. The girls wore fleeces, thermal jumpsuits, scarves, gloves and hats, the layers making them as deliberate in their movements as astronauts. The ground was carpeted with copper leaves, needles and fallen cones. It was as if winter hadn't yet penetrated the forest's edge. As he turned to watch the girls follow him up a rise, Robert believed he could live here, like this, forever. He would write in the early morning and take care of tasks around the property before lunch. In the afternoon there would be time to read, answer emails and run. He would be competent, patient and productive, every flaw – his negativity, his temper, his selfish need for solitude – sieved away, leaving only the good. He didn't know why he should leave this and return to those bleak, barrack-like streets and windswept avenues that weren't built to human scale, but for columns of tanks and Young Pioneer parades. The mess with Patrick only increased his sense of the city as a place to be abandoned.

He knew, though, that the rhythm of days beside the lake could be monotonous. Even this beauty eventually became dull because it was inevitable and unchanging, whereas beauty in the city was more valuable for arising, unexpectedly, from drabness. Here, beyond the lake and the forest, there was only the highway that ran to a town that was the same as a thousand other affluent European towns, with a dull square and a parade of shops and a mall somewhere on the outskirts. It wasn't enough.

'Pappa!' Nora was calling. They were a little way behind. Her glove had snagged on a bramble and been pulled off her hand. Sonja was laughing and pointing at it.

'No!' Nora said and stamped her foot, upset by Sonja's laughter.

'What's this?' Robert said, backtracking to where they stood. 'Is this glovefruit?' he said, leaning over and squeezing the glove.

'No!' Nora said, crossly but beginning to smile. A pennant of breath fled her mouth.

'I think it's ripe,' he said, bending to sniff it. 'And it smells delicious.'

Nora giggled. 'Pappa, no!' she said. 'It's my glove!'

Robert narrowed his eyes at her. 'I'm going to eat this glovefruit.'

'No!' she shouted.

He plucked the glove from the branch and handed it to her. 'All right, you have it,' he said.

She lifted it to her mouth and pretended to take a bite.

'Tasty?' he said.

'Disgusting.'

He nodded. 'Let's go.'

'How much further is it, Pappa?' Sonja said in her aggrieved voice, her arms dangling loosely in front of her in performed exhaustion.

'I think,' Robert said, pretending to carefully survey the terrain, 'it's just over the next hill.'

They had built the camp over a couple of days in July, a wigwam structure they made by leaning fallen tree branches against the trunk of a large beech. When it was finished, they came every day with blankets and food, colouring books and pens, and any other items the girls had woken up deciding were essential: a compact mirror, a plastic unicorn, Karijn's old flip phone.

As soon as the camp came into view Robert could see the girls hadn't been its most recent inhabitants. Most of the branches were still in place, but there was a litter of beer cans, cigarette butts and tiny brown bags of used snus spread around. A ring of stones surrounded the dark remains of a fire.

'Who's been here?' Sonja said, stamping her way around the camp. 'Who left all this mess?'

'Looks like teenagers to me,' Robert said, toeing a crushed can. 'It looks like they had a party.'

'It's not fair!' Sonja said. 'They should make their own camp.' She was almost crying.

'Yes, they should really,' Robert said, noticing Nora bending down and reaching for one of the golden cans. 'Leave that, Nora,' he said. 'But we can clean this mess up. It'll be good as new.'

Sonja looked around dubiously. 'It's ruined,' she said. 'I hate the teenagers.'

'That's reasonable,' Robert said. 'We can come back

with some rubbish bags tomorrow and tidy it all up, OK? Maybe some woodland creatures will help us.'

Sonja lowered her chin to her chest and smiled the exaggerated smile she saved for when he was being silly. 'No they won't, Pappa!'

'Maybe you're right. The ones in this forest are pretty lazy.' Nora had wandered off and was trying to climb a moss-smothered trunk. 'Careful, Norri!' he called. Thick cloud had covered the sun and the forest had darkened. The cold was beginning to bite. 'Who wants sausages?' he said.

'Me!' Nora cried.

'Me! Me! Me!' said Sonja, jumping up and down.

'I can smell them cooking, can you? Let's go.'

The wind had picked up and the pine boughs creaked above them as they made their way down to the house. Beyond the trees he saw the pewter smoothness of the lake. Two birds, black scraps against the sky, flew east to west above it. He felt his phone buzz. He thought it would be Karijn checking where they were, but the message preview showed an unrecognised number with a +34 country code. He opened it and stopped still. Hi Robert. This is the last you'll hear from me for a while, but I wanted you to know I followed you on your pilgrimage. Goodbye and best of luck. Robert looked up into the sky's glowing greyness. More snow, he thought. The wind gusted harder and the boughs thrashed. Nora was tugging at his arm. From further down the slope Sonja turned and looked towards them, angling her head back so she could peer out from underneath her hood.

'Are you OK, Pappa?' Nora asked, in a solicitous way that made her seem much older than she was.

'Fine, I'm fine,' Robert said, dropping the phone back into his coat pocket. 'Let's go get some sausages.'

'Yay!' Nora said and seized his hand and ran. He hurried down the slope beside her, leaning back to counterbalance and stop them both from falling.

Robert was mopping up the last of the mustard on his plate with a piece of bread when Karijn asked if he had checked the traps. In the summer they had left a few up in the attic, which was where the mice went when the weather turned cold. He hadn't checked them when he came in October.

The attic wasn't closed off from the rest of the house; it was a mezzanine that looked down on the living room and kitchen. It was bare except for a low table, a rolled-up yoga mat, and a lumpy futon Robert and Karijn slept on when they gave their bedroom to guests. A gust of wind thumped against the roof. Snow streamed past the porthole window. Robert looked behind the futon and saw that two of the traps were full. One mouse looked like it was asleep, the bar of the trap buried so deep in its nape that it couldn't be seen. The mouse lay on its side, as if it were using the trap as a pillow. The bar had crushed the other one's face. The small bodies drooped as he lifted the traps off the floor and dropped them into a bin bag.

'Anything?' Karijn called from the sink as he came downstairs. The girls were at the table, absorbed in colouring books.

'A couple,' he said, pulling on his coat. Outside it was almost completely dark. He felt the snow as a succession of wet shocks against his cheeks. He went to the carport, snapped on the light and looked for a bucket, then trudged across the lawn, glad of the morning's work. Looking at it now he realised that Lars must have mowed it since his visit in October, before the leaf fall. He had another bottle of whisky for him. He would take the girls and visit him in the morning.

He went to the edge of the spinney and shook the bag out. He picked up the first trap and lifted the bar. The mouse dropped to the ground. He picked it up by its tail and flung it into the undergrowth. He repeated this with the second mouse and tossed the traps into the bucket. Shivering from the cold, he left the bucket and traps in the carport. He would clean them later. He went around to the terrace. Across the water car headlights moved at a stately pace. The traffic made a faint, generator-like hum. There were the clustered lights of Sandared and over the hills beyond them, visible only as a reflection against the clouds, the diffuse glow of Borås. Here, at the other end of the lake, where each house stood distant and hidden from its neighbours, not a single light was visible.

He took out his phone and opened his texts. His breath showed in the light from the screen. He thumbed Patrick's message and wrote, You're right, I laughed. I hope things work out for you there. He sent the message and spent another moment in the stillness, then went inside the house.

Robert had bought a DVD of *Frozen* at the airport. Karijn made a fire and told Sonja and Nora they could stay up late to watch the film. She made popcorn, the girls squealing as the corn kernels began to ricochet inside the saucepan.

'Maybe tomorrow we'll go and look for Elsa's castle,' Robert said as the film began. The fire made the room churn with shadow and light.

'For real?' Sonja said.

'Absolutely.'

'Don't promise what you can't deliver,' said Karijn.

'It's tricky to find,' he said, 'but we'll do our best, OK?'

Sonja nodded distractedly, her eyes on the screen as men hefted blocks of ice from a frozen lake. Robert felt his phone buzz. He pivoted away from Nora, who was slumped against him, and pulled his phone from his pocket. He had been expecting to hear from Lars, but he always called. It might be Patrick, he thought. He hoped it was. The number was German, but he didn't know it. We are here Robert. We follow you, the text in the message preview read. He opened it. That was the entire message. The phone shook in his hand as another message arrived. If you love family come outside now alone. Robert looked to the window, expecting to see someone looking in. All he saw was the darkened terrace. Black trees against the purple sky. He stood suddenly, knocking Nora to one side.

'Pappa!' she scolded without looking away from the screen. He went to the door and pulled on his boots. As he shrugged on his coat Karijn called over, 'Where are you going?'

'Forgot the traps. Won't be long.'

'Do you have to do it now?'

'Just, peace of mind,' he said nonsensically. As he pulled on his hat and reached for the door handle, he felt as if he were operating within a dream and that the door might open onto anything: grasslands, a blank wall, a boiling sea. But when he opened it all he saw was the familiar driveway, the lamppost glowing beside the road. The wind had died. Flakes of snow fell slow and straight. He stepped off the porch. This isn't real, he thought. This is another hoax. Someone was fucking with him. He saw a white light in the spinney: it flashed in his eyes. He moved across the lawn towards it as if impelled. His legs were shaking. His breaths were no more than snatches of air. He felt lightheaded. Looking down, his feet seemed incredibly distant. The grass of the lawn crunched loudly. The light moved in a small circle, as if encouraging him. He stepped into the underbrush, frozen stalks of bracken snapping under his feet. Passing between the trees he felt as though he were moving through a crowd of people. He saw two men standing in a small clearing between three birches. One was short and slim, the other tall and thickset. The light went out. 'Robert Prowe,' the short one said. Russian, Robert thought. He couldn't speak. These men, the short one with a long, thin face, the large one with a black beard and a broad, misshapen nose, couldn't be real. They couldn't be here. He reached out a hand towards them. The larger one grabbed his wrist and turned his arm at an angle that made him bend down towards the ground. The man held Robert's arm fully extended. His other hand pushed painfully at Robert's straining elbow. The man's fingers were as rigid as metal bolts. A bit more pressure, Robert felt, and his arm would snap. Blood rushed to his face. The man forced him down onto his knees, the coldness of the ground spreading like ice water up his thighs.

The smaller man crouched down beside him. 'Phone,' he said, his hand extended.

Robert scrabbled at his pocket, trying not to alter the angle at which his other arm was held. He gave the man his phone. 'Who are you?' he said.

'It doesn't matter,' the man said. 'Look.' The man held up a phone and Robert saw his own kitchen in Berlin. His and Karijn's bedroom. The girls' bedroom. 'Rhinower Strasse,' the man said. 'Nice place.'

'What were you doing in my apartment?' Robert said.

'What we want, we do,' the man said. He nodded and Robert's arm was released. His wrist burned. His elbow throbbed. 'Now we are here with you and your family. To find something secret.' The man raised his eyebrows as if he had suggested something exciting.

'What secret?' Robert said.

'I ask questions,' the man said gently. 'You only answer. Where is Patrick?'

'I don't know,' Robert said. His stomach turned. He felt his bowels loosen.

'Where?'

'I don't know.'

'Where?'

'I don't know.'

'Where?' The man's tone was robotic. He spoke as if he would repeat the word until daybreak.

'I don't know,' Robert said. 'I don't really know him.'

The man sighed. 'You don't know Patrick Unsworth? You go to his house, Robert. You meet him in the cafe. You make party with him in the night. Maybe you fuck him, I don't care. But you know him. You know him.'

'I know him a little. I know he was thinking about leaving Berlin. But I don't know if he's gone, or where he's gone.'

The man rose, exhaling a little with the effort. He took something from his back pocket, raised it before him then snapped his arm down. With a rapid series of clicks a rod telescoped out. Robert tried to rise but his arms were gripped from behind and he was yanked backward. His arms were twisted and he was hauled over onto his front. He felt the rod whip down onto the back of his thigh. The man grunted and struck Robert again. One of his elbows caught the blow. It felt cracked in two. Nausea swelled in his throat, in his belly. He groaned and pushed his face against the cold ground. The man sat down cross-legged beside him. He said something in Russian, soothing words spoken quietly. He patted Robert as if he were a pet. 'Sit, Robert, sit.'

Robert felt the man tug at his shoulder and he rolled onto his side. He pushed himself up until he was sitting, one leg turned awkwardly beneath him. His thigh throbbed. His elbow felt as though it were alight. Waves of heat and cold shuddered through him. He gulped air, struggling not to throw up. 'I know it's not what you want to hear,' he said, 'but I don't know where he is.'

The man tapped at his phone. He raised a finger and read: 'You're right, I laughed. I hope things work out for you there.'

Robert didn't understand. 'Is that my phone?' he said.

'My phone,' the man said. 'I see all messages in, out. All calls.'

'How?'

'Robert,' the man said, waving his phone, 'this is not difficult. Little Sonja can do this.' He looked at the screen. '"I hope things work out for you there." Where is "there"?' You tell me now, or he' – he pointed to the man behind Robert – 'will go into your house. I promise you do not want this.'

Hands gripped Robert's head and twisted it around so he could see the house. Firelight danced in the windows. He had fallen into another life, or these men had risen up from deeper waters. 'And if I tell you?' he said.

'Tell us, never tell any people, happy family.'

He saw Patrick look up at him from the pavement, his closed eye and cut lip. 'Blanes,' he said.

'What?'

'Blanes.' It was just a word. He said it again. 'Blanes. In Spain.'

'Where in Blanes? Address.'

'I don't know,' Robert said, realising with a lurch that what he knew might not, after all, be enough. 'It's not big,' he said, pleadingly. 'That's where he is.'

The man stood. Robert tried to get up but was pushed down. 'When we go. Say you lost your phone.' They moved off through the trees.

'How do I know you'll keep your word?' Robert called after them. They stopped and looked back at him. The small man said something and the other one laughed. They turned and walked away and were swallowed by the darkness. Robert stayed on the ground cradling his arm, unable to move even if he had wanted to. He listened to his breath. For a time his world shrank only to that. He heard an engine start, its pitch shifting as the car climbed the hill away from the house, its light flickering through the trees. He could still hear the engine long after it must have been impossible to do so.

The film had finished. Karijn and the girls were asleep on the couch, curled into one another. Robert sat down on the coffee table. His body sparked with pain. His fingers throbbed painfully as they warmed. He stared at Karijn, at Sonja, at Nora. He was still staring, he didn't know how long later, when Karijn opened her eyes. 'There you are,' she murmured.

They carried the girls to bed. Robert told Karijn he would join her soon. He paced in the living room, the lights off, the fire burned down to embers. The night had cleared and the moonlight set the lake ice glowing. He took a pack of cigarettes from a drawer in the kitchen, put on his coat and went onto the porch. The security light made the night beyond it too dark, so he stepped away from the house and waited for it to turn off. The night was mostly silent, but at every noise – snow sifting from a branch, a rustle from somewhere in the spinney – Robert started and looked into the darkness to see if the men were coming back. He walked circuits around the house but the lake's vacant expanse troubled him, so he stayed on the wooded side. With each hour that passed the encounter felt less real. He let the feeling in. He welcomed it. It wasn't real. It no longer existed. He was the only one who knew it had happened and he would never speak about it. He promised himself that, standing in the darkness outside the house, lighting one cigarette from the end of another.

Acknowledgements

Thank you to Claudia Bülow, Eric Chinski, Rachel Cusk, Annette Excell, Emmie Francis, Edmund Gordon, Christian House, Traci Kim, Toby Leighton-Pope, Josefin Lindeblom and the Lindeblom family, Emma Paterson, Natasha Randall, Eleanor Rees, Julia Ringo and all at FSG, Leo Robson, Josephine Salverda, Siemon Scamell-Katz, Deepa Shah, Josh Smith and all at Faber, May-Lan Tan and Sarah Whitehead.

Thank you to Arts Council England and the Society of Authors for their financial support.

The following books and articles were a great help to me in writing this novel: *Putin's People* by Catherine Belton; *Putin's Kleptocracy* by Karen Dawisha; *The Man Without a Face* by Masha Gessen; *Mafia State* and *A Very Expensive Poison* by Luke Harding; *The Oligarchs* by David E. Hoffman; *Londongrad* by Mark Hollingsworth and Stewart Lansley; *The Invention of Russia* by Arkady Ostrovsky; *Nothing Is True and Everything Is Possible* by Peter Pomerantsev; and the 2017 *BuzzFeed* article 'From Russia With Blood' by Heidi Blake, Tom Warren, Richard Holmes, Jason Leopold, Jane Bradley and Alex Campbell.

Thank you most of all to Sofia, Astrid and Sigrid.